NORSEMAN'S REVENGE

GIANNA SIMONE

Rosavin Publishing
Contact: RosavinPub@optonline.net

Norseman's Revenge
Copyright ©2015 Gianna Simone

Cover Design: Gianna Simone

ISBN: 978-0692665008

Also by Gianna Simone

The Bayou Magiste Chronicles
Claimed by the Devil – Book 1
Claimed by the Mage – Book 2
Claimed by the Enchanter – Book 3
Claimed by the Zyndevine – Book 4

Medieval Warrior's Series
Warrior's Vengeance – Book 1
Warrior's Wrath – Book 2
Warrior's Possession – Book 3

Praise for Gianna Simone:

Warrior's Possession

BDSM Book Reviews: Gillian is keeping secrets and Royce will use everything in his sexual arsenal to make her tell him all of them. A BDSM bodice ripper... if you enjoy spanking, bondage, subduing and sexual interrogation you'll have plenty to enjoy.

The Romance Reviews: As a period piece, I was impressed with the author's research into all aspects of the story (language, clothing, food, activities, etc.). And in typical period fashion, Lady Gillian is treated more as an object to be controlled than a partner. Something she wants nothing to do with. Well, mostly. For the Panther has a knack for turning his lady inside out. The sex scenes and the BDSM scenes are scintillating as it's easy to imagine your own skin warming under the Earl's capable hand.

Warrior's Vengeance

The Romance Reviews: The plot is so captivating that the reader feels compelled to know more. The story, the development and the end are, to put it mildly, peculiar and original. This is my first Gianna Simone novel and I must say, she did a great job.

Goodreads: Impressive and totally hot bodice ripper!

Warrior's Wrath

BDSM Book Reviews: This story combines the richness of the 14th century history, meshed along with the stories of betrayal and the stories of love. There is a sweetness of Aeron as she is immersed in a sexual education she never knew existed.

Goodreads: The menage scenes were H.O.T.! Ms. Simone really does well with the heat and creativity of the triangle in action.

Claimed by the Devil

BDSM Book Reviews: The story leads you on an emotional rollercoaster, but it is well worth the ride. As Helene and Devlin get older their past is ever-present, but Devlin works at gaining what he desires. Devlin fed into Helene's needs giving her what she wanted. Sex is here, often and hot, well written and intense.

You Gotta Read Reviews: This is one intense and hot story that grabbed my attention from the start and would not let go. While we are treated to the romance between Helene and Devlin, we also get to find out about their lives outside of the bedroom, which include both friends and enemies. I loved watching the attraction between the two become so much more. Helene blooms with the help of Devlin and his love.

Claimed by the Mage

The Romance Reviews: Gianna Simone does an excellent job with Aiden's seduction of Lily. He reads her well and understands, most of the time, when to push and when to give. He takes care not to overpower or frighten away his healer as he carefully reveals her submissive side to her. My favorite parts of the book are those moments when he uses everything at his disposal to make love to her, and magic can allow for some sinfully erotic maneuverings.

Claimed by the Enchanter

BDSM Book Reviews: The author did a wonderful job of contrasting Regine's need to control and be dominated. She also showed how much trust plays into a relationship. Once Cameron and Regine get together, the sparks fly. The chemistry between the two is intense and the scenes between the two, and later with David, are very hot.

Coffee Time Romance: Claimed by the Enchanter is

published by a suitably named publisher, because it is a sizzler of a story. The struggle between self-perception and self-awareness is strong and the emotions it invokes mirrors the struggle between who a person thinks they are, and who they are afraid to be. The internal struggle was as strong as the struggle to solve the mystery. I absolutely fell right into the story and lived as the characters lived with every emotion magnified. I am happy to say I am a new fan of Ms. Simone and look forward to reading more from this talented artist.

Claimed by the Zyndevine

BDSM Book Reviews: This is a fast moving magical story with many twists and turns. I enjoyed this book with its feisty characters, spells and hexes, evil forces and new lands. The romance was inevitable and the sex was hot. Even though BDSM was the main element to all romantic encounters, the prominent feel for me was one of true love conquers all. If you like magic, fantasy and happy endings this is the story for you.

DEDICATION

To Janet Lane Walters and Liz Matis for all your help in getting this book together, especially in the technical sense, which trips me up every dang time! I couldn't have done it without either of you. Your guidance, knowledge and encouragement is more appreciated than I can properly say.

A special thanks to Lydia – you were the first beta reader for this book and I appreciate your honesty and cheerleading! And now - it's finally out here!

And I can't even begin to thank enough the ladies of my Tuesday Night Critique Group – you are the best critique partners an author can ask for. Receiving your honest reactions has brought out the best in me as a writer. I truly value every moment of your friendship, support, honesty and of course, the many accompanying laughs!

NORSEMAN'S REVENGE

THE NORSEMEN SAGAS, BOOK 1

BY GIANNA SIMONE

Getting kidnapped by a Viking raider on her wedding night might really be a blessing from the gods.

Geira Sorensdotter awaits her new husband, but she's filled with doubts about the man and the marriage. Those doubts are forgotten when the village is attacked, her husband is struck down and she is tied up and carried off amidst the raid.

Kori Thorfinnson has waited years to take revenge against the man who murdered his wife. But he soon finds the innocent young woman he's taken as his personal slave is not his enemy, despite her marriage to his foe. Her courage in defying him, her caring heart, and the fiery passion she shares stirs feelings Kori hasn't known since his wife died. Afraid to lose Geira, he binds her to him in many ways – not only with rope, but with his body, his collar and his mark.

Geira quickly learns just how despicable her

husband was, and despite her difficult circumstances, grows to care deeply for Kori, her captor. Still, dreams of freedom linger. But once she finds herself with child, she must plan her escape, to save herself and her baby. However, Kori has plans of his own.

Features A Kinky Twist on History! love scenes, including bondage, spanking, multiple partners and more!

CHAPTER ONE

Melodies from harps, punctuated by the sharper blare of carved wooden lurs cut through the raucous laughter and shouts filling the longhouse. With each blast from the long horns, Geira Sorensdotter's stomach clenched. She sat beside her groom, surveying the gathering of their clans. Mostly Einnar's clan, as few had traveled with her from her village. Just her father, brother and barely a handful of friends who would attend her tonight.

Her fingers clenched on the flagon of mead. She lifted it to her mouth and took a long swallow, hoping it would steady her nerves. Instead it only made her stomach roll more ominously. Einnar turned and gave her a leering grin. She forced a smile in return, relieved when he ignored her once again.

The bridal crown weighed heavily upon her, squeezing until her head pounded. When the crown had been presented to her that morning, she'd been well-pleased with the beauty of the headpiece. Made of ash branches and woven with flowers, she'd felt beautiful wearing it. But now, after all these hours, the crown had become cumbersome and uncomfortable.

From the moment her father had announced the marriage arrangements, she'd dreaded this day. Marrying outside of her clan had always been anticipated; she'd known she must make a match to better secure their survival. But she'd harbored a secret hope she would find her husband pleasing. While Einnar was a truly handsome man, Geira had been wary of him from the moment she'd arrived in this village a week earlier.

A shriek behind her drew her attention. Her eyes widened, her gut churning anew. Einnar's father forced a servant girl to the table, spreading her legs and using her in full view of the assemblage. While it was clear the girl had no liking for the act, her protests ceased amid the cheers and encouragement drowning out the music. Not that any would defend her, as a female slave, an *ambátt*, the girl had no choice. Warriors and women alike hailed the chieftain's actions, taking great enjoyment of the girl's brutalization. Geira's gaze slid to the chieftain's wife, seated beside her husband. The woman stared straight ahead, chin high, despite the spectacle beside her. Geira recognized the misery and resignation in the other woman's eyes. Would that be her, years from now?

Einnar leaned over. "You're a lucky girl. I learned much from my father."

He turned, adding his own ribald shouts to the chaos. Geira trembled. Unable to look away from the chieftain's exuberant rutting, she feared her new husband would treat her with similar brutality.

She looked for her father. His seat was empty. Where had he gone? Her brother also seemed to have vanished. A chill swept over her. Surely they wouldn't abandon her to this cruel debauchery.

One of the village skalds rose from his seat at the trestle tables filling the hall. Strumming his harp, he recited a humorous poem about Loki and how he was tricked by his fellow gods into trapping himself in a cave. Geira laughed with everyone else when the tale ended describing how the mischievous god had freed himself, though not without mishap, leaving him covered with honey and chased by bees.

She reached for a piece of beef, roasted to perfection, from the platter before her. She had to admit, Einnar's family servants prepared a fine feast. She reached for the plate of beets, surprised when Einnar turned, catching her hand.

"I will serve you, wife." He gave her a wink. For a moment, his courteous gesture dulled her worries. Then the heated lust returned to his eyes, rousing her doubts once more. Still, she said nothing, watching him pile the vegetables onto her plate.

The dancing continued, but all too soon, fighting contests broke out among the drunken revelers. Two of Einnar's warriors faced off, laughing and swaying unsteadily on their feet before charging each other. The men wrestled each other to the floor, shouts and curses filling the air as the onlookers chose sides. Finally, one of the men rolled to his back, eyes closed, while the other stood, raising his arms in victory.

Another contest began, this one between a shield maiden and a warrior. Geira grinned as the woman easily defeated the much larger man, using her lesser size to her advantage, surprising her opponent.

Once again, her gaze swept the smoky longhouse. Still no sign of her father or brother. No one else appeared to notice the empty seats on the other side of the chieftain and his wife. A tremor of alarm crept up her spine. Where had they gone?

A hand on her shoulder jolted her from her worry. She turned to see Dota, an expectant smile on her face.

"Come, Geira, it's time!"

The excitement in her friend's voice drew a smile, no matter Geira's uneasiness. Einnar turned. His gaze raked over her, returning to her face. The lust there drew a shiver.

"I cannot wait! I will see you shortly, wife." He grabbed her hand and pulled her close, lowering his mouth to hers, as he'd done a few times before. Despite her reservations, she felt no revulsion. In truth, she felt nothing. Maybe she could endure.

He released her and she stood, legs trembling. The sudden hard swat of Einnar's large hand on her bottom nearly made her stumble. She gave him a glare, which earned her only laughter in return. Lifting her chin, she turned, allowing Dota to lead her from the hall. As they made their way among the tables, past the dancers and several men engaged in an insult contest, Geira searched again for her father and brother. But they weren't anywhere to be found. She barely had time to focus on where and why they had disappeared before she was outside in the cool evening air, welcome after the oppressive and smoky heat of the longhouse. The soothing chill pronounced autumn had arrived.

Dota tugged on Geira's arm, pulling her close. Leaning over, she whispered.

"I've heard your husband is quite skilled in the marriage bed."

"I've not heard the gossip. What have you learned?"

Dota giggled, her gaze darting to the women surrounding them. The few who had accompanied them from her home walked alongside several other women. Part of her new clan. More laughter and whispers hovered around her and Dota, though most of the attendants hung back. Geira wondered at their sidelong glances and turned back to her friend. Dota continued to grin.

"Those who have lain with him say he is quite large and knows well how to wield his sword." Dota laughed again, dark eyes twinkling with merriment. "You're very lucky."

"Who said this? Is it one of them?" Geira gave a tiny nod to the women trailing them. Dota shook her head, her gaze darting away. Geira had the sense her friend hid something of import. What?

"Before now, he was unmarried. No one expects a warrior to ignore his urges."

Shouldn't the idea that her husband's past lovers could be attending her tonight trouble her? She found she didn't quite care. She looked to the heavens. Surely, Freyja would smile upon her, give her something to stir her emotions. Yet, no sign had yet appeared.

Passion. Geira wanted passion. Doubt her husband might spur such desire plagued her thoughts, rousing a moment of despair.

She stopped short, grabbing Dota's arm, forcing her friend to face her.

"How am I lucky? Tell me who can advise me on the best way to lay with my husband."

Concern about her husband's honor rose again. If only she could determine exactly why she worried. Mostly, Einnar had shown her nothing but kindness. While his cruel streak had been clear in his dealings with others, he'd always been properly considerate of Geira. Until tonight, when his attention had turned bolder. Harsher. Maybe it was the excitement of the celebration that changed his demeanor from respectful to expectant. Or maybe he'd simply been waiting until she could no longer deny him. Apprehension loomed, much as she tried to ignore it.

Dota quickened her pace, fingers tightening on Geira's arm, seeming in a hurry. "Trust him to guide you. He knows well how to please a woman."

Dota stared straight ahead, and a strange uneasiness shivered over Geira. Again, she had the sense her friend didn't share all she knew.

"How do you know this?"

The cloud-obscured moonlight made it difficult to clearly see Dota's face. "The whispers. I told you."

"Why did no one share this with me? Why did they tell you?"

Dota hesitated, clearing her throat. "To be honest, they worried they would frighten you. As your friend, they shared with me what they wish you to know."

Geira stopped and turned to face the women trailing them. "Which of you has lain with my husband?"

The giggles and whispers stopped abruptly. She peered at each of the women, but none answered her question. She folded her arms.

"I will not hold it against you. Until today, he was not my husband. But he is now. And if you can share anything with me that might make tonight... easier, please tell me."

More silence. Only the riotous sounds of the feast carried through the night air. Geira pressed her lips together and shook her head. She would get no help here. Dota tugged on her arm.

"Hurry or your husband will be at the hut before we are!"

Geira allowed herself to be pulled along, across the village square to the bridal hut which had been prepared for this night. She and Einnar would reside here for the next month, while the celebration and feasting continued. By then, winter would be near, and she and Einnar would move into the longhouse for the long months ahead. Another shiver at that thought. At least in the bridal hut, it would only be the two of them. The idea of sharing a home with the chieftain and his family left her anxious and unsettled. Maybe by the time the wedding celebration had ended, she would be more at ease with the change.

If only she could silence the voice in her head warning her of the misery her life might become.

***

Kori stood at the water's edge. Máni, the moon god, hovered behind wispy clouds, enough to soften the bright light, but not obscure it. Enough to allow Kori a clear view of tonight's journey, the end of the voyage begun a week earlier.

Across this inlet lay his enemy's village. He'd waited two long years for this night. Today's goat's blood sacrifice to Thor strengthened his confidence in success. Tonight, he would destroy his enemy and take everything dear to him. As had been done to Kori.

Word from a trader had come during planting time that Einnar of Fellskoger was about to take a bride. Kori's father, Jarl Thorfinn, had given his blessing for Kori's plan. The last months spent preparing for this raid before winter set in had been Kori's only focus. Each night, he wished his daughter sweet dreams, knowing his words did little to soothe the hurt and despair in her gaze, intensifying his anger. Avenging his wife would surely chase the misery he always found in his daughter's eyes. How he missed the mischievous sparkle.

His brother Hradi stepped up beside him. "Your honor will be restored tonight."

"Yes. The blood sacrifice will ensure it."

"The men are anxious." Hradi sucked in a deep breath. "It's a good night for a raid."

Kori gave a grim smile and nodded. His clan's warriors had not had the chance to raid for many weeks. They would be ruthless tonight. As would he. His body tensed in excitement. He imagined Borga watched over him, gave her blessing.

He studied the small rowboats bobbing at the shore. While not his preferred method for sailing, he'd carefully planned every leg of their journey to ensure no one would be able to find them once the attack was over. The rowed oselvars would be destroyed by the time the sun rose tomorrow and Kori and his men, and their bounty, would vanish into the mountains.

"Come. We go now." He signaled his men then strode to the boats.

CHAPTER TWO

Geira lay in the bed awaiting Einnar's arrival. After helping her into the sheer gown barely concealing her body, Dota and the other women had left to seek him out. They should have returned by now. Dread warred with excitement, neither gaining an edge. She should be thrilled with her new status, but the ominous chill still hanging over her muted her enthusiasm.

She thought back to Dota's earlier words. Her groom was a handsome man, and rumored to be quite skilled in the art of pleasure. Even so, she couldn't help thinking of the brutal way his father had used the slave girl. Einnar claimed to have learned what he knew from his father. She shivered, hoping her husband would be less vicious. She forced the recollection from her thoughts.

The match benefitted her in many ways and she would do well to remember that. Surely in time, she would come to feel fondness and affection for her husband, despite the uneasiness her fierce warrior husband caused when he looked on her. The concerns haunting her were likely due to his easily ignited anger, and the same stubbornness her brother possessed.

Once again, she remembered the first time she had met Einnar. Last summer at The Thing, the annual assembly of the local clans, she'd witnessed him win a brutal fight with an enemy. Afterward, her father's pronouncement that a marriage contract had been agreed upon between him and Einnar's father had left her surprised, especially since all had seen Einnar's dishonest tactics used to win the battle. (Yet), no one had demanded retribution for his actions. Over the long winter, she'd had much time to dwell upon it, finally convincing herself he'd done what he had to in order to defeat an enemy.

Another memory flashed, this one of what she had seen the other day. Was that truly Einnar with the servant girl? With his face half-turned away, Geira hadn't been sure, or maybe she had only tried to convince herself of her uncertainty, even as her heart told her the man taking the girl was her groom. The recollection compounded her concerns. She'd tried not to think about it again, but now, left alone with nothing but her thoughts, the uneasiness grew. She recalled the look in Einnar's mother's eyes earlier. The worry her own life would end up much the same knotted her gut. If only she could be sure. Instinct warred with reason.

A few days earlier, she'd mentioned her concerns to Dota about Einnar having concubines, but her friend had merely laughed, reminding her all men were the same, and there was little any of them could do about it. After she'd borne him several fine sons, Dota assured her that Geira might be glad for the concubines who would take her husband's attention from her. Considering the dark path her thoughts now traveled, she suspected her friend might be right.

Didn't matter anymore. She was now Einnar's wife and had to trust her husband. If only she knew his moods better, but in time, that knowledge would come. For now, she must hold onto faith her father's judgment of Einnar's worthiness would prove accurate.

Surely her father wouldn't sacrifice her happiness and well-being for this marriage, which brought a strong alliance to her clan. She'd voiced her concerns, but while he'd been reassuring, he had also been insistent. Accepting his wishes ensured the rest of her clan's security.

Where had he disappeared to? If her mother still lived, she would have attended Geira. But without the woman she missed dearly every day, she'd hoped her father would at least guide her into life as a married woman with a sign of his love and pride. Instead, he'd left her. His abandonment spurred a bitterness, followed by a guilty twinge of conscience. He counted on her to bring honor to their clan; surely his actions were not because he didn't care.

A moment's annoyance with herself raised the notion that maybe she should have protested this marriage more vehemently. Her wish to want time to know her groom better had not swayed her father. The alliance with Einnar's father was especially important this winter. Last spring, Geira's clan's crops had not been as bountiful as years past. Fellsskogar had fared better, even if only by a small margin. If Soren Sturlasson hadn't reached out to Fellsskogar's earl, offering the clan's ships and men for raids next summer, many in her small farm village would have died from starvation over the long winter months.

The final seal on the agreement came when she was offered as bride. A sacrifice to the virile heir, whose sons she would bear.

Her thoughts turned once again to the coming night. The earlier whispers and giggles of the women came back in a rush. Freyja surely smiled upon her, or so everyone affirmed.

Ha! She'd not felt the presence of the goddess of sensual delights once since her joining had been decided. Again, she wished for passion, knowing if she at least felt that, the marriage might be bearable.

Where was he? Frustration overpowered her uneasiness. Laughter and music echoed in the night. The celebration would continue for the coming days. Was Einnar still drinking and feasting? He would have plenty of time after tonight to partake. Why hadn't the women brought him yet? The pressure of the bridal crown on her head seemed suddenly too tight. A strange foreboding crept over her.

Her fingers twisted in the bedding. Finally, shouts and more laughter, louder and closer, broke her strange mood. Her heart raced. She recognized several of her attendants' voices. The time had come. The door banged open and Einnar filled the frame. His hair had again been neatly combed, his clothing adjusted so his sword could be seen in his belt. He grinned, his dark eyes hungry as they swept over her. Shouldn't she feel something, other than alarm?

"She'll give you a good ride!"

"Thor's teeth, you've got another feast for the coming night, Einnar!"

The shouts and laughter from his friends mingled with those of the women. Fire scorched her cheeks, but she forced a smile.

"Geira can tame the beast, can't you, girl?" Dota's laughing words drew more mirth. Geira gave a moment's thanks for having her friend with her on this momentous journey. Dota's silliness lightened her mood.

The teasing went on for several minutes while Einnar's friends removed his cloak and tunic. He paused, turning, his shoulders and chest swelling with pride. While her husband was indeed handsome, something about his gloating demeanor detracted from his looks. He gave her a sly smile, licking his lips.

Now his trousers pushed past his hips, Einnar took several more preening steps closer, to the delight of the onlookers. The roaring in her ears near drowned the giggles and ribald comments. He arched a hip toward her. She forced a laugh, feigning amusement, when the only true emotion in her body was apprehension. She tried to avoid looking at his shaft, instead focusing on his leering grin. A shiver crept along her spine.

"I look forward to teaching you the delights of marriage, wife."

Another shiver, accompanied by the earlier dread, now stronger. She tried, with little success, to ignore the flickers of recollection. Her fingers clenched. She knew what he wanted to hear, what words she was expected to speak.

"I… I also share your eagerness."

The scratchy whisper of her voice drew an arched eyebrow, followed by a knowing grin.

"Fear not, your maids have the right of it. I will be

gentle with you. At first."

He folded his arms, giving another turn of his hips that drew hoots and whistles. She kept her eyes focused firmly on his face, her efforts at ignoring the taunts and teases failing. Each sly comment stung like a hot poker into her spine. She resisted the urge to squeeze her eyes shut, resisted the image of his father's brutal conduct.

"Geira, you are a lucky girl!"

"If you can't handle him, I'd be happy to help!"

She should appear to be outraged, shouldn't she? Pretend to find humor in their words? Instead, she remained silent, surprised at herself for the lack of repartee. Too many suffocating thoughts smothered each other.

He stood beside the bed, the comments and laughter continuing. Somehow the noise faded, drowned by her thudding heart. Einnar held her stare, lust clear in his gaze. He leaned over and pressed a chaste kiss to her lips, amid more howls and whistles. She silently willed him to hurry, to remove her crown so the others would leave.

Instead, he continued to kiss her, the warm pressure of his lips calming her agitation. When he drew away, she found her fear had receded. Maybe her worries had been for naught. He stared at her for several moments then smiled.

"I now claim you in body as well as spirit." He reached up and gently removed the crown of branches and flowers. He set it aside and leaned close, running his fingers through her unbound hair. Another kiss stirred warm sensations in her belly and she found herself responding. This she could endure.

Einnar eased away and looked behind him. "We are alone now."

She peered over his shoulder and saw everyone had indeed left. A wave of relief came over her and she sighed. While some clans still insisted on having witnesses to the deflowering, she hated that idea and was glad his people didn't adhere to the old custom.

He sat beside her and reached for the pitcher on the table next to the bed. He poured the mead into a wooden cup and handed it to her.

"Drink, you'll be calmer."

That he showed concern now further perplexed her. The charming flirt he sometimes appeared to be made her curious. She peered closely into his face, finding only a troubling arrogance and expectation. Accepting the goblet, she took a large swallow. When she returned the cup, he did the same, then moved to climb under the blanket with her. His warm body pressed against her. Worry churned in her gut

"Geira, look at me."

She lifted her head, slowly, half-afraid at what she might find. Concern and tenderness softened his expression, though a strange gleam kept her worries roused. The knot in her gut tightened.

"I thank Freyr for his blessings. He clearly found my sacrifice worthy."

Geira recalled the gathering and spraying of the boar's blood. Her husband had shown great skill in the ceremony. The ease of the sacrifice assured a fertile marriage. Still, doubts about the joy to be found in the union lingered.

A gentle caress of her shoulder didn't stir further fear. It didn't stir anything. Her earlier yearning returned with force. Why didn't her husband inspire the passion she so longed for? Though her mother had been gone for several summers, Geira recalled the adoration her parents had felt for each other. Even if they stood just a few inches away, the love they shared had shone clear in their longing gazes. They always found a way to express their utter devotion, with a kiss, or a glance, or a sliding of their hands as they passed. That's what Geira wanted. But she didn't feel anything remotely similar to that now. Was that the root of her concerns?

Another stroke of his hand and she forced herself to concentrate, willing her body to respond to his touch. Surprisingly, it did, her nipples peaking into tight buds.

The sensation was far less intense than she hoped.

"We will share many pleasures in this marriage. Trust me on this."

His voice had thickened, deepened. His desire came easily. Why didn't hers? She took a deep breath, determined to hide her true feelings.

"I do, it's just –"

The door crashed open, screams of terror and pain now filling the air. In the doorway, a hulking dark warrior stood, sword raised.

Einnar leapt to his feet, diving for the pile of clothes where his own sword lay. He barely had a chance to raise it when the other warrior swung, forcing Einnar into a defensive position. Geira screamed, terror pounding in her head.

"Einnar of Fellsskoger, I claim my vengeance!" The invader's voice thundered within the small hut.

Geira scrambled out of the bed when the intruder fixed his furious stare on her. Cold fear pooled in her belly when he strode across the room. Another slice at Einnar sent her husband to the floor, clutching his gut.

"Einnar!" she shrieked and attempted to run toward him. The warrior caught her by the arm before she darted past. She kicked and pummeled him with her free hand, but he quickly captured her other wrist, forcing them both into his tight grip.

"Bastard! Let me go!" She looked over at her husband, who struggled to his feet, sword in hand.

"Unhand my bride!" His voice was not nearly as strong as before, blood seeping from the wound slashing his stomach.

Geira fought the urge to retch, focusing instead on pulling against the restraining grip of her captor. She swore at him, unable to free herself. His strength overpowered her, her attempts to escape futile. Hopelessness welled within, but she forced it aside, refusing to stop fighting, twisting and squirming against his hold.

"She is mine now, repayment for your crimes

against me!"

The booming words sent ice along her spine and Geira froze.

"What? No, I am not yours! Let me go!"

She caught Einnar's stare and her blood chilled. He knew exactly what this giant meant. Anger speared the fear, escalating her panic. What had her husband done? The earlier doubts flashed again in her mind. Had she been right all along, and everyone else so terribly wrong?

"Einnar, what does he mean?"

He took an unsteady step toward her, then another before collapsing to the floor. She screamed again, and tugged against her captor, surprised at how quickly he released her, making her stumble. Just as quickly, she was brought up short by the rope now binding her wrists.

"By the blood of Odin I will see you dead!" she swore. Fright left her limbs heavy and trembling. The strength to stand seeped from her legs, yet she somehow remained upright.

The warrior threw his head back and laughed. "You can try, but it's useless to fight."

"You killed my husband." She looked at Einnar's lifeless body.

"He earned it. He's lucky I killed him so quickly!"

Geira choked on a sob, drawn by fear of her own fate, rather than her husband's. "Please let me go. I don't know what this is about. I've done nothing to you. Please. Let me see to him."

A fierce stare accompanied a shake of his head. "He's dead."

Einnar's blood pooled beneath him, the puddle growing larger. Oddly, Geira felt no real sadness. Squeezing her eyes shut, she turned away from her dead husband.

The raider tugged on the rope, drawing her close, then bent, hoisting her onto his shoulder. She kicked and screamed, pounding his back with her bound fists.

He strode through the open door. Geira twisted and tried to free herself, lifting her head. She froze at the sight greeting her.

Everywhere, the huts and homes of the clan burned, the longhouse where the celebration had been taking place also eaten by flames. Judging from the screams, many people remained trapped inside. Her stomach rolled, sweat ran down her face, mingling with tears. Shrieks, shouts and the sounds of weapons clanging together filled her senses. Grunts and bellows of pain pounded her ears. The entire village was under attack. The acrid scent of smoke mingled with the bitter smell of spilled blood, nearly choking her.

Where were her brother and father? Perhaps their disappearance saved them from the slaughter now taking place. The urge to weep grew stronger. All around, bodies littered the ground. No! That wasn't... it was, she realized, recognizing one of the women from her village. An agonized howl escaped her. The warrior continued on his way and her clanswoman's body disappeared from Geira's view.

Terrified she was about to meet the same fate, she squirmed, searching the chaos, desperate to find someone to help.

"Papa!" she cried, hoping someone in her family would hear. But her voice was drowned by the sounds of battle, the screech and thud of weapons against flesh, shrieks of terror and agony, and wailing sobs. She offered a silent prayer to Thor to keep her father safe, wherever he might be.

As the giant continued to stride out of the village and to the water, she realized he carried her away instead of raping and killing her here. Why?

She fought again, pounding the man with her fists, trying uselessly to kick against the arm wrapped around her legs. His hand slammed into her ass, briefly startling her into stillness, but just as quickly she fought once more. Again, the giant's hand came down hard on her rear and she screamed her outrage. It did nothing to stop him. All too quickly, they were at the water's edge and he paused only to shift her before making his way to the boat anchored at the shore.

"No! Let me go!"

Her efforts to free herself failed again and soon she found herself on the oselvar, roughly shoved to a seat in the middle. Shocked at the speed with which she'd been captured, she fell momentarily still.

The calm of the water seemed a cruel joke against the sounds of the village's destruction. She looked around. Several more small oselvars sat nearby, bobbing eerily in the water. She wanted to scream her rage, but none would hear her over the din. The boat she found herself on was already manned and on the move when her captor gave the order to push away from shore. She started to rise, thinking to throw herself over the side, but the giant forced her to her seat once more, settling across from her. His legs surrounded hers, holding her captive. She looked around, but all other possible ways to escape were filled with men now rowing furiously.

"You are going nowhere. Disobey, try to flee, and you will suffer for it."

"Bastard! My father and brother will kill you for this." *If they still lived.* She forced the thought aside. Their disappearance from the feast offered a glimmer of hope that maybe they'd escaped the attack. If so, surely they would search for her.

He grinned, shaking his head. Her breath caught. Without the glowering fury in his face, she might almost think him handsome. Almost. If he wasn't such a monster.

"They'll never find me. Or you."

Fear chilled her heart. He reached out a hand to her face and she flinched away. The remnants of his smile faded.

"You can accept your fate and things will go much easier for you."

"What fate?"

His hand covered her cheek, sliding back to cup her head. He drew her close.

"Your new life. As my *ambátt*."

***

Kori watched the girl with fascination, pleased to find her pretty. He'd worried Einnar would take a sow to wife, but he knew he would enjoy this one. Odd though, that she'd only said her father and brother would rescue her. Did she not care for her new husband? Interesting. He remained silent, waiting for his words to sink through her obviously distressed thoughts. Her bright blue eyes widened, her mouth falling open in shock. She jerked free of his hold.

"I am no *ambátt*! I am the daughter of a fierce warrior, the wife of a chieftain's son."

"No longer. You belong to me now."

"You will never own me, even if you chain me, brand me and shear my hair."

He took that moment to run his fingers through her long honey tresses. Soft and silky, and shiny. The idea of cutting it away bothered him.

"I may let you keep your hair."

She sputtered and swung at him with her bound hands. He evaded the blow, his fingers fisting tightly in her hair. Her cry this time was full of pain. He tugged, twisting her head back and holding her in place.

"Do not make me punish you now, in front of my men. I have not the time to waste."

She scowled, but tears glistened in her eyes, shining under the moonlight. She nibbled at her lower lip, his gaze lured to the sight. With a muffled groan, he lowered his head, taking her mouth in a devouring kiss. She tensed and tried to break free, but he held her still, forcing his tongue between her lips.

She tasted of mead and delight speared him. To his surprise, her lips melted under his, her tongue tentatively dueling with his. Even better! When he released her, she seemed to protest. Her eyes darkened, horror lined into her face.

He leaned close once again, not surprised when she jerked away this time.

"You will do well, *ambátt*."

"My name is Geira."

He didn't tell her his, just nodded.

"You will pay for this!"

"Silence, *ambátt*."

He folded his arms, daring her to protest further. She didn't, but fixed a stare on him that if it contained daggers, promised he'd be in the grip of death throes. He'd best remember to keep any

weapons out of her reach.

CHAPTER THREE

Geira watched the shore and the burning village grow smaller in the distance. Her new home, and possibly her family, was gone.

She glared at the giant sitting across from her. He still refused to tell her his name. She knew why, she was no fool. She would never call him master. When she was saved, she would be the one to slice through his black heart.

Still, recollection of his kiss hovered in her thoughts, clouding all else. The notion that this raider inspired the passion she'd wished for earlier seemed the cruelest taunt of all. Had she actually enjoyed it? His lips had sparked an instant fire, her sex tingling with an odd anticipation. Maybe because logically, she knew he would take her innocence. Likely before the sun rose. Then why hadn't Einnar's kisses stirred such intense feelings? Her kidnapper's harsh touch shouldn't cause her to react in such a way, yet despite her fear and fury, lust had made its presence known.

Her fingers twined together. She could do little else, bound as she was. The water was too deep and they were now too far from shore for her to attempt to jump overboard. Not unless she wished to drown. She met her captor's gaze once more.

He leaned back, arms folded. His cloak and tunic were worn, but he brandished a fine sword, so his family must have some wealth. Why had he taken her? Vengeance against Einnar, clearly, but for what? Instinct warned whatever her husband had done, the deed must have been something terrible.

"Will you tell me why?"

He said nothing, increasing her frustration. He

simply kept his dark stare fixed on her. A shiver passed over her and it had nothing to do with the chill in the night air. Autumn had arrived and soon, winter would follow. If she didn't get free soon, she would be trapped with this giant for the long, cold season. Yet, the notion of sharing a bed with this man for the months ahead didn't inspire terror. Why not? The thought of Einnar claiming her body had terrified and repulsed her. Why didn't she fear this man in the same way? Some madness had taken hold of her and surely only due to the grave situation she found herself in. But she knew her predicament was only half the cause of her scattered and inane thoughts.

He shifted, one hand coming down to rest upon his knee. She recalled the feel of those long fingers twisting in her hair. Even though the pain, his touch had electrified. Freyja's teeth, the goddess surely played a cruel trick.

Her gaze lifted, settling on his mouth before she looked away, staring out over the dark water, a strip of moonlight shining with unnatural brightness. Fingers on her chin turned her to face her captor.

"I am Kori."

She said nothing, too distracted by the feel of his calloused fingertips stroking along her jaw and neck. She fought to keep her breathing steady, but only half-succeeded. How could she want him to kiss her again? Had there been herbs in the mead that had caused this peculiar acceptance of what was happening?

"You are very pretty, Geira. I will be the envy of my clan with you for an *ambátt*."

The taunt dashed cold water on the heat his soft touch and intense stare stoked, bringing clarity with it. The bastard sought nothing but her humiliation. Anger pricked her, along with a hint of an unusual disappointment, but she forced the feelings back, needing to stay calm. Keep her wits sharp for a chance to break free. Exhausting herself would dull her senses as well. Still, she didn't have to accept his demands without some resistance.

"I am no slave."

"You are now. Einnar killed my wife, the mother of my child. You have been claimed in recompense."

"You lie!"

She shook her head. What he said wasn't possible! Even as she tried to deny it, she knew there could very well be truth in Kori's words. The knowledge seemed a cruel confirmation of her earlier fears.

Her reluctance to bring dishonor to her family had led to this. If she'd shared the depth of her misgivings with her father, would he have given in and broken the agreement? Likely not, no matter how powerful her worries.

Through the days leading up to the wedding and feast, Einnar had shown hints of kindness. Surely that indicated he had some honor. Didn't it? Geira gnawed on her lower lip, trying to make sense of the conflicting man she'd wed. As much as she hated acknowledging it, she'd witnessed more cruelty than those few traces of decency.

"You do believe it."

She met Kori's knowing stare. The words seemed a taunt, even though no malice laced his tone. Still, she'd not give him the satisfaction of admitting her own doubts. Again, she shook her head.

"No, I don't." Her family's honor rested on her shoulder now. To deny any of them, even Einnar, would give her captor more power over her.

"Now you lie." He arched an eyebrow, daring her to refute his words.

She lifted her chin. "Do you have proof of what you say?"

"You can ask my daughter. She was there. She saw everything."

"A child's word to prove that of a kidnapper and murderer?"

"If my brother had not arrived, he would have raped my daughter before killing her, as he did to my wife. Thora is lucky to have been saved."

Geira's stomach rolled. Would Einnar rape and murder a child? Was he that savage? She didn't want to believe it, but the idea refused to be completely silenced.

"She must be mistaking him for someone else." Yet, another flash of recollection eroded her denial.

"Does your husband bear the mark of Thor on his wrist?"

Geira feared she might lose the meal she'd eaten so many hours ago. She took a deep breath and willed her jumpy stomach to settle. "So do many other warriors. That is not proof."

"You refuse to see the truth. No matter. You are mine now. And you will perform the duties of my wife and provide for my needs. In every way."

She gulped, dread tightening her chest. At the same, his meaning stirred the earlier heat. Her breasts felt heavy and hard, nipples poking against her gown, the one made for her wedding night. Now it was dirty and torn. Lowering her head, she choked on a sob. How had everything gone so terribly wrong? Mayhap she should have refused Einnar more vehemently. Then she wouldn't be trapped on this boat, with a hulking man who sparked more emotions than she'd ever thought to feel. She was tired, exhausted from the ordeal. That explained her scattered senses.

She looked back once again at the fading shoreline. Flames continued to burn, lighting the night sky. Had Kori's men killed the entire clan? Fear for her family's safety once more brought the hope they'd escaped the carnage. Still, the reality of knowing so many died in the raid cooled the fire of her captor's words.

***

Kori studied his slave, remorse slicing through him. She was an innocent in this battle and he would do well to remember that. She defended Einnar as he'd expected she would, but he'd seen the realization in her eyes. He admired her loyalty in supporting his enemy and hoped someday she would feel such loyalty for him. Not that it mattered. She was his, claimed in revenge as was his due. Besides, with her husband dead, she no longer had a home to return to. She'd mentioned a father, and brother, but if they survived the attack, they would not know where to begin their search. If, by the tiniest chance, they succeeded in finding his village, Kori knew it would be too late. She would be his in every way, caring for him, his daughter and his home. He looked forward to the months ahead, when he'd secure her to him. Her husband had aligned her family with his, making them his enemy as well. Watching her renounce them would bring him enormous pleasure.

He also sought another sort of pleasure, one he would indulge. Soon. Thor's blood, he wished to take a more direct route and return to his home now. His attractive *ambátt* had stirred him in ways he hadn't been since Borga had been killed. While he had taken advantage of slaves and other women to satisfy his carnal desires, none had enthused him as this fair woman before him. Her wide blue eyes, her flaxen hair, the curve of her bosom, all lured him in ways he thought he would never feel again. He would slake those desires. Before the sun came up.

The urge to kiss her again came upon him with such force, he had no thought to resist. He captured her face with his hands, holding her still. The clarity in her eyes told him she recognized his intentions, yet he detected no resistance, merely curiosity and eagerness. Did she know the power of her innocent allure? He considered the thought for half a heartbeat then took her mouth with a hunger that threatened to consume his very soul.

He tasted, he teased, stunned at her response, willing and full of heat. Her lips burned against his and the urge to throw her to the deck and take her now nearly overcame him. He fought the compulsion, knowing in a few short hours, she would be in his arms, and he would be within her body, no matter her choice.

The idea he wanted her to enjoy their coupling startled him. He never slowed his assault on her mouth, driving deep to taste the heat that was solely hers, his mind whirling with the ways he would bind her to him, more than any ropes or chains. The ultimate revenge would be to make her crave his touch, make her want him over any other.

He drew away, pleased with the way she tried to follow, her moan of disappointment telling him more than she likely wished. While she was a weapon to be wielded against his enemies, she posed a very real threat to his soul. How he knew, he couldn't absolutely be sure. He prayed to Odin for the strength to survive the maelstrom he feared this woman would bring to his life.

Kori glanced over his shoulder. The flames burning Einnar's village grew smaller. The knowledge his enemy now lay dead eased a pressure in his chest he'd carried with him for the last two years. The threat there had finally been put to rest. She warned of her father's wrath. First, the man had to survive. Odds were slim. Yet, he knew little of her father. He must remedy that immediately.

Would her sire be able to launch a raid to rescue her? She'd declared him a chieftain, and as the son of an earl himself, he knew well the resources and allies available to someone of such stature. He should have stayed to ensure his orders to leave no one of import alive had been completed to his satisfaction.

He turned back to the woman before him. She watched him warily, but he expected that at the very least. She'd been stolen away, on her wedding night, and claimed as an *ambátt*. Fear and distrust likely had a solid hold on her. He grinned, thinking of the fight she'd give him. He looked forward to it, perhaps turning her over his knee and reddening her ass first. He glanced at her bound wrists. For now, she would remain thus.

"Where are you taking me?"

"You will see."

"When will we get there?"

"Soon enough."

He could swear she growled, and he chuckled. "You have fire, girl. I'll enjoy that."

"I'd rather die than let you rape me."

"It won't be rape."

She lifted her chin. "I'll not lie with you willingly."

"We shall see."

He leaned in again, and at almost the moment his mouth pressed against hers, she reacted eagerly, lips parting without any effort from him to compel her. As if she realized her response, she attempted to jerk away, but he cupped her head, holding her still as he swept her mouth once more. His cock hardened, much too quickly. He shoved her away, chest heaving. She drew her arm across her mouth, as if wiping away his taste. Then she spit in his face.

"Pig! You will pay for that."

He wiped his cheek and slowly shook his head, fixing his fiercest glare upon her. Fear returned to her gaze.

"No. You will pay. In more ways than you can imagine."

"Are you going to make her a public slave, Kori?"

He found himself forcing a laugh at Geira's reaction to Bjorn's question. For some reason, her wide eyes and the panic lining her face sparked an urge to pull her close and reassure her he had no such plans. He didn't. Showing such weakness was unacceptable.

"Haven't decided yet. You'll be the first to know. After I've sampled her."

He held her gaze steadily while he spoke, savoring her snarl. Her eyes sparked with anger and hatred. Aye, this woman would be a delight to tame.

***

The thought of being a public slave, lent out to anyone, for any use, had not entered Geira's head. She knew he meant to take her himself, but she had no idea what he was truly capable of. Would he let her be used by all the men in his clan? She shuddered and looked at the men frantically rowing them further and further away from her home. No, her husband's home. She thought of Einnar, lying motionless on the floor of the wedding hut. A bride and a widow, all in the same day.

Another glance at the burning village reaffirmed she had no one but herself to depend on, To survive, making him desire her enough to want to keep her for himself was her only hope. That and to pray to the gods to spare her family and send them to find her.

The knowledge of what she must do brought a moment of shame, but she tossed the thought aside. Surviving with as much dignity as she might manage must be her only goal. She was the daughter of a powerful warrior, and her marriage had aligned her with another powerful clan. For her people, and those she had sworn to take as her own, she must show the strength expected of her, endure whatever trials she faced. All the gods in Valhalla would be proud of her, living with whatever semblance of honor her sacrifice would bring.

Still, she must use caution. Giving in too easily could work either for or against her. She'd fought him until now; to suddenly acquiesce to his demands could make him wary. He likely expected rebellion and resistance. He certainly made it easy to give both, his constant attempts to humiliate her rousing her anger. If only he didn't rouse her body as well. In his bed, she would surrender to whatever he wished. Outside... no one would ever know her plans.

"We'll reach shore soon."

Kori's statement broke through her concentration. She remained silent. Despite her calm planning, panic lurked beneath, threatening to burst free in screams of terror. She shouldn't enjoy the firestorm of sensations her captor stirred. But to act on those feelings might be her only hope of survival. Should she not find some taste of pleasure?

"Where will we go?"

"My village. In the mountains near Albura."

She knew nothing of the area he spoke. While her father and brothers had gone a-viking many times, she had never ventured further than Einnar's village, only a few day's wagon ride away from her own. She wished she had listened more closely to her father's plans before they'd departed for their adventures. She couldn't see the shore anymore. Nothing surrounded them but deep, dark water. She stared at the waves, illuminated by the moon. The splashing of oars in the water grated on her ears.

The murky water seemed to send a message, one she didn't fully understand. Or perhaps she didn't want to understand. The one sure way to avoid shame and slavery fought to be heard over the roaring in her ears.

Could she? She swallowed a jagged lump. She didn't want to, truly she didn't, but the idea of her life spent in an endless cycle of abusive slavery spurred a despair she'd never thought to know. If she ended her life now, she could save herself that. Yet, fear battled against the call of the sea. She didn't want to die, not really. Would she be viewed a coward if she leapt from the boat and allowed herself to drown?

A hand on her arm stopped the chaos in her head. She met Kori's dark stare. He shook his head.

"Don't even think it. You will not succeed, should you try. If you jump into the water, I will pull you out myself."

She had no doubt he would do exactly that. He wouldn't allow her the mercy of a quick death.

"I had no plan to jump."

"Didn't you? One thing I will not tolerate, *ambátt*, are lies. Each one you tell will earn you punishment. And I am not a kind master."

"No, you're a monster. But by Odin's will, I will free myself."

He grinned again and she had the odd thought he

was attractive, for a savage. More ideas sprouted, and she knew it would only be a matter of time before she fled him. She would likely need all of the days of the upcoming winter to plan, but by spring…

"You'll be a fool to try."

"I am no fool. But I will prove you one."

Behind them, one of the men laughed.

"Kori, careful with her. She'll strike when you sleep."

"She'll not be given the chance."

His grip on her upper arm tightened, a warning, or to ensure his words were believed? Either way, she must use caution and never give a hint of what she planned. This ordeal would end with her on the victor's side. Her chance would come one day and the less she resisted, the easier and sooner her escape would come. She held back a smile, recalling how her brother Brosa had taught her to creep through the forests without making a single sound. That skill would serve her well. And if she ever got her hands on an axe or dagger… she was no shieldmaiden, had none of her brother's experience, but she could manage if need be.

She eyed his sword. Clearly, he possessed wealth, though how much she couldn't be sure. He'd claimed himself a chieftain's son. Whose? Could his clan possibly be an ally of her father's?

Aware her captor still studied her, she lifted her chin. "You'd best heed your man's warning. I am not without my own power."

The sly smile parting his beard sent a shiver along her spine.

CHAPTER FOUR

Kori's men drove the boat to a halt in shallow water. Leif jumped into the lapping waves with Erik and pulled the boat onto the sand. Kori waited until the others jumped to the shore before rising from his seat. He reached for his *ambátt*. She jerked away, but had nowhere to go. His grip firm on her arm, he pulled her from the seat. He bent and slung her across his shoulder again. She shrieked in outrage, legs flailing, despite the way he held them tight. He slammed his hand against her ass. Another shriek, but she momentarily stilled.

"If you wish to find yourself in the water, keep fighting."

He didn't wait for a response, leaping from the boat into the sands of the receding tide before she once again tried to free herself. He pulled her down to stand before him. She swayed a moment then straightened, chin tilted up in defiance. He grinned.

"We walk from here. You can go along willingly, or I will carry you."

"Don't touch me. I'll walk."

She sneered, her eyes sparking with anger. With a toss of her head, her mane of fawn-colored locks floated like a cloud. He fought the urge to bury his hand in the tresses and haul her mouth to his. He couldn't afford to waste the time.

Her fire delighted him. Anticipation to make camp took over his thoughts, his body aching to take hers. He forced himself to quell his excitement. They had a ways to go before he could indulge in pleasure. He caught the trailing rope from her bound wrists and headed into the trees. The trail that snaked through the forest was barely visible, but he and his men knew it well enough now. He pulled his slave behind him as he wound through the trees. A moment's resistance quickly faded and she fell into step.

Several times during the long trek, he looked over his shoulder to check on her. Her flimsy bridal garment did little to keep out the chill of the late summer air. She made no complaints, keeping up with his stride, but every now and again, a pain-filled grimace creased her face. Thor's bones, how could he be so careless? He glared at her bare feet. No wonder she'd been slowing. He moved closer.

"You have no shoes."

"Because you kidnapped me while I was preparing for my wedding night, you stupid beast!"

He chuckled. "We have no time to stop now. I'll carry you."

She shook her head, backing away. He held tight to the rope, preventing her flight.

"You have no choice. We'll make camp soon. Besides, I'm anxious to see just how valuable a slave I now own."

Her outraged protests only drew more laughter from him, as well as from his men. He bent and once more slung her over his shoulder. Within moments, he resumed his venture into the forest.

The moon had moved further across the sky when Kori gave the word to halt. He lowered Geira to her feet and she swayed unsteadily. He caught her as her legs gave way. A call to Leif sent a blanket tossed his way. Kori caught it and wrapped it about Geira's shoulders. Then he settled her at the base of a sturdy pine.

"Thank you."

Her soft words were almost lost on the breeze that kicked up at that moment. She met his gaze. Confusion wavered in her eyes. Though he'd explained it, she really had no idea what he expected of her. And while he knew part of her role gave her more power than she had yet to realize, since he'd laid eyes on her, his intentions had shifted.

Perhaps it was the time without Borga, but he knew

the idea a lie. He'd enjoyed several women, enthusiastically and with great satisfaction. Some had even shared his liking for the darker side of pleasure. Still, he'd been lonely. He must be careful, or this slave of his could undermine his entire life.

"Stay here. Don't try to run." He forced ice into his words, angry she made him feel things she had no right to. "You won't get far anyway. It will only get you punished, *ambátt*."

He turned away at the shocked anguish in her expression. His men expected him to act the chieftain and treat all bounty as goods. His *ambátt* was no exception. She was a tool, to be used in ways he still hadn't fully planned. It seemed the only sure path to supremacy. Revenge. His daughter demanded the repayment, she would have it.

Yet, when he gazed upon the beauty he'd taken as *ambátt*, he found himself imagining things he never should.

He turned to his men. They awaited his orders. He looked up at the moon hovering overhead. He would give his brother until Máni reached the trees near the shore. If Hradi didn't come then, he would travel onward, deeper into the forest, before setting up camp for the rest of the night. If his brother had led the rest of the men successfully, nothing remained of Einnar's village. Hradi would be sure to gather anything of value before departing. Kori calculated the time necessary for the task.

Maybe they should just set up camp here and wait for his brother and daybreak before continuing. He glanced over at the girl under the tree. She shivered, despite the blanket. The urge to warm her had his cock harder than he'd been in a long time. He made his way toward Erick, his gaze focused squarely on his slave.

"Tell the men to take a rest. We may make camp here. First, I need to tend to my slave."

Erik laughed. "Of course! Wish I could join you."

Kori shook his head, chuckling. "Not tonight. But

I'll let you know when I'm ready to share."

He strode over to Geira and picked up the end of the rope. He tugged, drawing her to stand before him. She met his stare evenly. He fought the urge to take her there. Instead, he turned and pulled on the rope, urging her to follow him deeper into the dense forest.

A cry behind him reminded him again she was not prepared for such a trek. He heaved a sigh, turned and lifted her to his shoulder.

"My head hurts like this!"

Her pained words halted him. He shifted her so she nestled against his chest. She'd seemed bigger before, somehow, but like this, she felt like a waif. He ignored the hint of contentment that arose and continued walking until he spotted the ideal cluster of trees. It made almost a perfect circle, near glowing in the moonlight, dappling the underbrush and blankets of leaves and pine needles. Once inside the grove, he lowered her to the ground. He released his hold on her rope and smiled when she inched away from him. A shaft of moonlight illuminated her face and he recognized the knowledge in her eyes.

He took two steps and stood before her. Thor's blood, the way she looked up at him had him ready to explode.

"Are you a witch?"

"What?"

The rasp of her voice sent another shiver of need to his cock. He bent and grabbed the end of the rope. He tossed it over a low branch, ignoring her protests. With slow and precise movements, he drew her up. Each tug drew another cry, her outrage more intense. Finally, she stood on tiptoe. Her eyes blazed with anger.

"Will you sacrifice me now?"

"I have no intentions of sacrificing you. I merely wish to make it easier to inspect my goods. Máni has smiled on me tonight."

Geira tugged at the rope, but he'd secured her well. He stepped up close. She tried to back away. He moved closer still. After several moments, her struggles to avoid contact ceased, and wearied by her efforts, she fell against him.

Her head tilted back and she met his stare. "I am not an animal to be inspected."

He grinned. "No. But that's why this will be so much fun."

She pressed her lips together, but when he ran a finger along her throat, she gave a sharp gasp. His other hand quickly moved to her breasts, not surprised to find her nipples hard and tight. He stroked her leisurely, pausing to examine her more closely. The garment she wore was tattered and it took a mere tug before the rest of the fabric fell away.

She shrieked. "I have no other clothing!"

He chuckled. "I know."

He resumed his exploration of her breasts, noting the way she struggled to contain all sound as he stroked and patted her creamy flesh. He gave each of her nipples a sharp pinch. That time a cry escaped, and he recognized passion in the guttural shout. He grinned, repeating the action and savoring the quiver that assailed her.

He took his time, running his hands along her body, noting each tremor or shudder she gave. After a bit, her skin grew damp, her breath quickened. He paused, catching her chin to hold her still. She cried out just as his mouth covered hers and the sound echoed within him. His cock ached, desperate to come. The feel of his slave's soft skin inflamed him further and he drew away, quickly stripping off his tunic and hose.

He resumed his position against Geira, groaning at the feel of her bare skin against his. He stroked himself, gritting his teeth to hold his climax back. He wanted to be inside her for that. Soon.

***

Geira tugged against the ropes holding her helpless before her captor. How she wished the heat coating her insides would recede. Instead, her nipples remained hard, aching for more of his touch. How could she like this? She'd known he would take her, but she hadn't expected to enjoy it so much.

His hands gripped her hips and he rubbed his hard shaft against her cleft. Her flesh slickened and swelled at the contact, intense sensations gathering and throbbing. His fingers slid alongside his cock, stroking her folds and she bit her lip to suppress the moan of pleasure. When he caught the hardened bud of flesh where need gathered and gave a gentle squeeze, she could no longer hold back. A loud cry escaped, despite her efforts to contain it.

His hoarse chuckle roared in her ears. "You like this, don't you girl?"

He continued to stroke her swollen and moist flesh. Geira had never known such pleasure. His cock rubbing against her, his finger tormenting her, whipped up a frenzy of longing that left her gasping. Her hips thrust toward him, seeking greater contact. Higher and higher, he drove the fire, until she feared she'd be reduced to ash. Still, the pleasurable pressure grew, until nothing else mattered but the sheer delight. She sensed an impending explosion, a frisson of fear at what might happen mingling with the excitement. But the yearning only intensified, and she found herself moving in time with Kori's cock and hand, anxious to reach the peak she soared to.

He stopped then, moving away. Her eyes fluttered open, her vision hazy with need.

"Not yet. You will receive your pleasure after mine."

She barely had a moment to consider what he meant when he resumed his casual inspection. She shivered, the loss of the heat of his body chilling her. He stepped behind her, his hands resting on her hips. Excitement at the searing touch sapped her will to remain aloof. His finger sliding along her spine drew a quiver, the tickling sensation as maddening as it was delightful. She bit her lip to hold back the plea for him to touch her that way again. Her sex ached, hungry, slick, nearly painful with need. She pressed her legs together, the pressure offering a modicum of relief. A moment later, Kori used his foot to spread her legs once more.

"Not yet, *ambátt*."

The hand on her hip squeezed. A warning? His other hand continued to stroke along her back and her frustration grew.

"Beast! May Odin strike you down for what you're doing!"

He said nothing, though a hint of a laugh echoed around her. Heat from his hand spread. A breeze across her bare flesh left her nipples harder than ever. He moved in closer, brushing her hair over her shoulder, his breath hot on the back of her neck. The scorch of his mouth there a moment later reduced her to shallow breaths and she twisted in his hold.

Fire from his lips cascaded over her and when he reached around her to cup her breast, she cried out, pushing herself into his hand. Her body had taken over all thought, and sought only the pleasure he stirred. The warning that she should protest, resist harder, faded until barely a wisp remained.

Freyr's blood, she wanted this, wanted the fury his caresses promised. His bare chest rubbing against her, the hard shaft pressing into her ass, his hands and mouth, soon had her writhing against him. His teeth caught the curve of her neck, biting, the sting adding to the tumult.

A sudden movement and she found herself falling, her arms now cut free. She barely had a chance to blink when Kori caught her, turning her to face him. He grabbed her still-bound wrists and hauled her against him. Her dazed senses had no time to react to anything but the force of his mouth as it crashed onto hers. Her fingers curled, fire swept down on her and she met his seeking tongue with her own, need and lust the only things she cared about.

A low groan rumbled from his chest. He caught her shoulders, pushing her down to her knees, spreading her out before him. All too soon, he rose above her, his silhouette blocking the moonlight. Geira held her breath, a moment of alarm creeping into the fog of passion. His finger stroking her sex chased the fear and her hips arched toward his touch. He took his time caressing and pinching, finally daring to slip into her moist tunnel.

"Oh, yes!"

The words escaped her before she even knew they'd formed. Kori gave another chuckle, his thumb catching her clit, circling until it ached with desire. Higher and higher, the pressure inside built, and she arched her back, anxious to taste the pleasure she could only imagine now.

"You are a surprising treasure, girl."

His words tempered the flames and she tried to comprehend, but he'd taken his hand away. She whimpered in frustration. Her body trembled, her pussy clenched almost painfully and her breasts felt full and tingly. She shouldn't like what he did to her, but she'd never imagined mating could feel this good. She wanted more.

As if he understood her thoughts, he lifted her legs, holding them wide. Exposing her sex to his cock. He inched closer, guiding her thighs around his waist, his hard shaft once more rubbing against her pussy. The fire grew into an inferno. She couldn't find her voice to tell him she wanted him to continue. Another moment's shame surfaced at how easily he had seduced her and was quickly chased by the feel of his cock easing against her flesh. He paused, then with one swift stroke, entered her fully, breaching her maidenhead and taking her innocence.

The sharp pain cooled the storm, and she cried out, gasping with the sudden invasion. If Kori hadn't been holding her so closely, trapping her within the confines of his body, she would have broken free and fled.

He stilled, raising one hand to brush her hair from her face. He held himself motionless, and she felt his gaze upon her. After a moment, her body adjusted to his penetration. The tension holding her eased. Her hands, caught between their bodies, reminded her of her helplessness. Yet she knew if she were free, she would be holding onto him, offering herself. She couldn't. He held all the control. She was nothing more than a vessel, to be filled at his whim. The notion brought angry tears to her eyes, even as the lust rose once again.

"It shouldn't hurt so much anymore."

Oddly, his gruff, almost careless words soothed her rising agitation. As if sensing her acceptance, Kori began to move. Geira's eyes widened. Almost instantly, her body returned to the peak she'd been floating atop before. But this…

If she had enjoyed his touch before, this was beyond pleasurable. He maintained a leisurely pace, and each slide within her body set off new tremors of tumultuous delight. He caressed her breast, pinching the nipple, harder and harder until she cried out. He repeated the motion on her other breast, making her flesh more sensitive than ever. He seemed to know exactly where and how to touch her to extract the most delicious sensations. She held her breath the moment he lowered his head to her breast, her sex clenching on his cock, still moving slowly within her. The rasp of his tongue against her hardened flesh added to the maelstrom and she tossed her head, afraid she would explode.

She realized she had locked her legs around him, her hips undulating against his, keeping pace with his increasing rhythm. He lifted his head, his eyes seeming to glow. Her heart pounded still harder. Her body strained, toward what she couldn't say, but she was too caught up in passion to think clearly. The knowledge she gave herself so willingly should outrage her, but the rising waves of bliss made her care naught. She would take her enjoyment from him, just as he took from her.

Sensation assailed her from everywhere, his fingers squeezing her nipples, his cock thrusting into her body, his mouth moving along her neck. It all left Geira breathless, anticipating the awaiting pinnacle. At that moment, Kori stiffened, his loud bellow echoing around them. His large cock throbbed and pulsed within her, and she knew he had reached his climax. He stilled his motions, breath heaving, and leaned against her.

Her body still raged, frustration and desire making her want to weep. He lifted his head, peering into her face. A brief smile lifted the corners of his mouth.

"You will do nicely."

The reminder of what she was to him dampened the flames, but desire still had a firm hold on her. Damn him! This was why she shouldn't give in so easily. He cared naught for her pleasure. She would not tell him of her need, lest he think she begged. But when he slowly withdrew from her body, a protesting groan escaped her.

He grinned. "I know what you want, girl. How badly?"

She clenched her jaw, refusing to respond to his taunt. He stroked a finger along her sex, and despite her intentions, her body betrayed her, moving closer to his hand, seeking more. He *had* made her a slave – a slave to passion, and in less than a few hours. A sob rose in her throat, choking her with the effort of holding the cry back. She *was* weak.

His fingers continued their torment, his other hand reaching once more for her breast. His stare burned into her. She squeezed her eyes shut, not wanting him to see the hunger she knew he'd find. A harsh squeeze of her nipple, a pinch of her sex and she once more rode a fiery crest that promised ultimate delight.

He continued his teasing caresses, the warmth of his body and the spark of his touch holding her at the edge of something glorious, something decadent, something... Fire exploded in her brain, in her sex, in her very spirit and she cried out, unable to contain the bliss cascading over her. Her body bucked in the whirlwind, lost to ecstasy none had warned her existed. Such delights were only for the gods, not for mortals and yet... Wave after wave flooded her trembling body, her only focus Kori's fingers moving rhythmically on her clit, making the tempest last until she couldn't see, couldn't hear, couldn't breathe.

The haze engulfing her took what seemed hours to dissipate. She fought the heaviness in her eyelids, catching his gaze in the moonlight. Her blurred vision slowly cleared, but she could only make out his outline, dark and overpowering. The intensity of his stare still burned into her thoughts. She turned away, uneasy about revealing how much she had enjoyed their coupling.

He slowly moved away from her and she shivered in the ensuing chill. He reached for his clothes and tugged them on. As the clouds in her head cleared, she recalled she had no clothing. He'd torn the remains of her bridal garb off her. She sat up, wincing at the prickle on her skin from being crushed against the twigs and leaves of the forest floor.

"Cover yourself with this."

He tossed the blanket to her and she caught it with trembling hands. But with her wrists still bound, the cloth proved difficult to wrap herself in. He gave an exasperated huff and tugged her to her feet, taking a few moments to adjust the cloth around her body

"Perhaps I will give you one of my tunics."

She nodded, her mind awhirl with all that had passed. A tenderness between her legs reminded her of the pleasure he'd given her. Her nipples tightened at the memory, too. He had ensured her enjoyment, known what she wanted, needed. Her worries had been for naught. His slave she might be, for now, but a common bond, one of physical delight, had been forged, giving her an advantage. Denying their passion was a waste of her time. She only hoped he felt the same and wouldn't share her. He tugged on the rope and pulled her to him.

His arms encircled her, his mouth taking hers again. In an instant, the inferno raged once more. When he drew away, she held back her moan of disappointment.

His studious stare seemed almost a tangible caress, but she kept her eyes closed, fearing he might detect the contradictory emotions battling for supremacy. Freedom must remain her only goal. Attaining it required her to behave carefully. Anticipate what he expected from her, rebellion or obedience, and give him what he presumed. He'd let his guard down sooner or later.

CHAPTER FIVE

Kori lifted his slave into his arms, his mind still fogged by the lust that had overtaken him. Being inside her seemed a taste of what living in Valhalla must be. Caution should be his guide. She had ensorcelled him somehow, in only a few short hours. Caring for her needs shouldn't matter, except for what he required of her. He needed someone to tend his home, help with the farming and take care of his daughter. She would slake his physical desires and her response to his touch had already proven he would much enjoy her passion. Often.

But he needed to keep her at a distance. The way she'd so easily drawn his affection alarmed him. He didn't understand it. He'd never feared his feelings for Borga, had reveled in them. But this woman, his enemy's bride, left him experiencing those sensations in ways he'd never imagined. She'd surely cast a spell on him, and he would need to make a sacrifice to convince the gods to break it.

He approached the small fire his men gathered around. They laughed and drank, waiting for Kori's orders. His grip tightened around the woman he held. Dark circles under her eyes betrayed her weariness. If the gods smiled on them, his brother would catch up soon and she could rest. A moment later, he silently cursed himself for caring for her comforts. Straightening further, he stepped into the glow of the flames.

"Set up camp for the night. Hradi and the others will be along soon enough, with more food and drink."

"Sure, they've got Gunnar to make sure they bring all the ale. With the celebration in the longhouse, he's sure to bring us a feast!" Leif lifted his skin and squeezed ale into his mouth.

Kori grinned as laughter echoed in the forest. His slave stiffened in his arms. The merriment had been for her marriage. Now she was here, no longer reveling in a happy occasion. Instead, she'd become a slave to a stranger. He didn't want her to fight him, well, maybe he did, thinking of how he could use her rebellion to his advantage. He tossed the thought aside. A large part of his satisfaction in owning her was earning her loyalty. Cultivating that required intricate planning.

He sat before the fire, shifting Geira so she sat between his legs, resting against his chest. He rather liked the feel of her warmth. Fatigue threatened but he held it at bay.

He looked up at the sky. Smoke from the inferno of the former village caused a haze around the moon. He heaved a deep breath. Tonight had been more successful than he'd hoped and he finally felt as if he neared the end of a long journey. He thought of Thora, crying for her mother, waking in the night with terrifying dreams of that awful day. His slave chose that moment to shift against him, snuggling closer. He glanced at her. She'd fallen asleep. Good. She'd need her rest. And perhaps, once she had been entrenched in his home, he and his daughter could find some peace as well.

The men still laughed, sharing their experiences of tonight's raid. Kori grinned too, listening to his friends and clansmen describe their victory.

"How was she, Kori?"

Leif's question silenced the men. They all turned expectant stares to him. He tightened his embrace around the sleeping woman.

"As sweet as ambrosia."

"I'd like a taste of that!"

Roars of laughter echoed in the forest. In his arms, Geira shifted, her eyes opening as she woke. She pushed against him, her efforts halted by Kori's arms.

"Easy, *ambátt*. We are still camped in the woods."

She shook her head, turning to look at him.

Confusion and sleep glazed her eyes, then cleared. She struggled more fiercely against his hold, but he squeezed her tighter until she stilled.

"Don't fight."

He barked the words, aware his men, though sharing tales amongst each other, watched him closely. She dared a look around and shrank back against him upon discovering his warriors ogling her. Kori knew they wanted him to share, but he found himself unwilling. Would they think him enamored of the girl, think him weak? The dilemma taunted him. He must address this now.

"Sorry, Leif, but for now, the girl is mine. If I change my mind, you will be among the first to have a go."

An outraged gasp escaped his slave. He held back a chuckle. When she squirmed again, he cupped a breast, squeezing. Another cry echoed around him, this one laced with a hint of desire. His cock stirred, the feel of her soft flesh under his hand tempting him. He continued to caress her, noting the shivers sweeping over her. He shifted her so she lay across him, giving him more access to her luscious body.

"Stop!"

He ignored her, watching her intently as he stroked her, her nakedness barely covered by the blanket. Despite her demand, her body quivered, instinctively moving toward his touch. He expanded his exploration, moving under the rough cloth to find the warm skin beneath. He trailed his fingers along her sides and belly, the softness of her skin an allure he worried might pose a danger to his wits. Her outraged gasps turned to moans and she bit her lip in an attempt to hide her desire. Kori saw well the effect of his touches. To confirm his suspicions, he slid his hand to her pussy. Sure enough, her sex was soaked with her juices. Catching some of her essence with his fingers, he circled her clit, noting the way her entire body stiffened. Her bound hands came up, fingers curling tightly into his arm.

"You like this, girl, don't you?"

She squeezed her eyes shut. He continued to stroke her pussy, savoring the hot moist flesh trembling beneath his hand. Her hips moved toward him, her breathing hard and fast. His cock had grown hard as iron. He needed to be inside her again. Soon.

With a groan, he withdrew his hands, hiding a smile at the moan of disappointment Geira failed to hide.

"Not now, girl. No more distractions, until after my brother arrives."

A soft sound erupted. A sob? He couldn't say, but it stirred a mass of conflicting emotions he didn't want to think about. He shifted her again, breathing a sigh of relief when his cock finally calmed.

"Don't fret. When we get to my village, I will let you savor the pleasure you seek."

"You are a pig."

"Aye, I suppose to your eyes I am. But you like it, too."

She remained silent, but the shivers running along her body told him all he needed to know.

An eagle's cry drew his thoughts away from the desire his *ambátt* stirred. But that cry didn't come from an eagle. He recognized the sound. His brother Hradi. Kori tilted his head back and responded with a call of his own, pleased when two more sounded in response. He grinned.

"Hradi returns! Our victory is complete!"

He eased the girl away and stood. She refused to look at him. The disrespect didn't bother him. It would likely take several more weeks before she fully accepted her lot and gave her loyalty to him. Anticipation of the coming days and nights of breaking her resistance roused an eagerness to be home.

Hradi, surrounded by a throng of warriors and shieldmaidens, came into the clearing hauling sacks of goods pillaged from Einnar's village. The gold and other bounty would bring his clan much wealth, enough so all of the men could have a decent share. He felt strongly the goods should be divided among his people, so all would have success and luxury, not just his family. His father had taught him the best way to maintain his people's loyalty was to show them respect. Not leave them struggling in poverty as many chieftains did, hoarding all the treasure for themselves. Kori had to agree with his father. Their clan suffered very little strife and dispute. Sharing rather than hoarding. It had been their way for generations. When an enemy struck against any one of them, they all rallied together. Just as they had tonight, to avenge Kori's wife, and restore his honor.

He gave his slave one last glance and strode over to his brother. After much embracing and congratulations on the success of their raid, he turned his focus to the pile of loot. He gave an approving nod.

"This will bring much prosperity to our clan. You've done well, brother."

Hradi grinned. "I think you've done well yourself. Is she worth it?"

Kori chuckled and turned to look over at his slave. His humor faded. She no longer sat where he'd left her. She dared try to escape? His anger rose as he searched the area, quickly spotting her. The dark blue blanket made it difficult to find her in the darkness, but the moonlight glinting off her fair hair betrayed her location. She moved quickly, and he took off in a run.

He gained on her rapidly, more familiar with the forest than she. She must have heard him near, for she turned, her eyes widening as she gave a little shriek, then with a burst of speed, hastened her pace. The girl was quick, but he was quicker and soon overtook her.

She screamed when his hand caught her arm, pulling her up short. She struggled and fought against his grip, but he didn't release her. She tried to swing her bound hands at him, but had little leverage to complete the task. He hauled her against him, lifting her so her eyes were level with his.

"You dare!"

"Bastard! Let me go! You've had your revenge, you killed my husband! You have no need of me!"

"*You* are my vengeance! *My* slave! To punish for daring to flee." He sat down on a fallen log, dragging her across his lap. She continued to kick and scream, cursing him so furiously, he swore she blistered his ears. Ignoring her protests, he caught her flailing legs between his, securing her. He moved aside the blanket, baring her ass. The outrage in her cries intensified. He gave a grim smile and lifted his hand.

***

Geira struggled against Kori's grip, but he held her securely. The bastard intended to spank her, as if she were a child! After a few more minutes of ineffective squirming, she turned her head, sinking her teeth into the hand holding her bound wrists. He let out an angry curse and clamped his hand on the back of her neck, immobilizing her further.

"Foul monster! Let me go!"

The sudden strike of his hand on her ass shocked her into stillness. The bite of pain drew a yelp, and she heaved a deep breath. Again and again, he brought his hand down hard on her flesh, and she pleaded with him to stop. Yet at the same time, the heat from the blows sent a strange tingling through her body. Oddly, her breasts ached, similarly to the way they had earlier, when he'd taken her. Her sex also responded in the most baffling way, swelling and slickening, hungry.

At the next strike, she found herself lifting her ass to meet his hand. This must have surprised him as much as it did her, for he paused, loosening his grip on her neck. She turned to stare at him through tear-blurred vision. She opened her mouth to speak, but the words fled when he abruptly slipped his fingers to her pussy. A dark eyebrow lifted and he gave what seemed an evil smile.

She lowered her head once more, ashamed that he

knew how his spanking had affected her. The disgrace faded under his devilish touch, sliding over her heated flesh and finding the hard nub of her desire. He squeezed and she cried out, more from frustration than anything else. He had driven her body back to the fever pitch of earlier, and logic eluded her. All that mattered was that he kept touching her, bring her that delirious pleasure he'd given her before.

Just as abruptly as he'd begun, he withdrew his hand. She bit her lip against the protest desperate to be heard. Another slap on her bottom drew a gasp. Her head spun, lost in the sensations of pain and pleasure, mingling together to create a fire she'd never imagined could burn so hot.

He continued spanking her, the heat in her ass intensifying with each strike. Another pause and he returned to her sex, stirring her as he had before. Her body moved of its own accord, pushing closer to his seeking hand. His chuckle sounded like a roar in the quiet of the forest. The bastard delighted in tormenting her this way. If only she didn't delight in it as well. Flames licked at her skin, and she strained against him, urging him without words to continue. She was close, so close, and her mouth watered at the idea of reaching the awaiting bliss.

But he stopped again. She whimpered and tensed, expecting him to spank her once more. Her bottom burned and throbbed, oddly in time to the clenching of her pussy, as if both sought more of whatever Kori chose to give her.

Instead, Kori eased her up. She swayed, the sudden upright position making her dizzy. He caught her before she fell and drew her onto his lap. At the first touch of her bare and inflamed ass on his leg, she cried out and tried to stand, but he refused to release her, holding her firmly in place.

Geira choked on a sob, holding it back. Did she cry for the pain or the fact that the need sliding along her veins nearly scalded her? Why had he stopped?

"You receive no pleasure for disobeying me."

"How can you expect me not to try to free myself?" Her shaky voice made her wince. She hated showing such weakness.

His chest heaved with his breath. "I suppose I should expect you to try and escape. But you are a slave, *my ambátt*, and I will not allow you to shame me this way. Besides, it's dangerous in the forests. You have no defense against any enemies or wild animals who will tear you apart. I won't let you deprive me of my slave."

"You are the cruelest bastard I've ever encountered."

"I'm sure you believe that. But if you obey me, you will be treated fairly. I need you healthy to tend my farm and home, and care for my daughter. Continue to disobey me and you'll not be able to sit for Máni's cycle."

Geira remained silent. Deep down she agreed she was likely safer with him than without, but she'd had one chance to get free before she suffered anymore, and had to take it. Besides, he would expect that of her, and she must be careful to behave exactly as he anticipated.

"Continue to cause trouble for me, and I'll punish you in such a way you'll never dare it again."

Ice slid along her spine. What did he mean? Various ideas flitted through her thoughts, each one more terrible than the last. He could give her over to his men to be used brutally, he could whip her to within an inch of her life. He could cut off fingers, or toes, or worse, to keep her from fleeing again. Caution must guide her as she enacted her plans to lull him into trusting her. After her flight, achieving that goal would take even longer. Still, she had to remain alert for any chance to escape.

When he stood, setting her on her feet and wrapping the woolen cloth securely around her once more, she fought the urge to burrow into him and seek comfort. Instead, she allowed him to grab the rope still keeping her bound and dragged her back to the camp.

They neared the group of men around the fire, the voices and laughter growing louder. Kori stopped beside his brother. What was his name? Hradi? Geira noted the resemblance and the warmth in the other man's eyes when he smiled at Kori.

"You've got yourself a fine slave, there Kori!" Hradi stood. He peered down at Geira studiously. An appreciative lust crept into his eyes.

Geira met his stare boldly. He wanted her. The notion sent a thrill skittering along her spine. Would Kori share her with his brother? Heat scorched her face at the idea, but oddly, the thought didn't terrify her as it had when she'd considered being given to the other men. The taunting voice in her head mocked her, her wish for passion now cruel trickery. Did Freyja conspire with Loki to torment Geira this way? Aware of both men studying her with desirous intent left her flustered and oddly impatient. Still, she fought the urge to flinch when he reached out to stroke his hand along her hair.

"She's lovely. You know, if you decided to sell her, you'd fetch a fine price."

She narrowed her eyes, clenching her jaw to silence the retort that hovered on her tongue. Her bottom hurt enough and she feared disrespecting his brother might tempt Kori into spanking her again. Her pussy heated at the notion. She shook her head, trying to clear the mad thoughts. Exhaustion played with the ideas running through her head, plaguing her wits as surely as Kori.

"I'm not selling, Hradi, don't even try to bargain. Thora needs tending, and she will do it. I haven't the time to find someone else."

Hradi chuckled. "Surely you'd let your brother have a taste?"

Geira gaped at Kori when he grinned. Surely he wouldn't go along with his brother's suggestion. The intriguing idea tried to force its way into her thoughts.

She tamped it down.

"Maybe. I'll think on it."

"You're going to make me pay, I can see."

The teasing words continued between the two men as they took seats with the others. Once more, Kori settled her against him, one arm carelessly slung across her chest. Yet she knew should she attempt to move away, he would tighten the casual grip.

Her lids drooped. The men's voices faded and she let herself relax against Kori. Despite the madness of the last day and night, she felt secure.

***

The telltale relaxing of her body told Kori his *ambátt* had again fallen asleep. He hated to admit having her here in his arms like this felt good. Right. As if the gods smiled on his decision to take her. Aware of his brother studying him, he turned.

"You are taken with her."

It wasn't a question. Still, Kori gave a terse nod. "I find her pleasing. She will warm the nights and take over Borga's duties in my home."

"Use caution, brother. One such as she could be seen as a weakness. One to be exploited. Watch your back."

"I have no worries. Einnar's clan is all dead." He fixed a pointed stare on Hradi.

His brother nodded. "We've brought a few slaves of our own, but otherwise, all are dispatched. I set fire to Einnar's hut. He is nothing more than ash now."

Kori gave a grim smile and raised his eyes to the heavens. "Thank you Odin for guiding me. My wife is avenged. May she wait for me at your side."

"In the meantime, enjoy your new slave."

Hradi's sly comment drew more laughter from the men. Kori grinned, caught up in their good mood and the success of the night. The woman in his arms shifted, snuggling against him, as if seeking warmth. He suddenly had plenty to share.

CHAPTER SIX

Geira fought the dark shadows keeping her in slumber. She shoved at the shrouds obscuring her vision, sucking in deep breaths as she struggled against the last vestiges of sleep. Warmth surrounded her, cocooning her, tempting her to stay. She forced her eyes open and blinked in the bright morning light.

A moment's confusion cleared, the events of the night before reminding her with sickening force where she was. The large body surrounding her held her captive, though she had to admit, there was nothing threatening about Kori's hold. Her back rested against his chest, his arms wrapped around her. He'd slung his leg over her hip, holding her lower body close to him. With nothing but the thin blanket covering her, his shaft, hard and hot, pressed against her bottom. She held her breath, startled at how her own body reacted. If she had been warm before, she sweltered now.

He shifted against her, his leg sliding between hers and spreading her. The bastard was awake, doing this apurpose! She squirmed in a vain attempt to break free of his hold.

"Shh, *ambátt*. I wish to enjoy you." His gravelly voice beside her ear was a caress of its own, sliding along her skin. "I'd not wake the others yet."

Her eyes widened. He would do this in front of his men? His hand slid along her belly, closer to her sex, and her worries fled on the excitement building within. His lips trailed on her throat, to her shoulder. She bit her lip, drawing blood in the effort to remain silent. He'd grabbed one breast now, kneaded it until a low moan finally escaped. He gave an odd sound, but she noted the pleasure in it just before he bit lightly at the base of her neck. Fire shot through her veins.

Fingers sought her pussy, and her hands clenched

in response, an attempt to keep some control over her response. He kept his touch light, building the storm slowly, until she trembled in his hold. Barely coherent warnings flashed, but she paid no heed as he explored her slick flesh, now swollen and hot. When he drew away, she whimpered, both hating and delighting in the way he tormented her. When he gripped her hips, pulling her still closer, she barely had a moment to consider his intentions before the head of his cock rested against her pussy. The heat from his swollen shaft sent her hunger soaring, even as admonitions strained to be heard in the maelstrom of passion. Eagerness had hold of her now and she found herself spreading her legs even wider, giving him better access.

Revealing her own delight should shame her, but she was past the point of caring. His lips and tongue still meandered over her shoulder, the rasp of his beard an added layer to the uproar assaulting her senses. She arched back against him. A swift thrust and he filled her, the sensation bringing a completeness that stunned her. No time to dwell on that as Kori began to move. At the same time, he reached around and stroked her clit. Starbursts exploded, her body bucking with the force of the crashing bliss, shocked by how quickly it had overtaken her. The pleasure never ceased as Kori continued, driving her to another peak, and another, until all she could do was quiver and moan and ride the torrents.

A hoarse grunt preceded the pulse of Kori's cock. She trembled and writhed against him, helpless against the whirlwind he continued to rouse. When the tempest passed, she lay gasping in his arms, her wits as dazed as her body.

"I think I shall wake you like this every morning."

His hoarse words shivered along her spine. She had no thought to respond, still trying to weave together her frayed senses. Kori's sudden withdrawal from her body startled her into awareness. Her gaze swept the camp, relieved he at least shielded her from his men. She remained still as he disentangled himself, then wrapped the blanket around her once more. He stood and held out a hand.

She reached for him then withdrew when the glint in the sunlight revealed the knife in his grip. She shook her head, backing away.

With a huff of annoyance, he reached down and grabbed her wrists, slicing the blade through her bonds. She stared blankly at him for a few moments, then cried out when the blood flowed back into her arms. This fire hurt, searing and tearing. Tears burned her eyes and she rubbed her wrists with stiff fingers, trying with little success to ease the sharp hurt. Kori knelt before her, pushing her hands aside to gently rub her tender and chafed wrists. Under his ministrations, the pain slowly receded but her hands still hung heavy and numb. No matter how she tried, they refused her commands to move.

"We travel to my village now. Come and eat something."

He helped her stand and guided her to the dying fire. The men were much quieter this morning as they broke their fast. Kori positioned her before him as he had last night and handed her a piece of flatbread and some dried herring. Her still-weak fingers almost dropped the food, but she forced her grip to tighten. After her first bite, she realized just how hungry she was and devoured the meager allotment quickly. Her captor gave her another portion, and she savored the salty fish, strength slowly returning to her fingers. A horn with ale was pressed into her hand. She quenched her thirst and handed the empty horn to Kori. She caught his gaze, startled by the amusement in his expression.

"You mock me," she accused.

He shook his head, his smile broadening. "No, I merely enjoyed watching you eat. I am thinking what it will feel like when your lips close around my cock."

Her eyes widened, an image of his suggested act

scorching her thoughts. The idea sent excitement slithering through her veins. Her voice refused to cooperate, so she turned away. His chuckle stirred heat in her cheeks.

He stood then, drawing the men's attention. Geira looked from one to the other. Most ignored her, but when her gaze laded on Hradi, she found Kori's brother watching her with interest. He looked much like Kori, but his dark beard was longer. His eyes, dark and intense like Kori's, also possessed a similar lust. Try as she did, she found herself unable to look away, captivated by his silent promise.

"We will divide our bounty when we return to the village." Kori's voice rang through the forest. "We are to meet Galinn and the other men tomorrow. They await us near the top of the mountain. From there, we'll reach the village in two suns."

Geira managed to focus again on Kori, unsettled by the way her body reacted to Hradi's stare. She should be disgusted, instead of wondering if his kisses tasted like Kori's, if his hands were as knowledgeable as his brother's, and if his cock was…

She shook her head. She'd surely gone mad! A rumble of laughter drifted to her, but she didn't dare look. When Kori grabbed her arm and pulled her up, she forced thoughts of his brother aside. She had more important things to worry about.

"Put this on."

He held out a dress. She knew he'd gotten it from the village, and nausea rolled her stomach when she recognized it as belonging to one of her husband's cousins. The poor woman surely now lay dead. Geira offered a silent prayer of thanks, and another for the woman's soul, wishing her peace in the afterlife. She tried to shield herself from the other men with the blanket, with minimal success, judging from the sounds of appreciation made as they strode by. She finally managed to pull the dress over her head.

A sense of relief soothed some of her worry. Her

hands remained free, she had clothing. At last, some dignity had been restored. Her bare feet poked out from under the dress. Before she could voice her question, Kori handed her a pair of laced shoes.

"Thank you." She accepted the shoes and sat down to put them on.

"I can't carry you all the way. A slave needs to walk behind her master."

Why must he always be so cruel? He'd shown her kindness this morning, as well as passion. Now he was her cold and aloof captor again. Just as well. She couldn't let herself be swayed by the times he seemed concerned for her welfare. She had to focus on her goal of finding a way to escape.

He caught her wrists in his hand. Disappointment flooded her when he once again wrapped the rope around them and tugged on the trailing end. He gave her a stern look before turning and walking along the trail. He kept a quick pace, taking a place at the head of the group. Geira stayed a step behind him, flanked by his brother. She stumbled once on the unfamiliar terrain, regaining her footing just as Kori turned to pierce her with a stern look.

"If you fall, I will drag you."

She glared at his back, imagining all of the ways she'd like to repay him for putting her though this.

***

Geira trudged behind Kori, trying not to fall far enough back that he needed to tug on the rope binding her sore wrists. While grateful for the clothes and shoes, her feet and legs still ached. After breaking their camp, Kori kept his men moving at a rapid pace, though that pace now slowed as they moved further up the mountain. Several times she had turned to look at the men following. She hadn't realized just how many there were, the line of warriors and shieldmaidens stretching farther back than she could see. There had to be close to one hundred in the band Kori led. Had he brought his entire village?

Where did he take her? He'd mentioned Albura, but where was that? Unsure of their current location, and with the sun hidden by the trees of the thick forest, she had no idea how long they'd been traveling. Hours at least. Weariness consumed every part of her. She wiped sweat from her brow with her arm, wondering how long this journey would take. Exhaustion made it more difficult to notice anything remarkable that might lead her back the way they'd come, should the chance for escape present itself. If only she could free herself from this damnable rope. In the beginning, she'd fisted her hands repeatedly, but numbness had set in some time ago, and she no longer possessed the strength even to wiggle her fingers.

Geira bumped into Kori's back when he stopped abruptly. He turned, catching her arms to keep her from falling.

"Ease, *ambátt*. We are taking a rest."

At his words, her legs buckled. Kori swept her into his arms and carried her to a large oak, settling her at the trunk. He searched her face, his eyes dark with concern, his hand sliding through her hair to cup the back of her head.

"Are you ill?"

She blinked. The urge to reassure him she was merely tired hovered on her tongue. She forced it back, her wits again sharpening. Remembering her plan, she lifted her chin.

"Ill with what you've done to me!"

Amusement softened his features and he chuckled. Before she realized his intentions, he hauled her close, covering her lips with a harsh kiss. She had no thought to resist, his demanding mouth coaxing fiery sensations that left her weak for different reasons. How did this man provoke her passion so easily? The brush of his tongue drew a sharp and immediate response in her core, her entire body roused under his onslaught. He near pulled the breath from her lungs when he withdrew.

She gulped past the lump choking her and looked away. For several moments, he remained kneeling before her, but she refused to look at him. Finally, he stood, fastening the end of her rope to a branch out of her reach. Her attempt at flight had made him more cautious. Which made her awareness of the journey more important. She must hold back the fatigue in order to properly concentrate.

"Stay here."

Keeping her face averted, she resisted the urge to rail at him for his inane words. He'd left her no choice but to remain leaning against the oak. Her numbed fingers finally clenched, the combined force of the passion he stirred and the anger he elicited giving her a modicum of strength. He stirred every emotion - anger, fear, desire - to its highest peak. She lifted her eyes to the sky, asking Freyja to explain why her captor inspired such acute feelings.

Several of his men passed near Geira, pausing to study her. She ignored them all. Her lips moved as she quietly prayed for her father's survival. Though all the recollections now blended together in a weird dream, she distinctly recalled the moment she'd first noticed her father and Brosa had disappeared. When Einnar's father had…

Had he left because he'd found the chieftain's conduct dishonorable? Why did he abandon her to such debauchery? And did the disappearance mean hope remained that her family lived? She must find some way to make a sacrifice to the gods, to earn their favor and perhaps a message about her father.

Shouts and laughter drew her from her thoughts. One of the men held a handful of coins, releasing them onto his head amid hoots of encouragement. Another raised golden pitchers. Still another held a jeweled necklace. Geira gasped. Einnar's mother had worn that necklace. While she shared no bond with the woman, Geira still mourned her death, hoping it was quick and that she now resided with gods, serving them and her husband.

"He had no part in that. He went straight for you."

She looked up to find Kori's brother standing before her. Again, the resemblance struck her, though Hradi was broader in the shoulder, yet shorter in stature. His words sunk through her confusion.

"What do you mean?"

"All he wanted was Einnar's bride. You. The rest…" He crouched before her. "Has he explained?"

She nodded, searching his face. "His wife was… murdered."

Hradi looked away for a moment. When he faced her once more, his expression tightened with anger.

"I arrived too late. Borga was already dead."

Geira stared, recalling Kori's words. Until this moment, they'd seemed a story that wasn't quite real. Looking into Hradi's eyes, Geira no longer doubted.

"The son of a dog was about to…" He growled, his lips curling in a sneer. "We hunted the vámr through the forest, but he escaped."

"When?"

He seemed surprised by her question. "Two summers past. His father protected him. We gained no retribution from the council at The Thing."

Hradi gave a grim smile, his eyes ablaze with a frightening satisfaction. "Now, Kori is avenged."

"But that was… I wasn't… I am not to blame!"

Hradi studies her for a few moments before nodding. "I know."

"Yet, he's taken me! Killing Einnar wasn't enough?"

"Kori has a daughter to raise. He needs a woman to help him."

Geira almost laughed, the idea ludicrous. "Surely there are others who can help that he didn't need to steal me away, turn me into a slave!"

"He did what was done to him, he took a man's wife."

"I am innocent in this war! I was given to Einnar. It

wasn't my choice!"

"Borga didn't have a choice either." His pointed stare held a message Geira hadn't yet dared to face.

Silently, she conceded her gratitude that she still lived. Hadn't been brutalized, despite her capture. That she shared similar sentiments about her husband as the man who was her enemy. No, that didn't seem right, somehow.

"You may find him a fair master." Hradi pierced her with a stare. "If you heed his orders."

"I am no slave. And I will be free!"

Hradi grinned, the smile transforming his scowling features into a handsome warrior. Her heart quickened.

"You've got fire, girl. I like it."

His low voice sent shivers along her spine. She clenched her jaw, horrified to find herself drawn to the twinkle in his eyes. Truly she'd gone mad to consider any kind feelings toward this man. At that moment, Kori walked up and untied the rope holding her bound wrists to the branch. Despite her efforts to resist the yearning he seemed to always inspire, heat raced in her veins. She looked from one brother to the other, unable to take a steady breath as the implications of these feelings sank into her consciousness.

She looked away from both sets of probing eyes, determined not to reveal the conflicted emotions knotting her gut. Was it really almost two days since she'd been wed? To her exhausted thoughts, it seemed as though months had passed. Worse, she found herself unable to clearly recall her husband's face. Every time she tried, Kori's smiling visage took hold in her thoughts. She bit hard on her lip, hoping the pain would distract her from these shameful feelings.

A waterskin appeared before her. Surprised, she met Kori's gaze. He nodded, urging her to take it.

"Drink."

Several moments passed as she debated why he toyed with her. The moments he showed kindness further muddled the conflicting sentiments she felt toward her captor. Still, her thirst was greater than her need to defy him, at least at that moment. She accepted the skin and raised it, her lips curling around the spout. Warm and musky from the warmth of the day, the water still tasted sweet as mead.

When she lowered the skin, it was yanked away, at the same time a tug on the rope drew her to her feet. She raised her gaze, meeting Kori's. His face no longer held no emotion, but the heat in his eyes served only to confuse her further. Without a word, he turned and led her back to camp. Hradi followed close behind.

When he reached the fire, Kori pointed to the ground. Fearing retribution, she held back a retort and lowered herself to her knees. Kori sat on the log behind her, his legs surrounding her. Any chance to flee was gone. For now.

She looked up at Hradi standing before her. He gave her a wink, then looked over her to his brother. With a nod, he took a seat beside Kori.

"We camp here for tonight."

Kori's pronouncement rang out through the clearing. Geira looked up, realizing the sun had moved almost all the way across the sky and soon, Máni would take its place when darkness fell. An entire day since she'd been taken. How many more before the journey ended? She both feared and longed for the answer. All she did know was that each step further into the forest, the harder it would be for her father to find her.

Kori leaned over and the glint of a knife drew her focus. She flinched away, but caught as she was between his legs, did not get far. She held her breath, letting it out on a rush when he merely sliced through her bonds. Her relief was short-lived, however, when her numbed fingers came back to agonizing life. Tears burned her eyes at the sharp pain and despite her intentions to conceal her discomfort, a cry went unchecked.

Two pairs of large hands closed over hers, Kori and Hradi each taking one and massaging it gently.

Slowly the pain receded and her breathing steadied.

"Next time, I won't bind you as tightly."

Was she supposed to thank him for that? She remained silent, holding back her angry response when he laughed. He ran a finger along her lips, pressed tightly together.

He looked away, a smile lighting his face at two of his men arguing, which soon escalated into the two warriors shoving each other. Hradi intervened, settling the tussle before it evolved into a true battle. Soon enough, a large fire burned and ale was passed around to all.

Once again, she marveled at the number of men accompanying Kori. She realized as their crude jokes and taunts flew through the clearing that her captor seemed the sanest of them all.

She leaned her head against his thigh, the weariness now impossible to resist. His hand on her head, fingers sliding into her hair, brought a strange sense of solace.

***

The sight of Geira's head nestled so close to his aching cock stirred a pain in his gut Kori had never known before. Despite the hardships she'd endured in the last night and day, she'd not once faltered, until he assured her they would walk no further today.

Hradi took a seat beside him on the fallen tree. "They've plenty of ale now. Convinced them to save the full celebration until we return to our village."

Kori grinned. A successful raid was always cause for festivity, but a long journey still lay ahead. Kori didn't want his men's wits addled by too much revelry. The welcome feast would last for days. His brother was a wise politician and knew well how to placate hot tempers, even if he possessed the fiercest of them all.

He glanced at his brother, but Hradi didn't pay him any mind. Instead, his gaze focused on the woman kneeling between Kori's legs.

"What is it?" he asked.

Hradi raised his gaze to Kori's. "Nothing. Just… she is innocent in this. As Borga was."

Kori looked away, jaw clenched tight. "I know. And she is lucky I have more honor than her husband. She'd do well to remember that."

He could have killed her outright, left her body beside her husband's. His plans dictated otherwise.

He'd sworn to drive Einnar's bride to her doom, but the fierce need to break her had changed somehow. He didn't understand it, and resolution remained elusive.

Aware his brother watched her with keen interest, Kori recalled the way his *ambátt* had looked upon Hradi. While apprehensive, he recognized an appreciative gleam in her eyes that shone through despite her exhaustion. This required further study. Her hair, soft beneath his fingers, tantalized him, distracted him. His divided focus narrowed to the woman between his legs.

She stirred, rousing from her light slumber. Kori kept his fingers tangled in her hair, knowing the exact moment full awareness brought her from her dreams. Her body tightened. He stroked her hair, an attempt to soothe her. For a moment, worry his men might see him as weak for taking care with her rose up, but he forced it back. Better to keep her calm and biddable, if possible. He smiled. He wondered how long it would take before she completely accepted her lot. Judging from the fire she'd so far displayed, he doubted it would be anytime soon. He leaned close to her ear.

"Are you hungry?"

She gave a little start, then nodded, still refusing to look at him. That would change soon enough. He ordered Hradi to fetch some of the hares and ducks the men roasted over the now blazing fire. While he waited, he continued to slide his fingers in her fair tresses. The fierce need to possess her again left him confused and wondering how a woman he barely knew, one who was merely a tool in his plan for vengeance, could inspire such desire.

Hradi returned with enough meat for them all. Kori looked forward to returning home and the feast to follow.

"Won't be any left soon." Hradi bit into a leg, juices running down his chin.

Kori pulled a piece of meat from the bone and handed it to Geira. Her fingers shook as she accepted the morsel, shoving it into her mouth. As he alternated between taking bites of meat and handing her pieces, he studied her. His longing only increased. He turned to Hradi.

"Tell me more about the raid."

Hradi relayed the success of the attack. All of the buildings had been burned to the ground, though not before every item of value had been removed. The village's warriors had been too deep into their cups to put up any realistic defense. Hradi estimated the raid had taken all of a few hours before the last of the clan had been silenced.

Kori sensed Hradi did not tell him everything. He folded his arms and gave his brother a probing glare. Hradi chuckled, looking away sheepishly.

"We've taken some slaves. Women, though I took none and warned against it. Bjorn and Hersir will likely sell after the winter, but it's Muli I worry about."

Kori nodded in acknowledgement of Hradi's mistrust of the cruel man. Muli's reputation for abusing his women, slave or otherwise, was known by all. If the woman he'd claimed survived until next spring, it would be only by the mercy of the gods.

Kori stared at his own slave. Her head now rested against his thigh, the softness of her body indicating slumber once more lured her. Despite his intentions to taste her passion again, he suspected his desires would not be met this night.

Despite his yearning, he knew it was better to let her rest. She'd endured so much in only a few days. As had he. His original plans seemed hazy and unclear, replaced with different intentions.

He stroked her hair. This growing affection could be a blessing or a curse. Kori hoped to decipher the puzzle before it was too late.

CHAPTER SEVEN

Thunder boomed overhead. Kori looked up at the darkening sky. What had angered Thor that he would reveal his displeasure during their journey? He'd hoped to cover more ground on this third day of their journey, but clearly the gods had other ideas. He summoned Hradi closer.

"Set up camp, we need shelter during the storm."

Odin's firebolts rent the sky, the sound of Thor's hammer rolling more ominously, louder. Growing closer.

"Hurry!"

Despite the danger of the imminent storm, no rain fell, but the men quickly gathered sturdy branches and logs to create rough lean-tos to shelter them and their goods. Kori tugged on Geira's rope, urging her closer. He pulled out his dagger and sliced through her bonds, watching her closely. Her only reaction was a slight wince, and she caught her lower lip between her teeth, as if to silence any cry of pain. Admiration grew to see her determination and strength to endure what he put her through.

"Gather wood for a fire before the rains come. We will need it when the storm passes."

She said nothing, merely stared at him. Sensing her thoughts, he caught her chin in his hand.

"Do as I order and do not try to flee. I will be watching you."

She gave a nod as best she could held in his grasp. He released her and she began her task gathering kindling. He spent a few minutes watching her, pleased when she set the branches and sticks in a pile nearby before resuming. Every now and again, she glanced his way. He folded his arms and waited a few more minutes before, assured she would not try to run, turning to help his men set up the shelters they would need for the next few hours.

"Thor isn't happy," Hradi remarked as Kori neared.

"Wasn't our doing."

Kori set to work with Hradi, driving long branches into the ground. The upright poles formed the outer frame of the lean-to, and several similar branches ensured sturdy support for the covering of the shelter. Kori held one end of a long branch still while Hradi maneuvered into place and tied it off with vines pulled from the forest floor. Every few minutes he looked up, to ensure his *ambátt* remained close and continued her task. Finally, his men dragged boughs they'd cut from the pines and in minutes the structure was complete.

There was more than enough room for himself, Hradi and several others, if Kori chose. And of course, Geira. He turned, his gaze again scanning the area. Geira still gathered wood as he'd ordered. She paused, lifting her head and meeting his stare. Even from this distance, a question shone clear in her eyes. After checking the pile she'd created, he determined they needed still more wood. He shook his head, motioning with his hand for her to continue. The acknowledgment also served as a silent statement that he had been watching her. She scowled and resumed her search for kindling.

The wind kicked up and Kori ordered his men to quicken their pace. He needn't have worried. They were speedy and efficient and before long, several shelters had been erected, some free-standing, some secured between sturdy trees. The valuables they'd gained in the raid lay safely tucked away, safe from the storm. Kori looked at the sky, dark clouds roiling above, pierced by lightning. The loudest thunder of all left his ears ringing. The first drops of rain began to fall. Kori turned, seeking his *ambátt*. A menacing growl carried on the wind and Kori froze. What was that?

Several feet away, Geira stood immobile, eyes wide, fingers tight on a small cluster of twigs. Kori followed her gaze, his heart slamming into his chest at the sight of the wolverine staring at Geira. The forest suddenly seemed to fall completely silent as Kori drew his sword and ran toward her.

The bear-like beast leaned back on his haunches, clearly ready to pounce. The roaring in Kori's head drowned out his war cry and he pushed himself to greater speed in an attempt to draw the creature's attention to himself.

Thunder clapped violently overhead, but he barely noticed as he forced his legs to race through the sudden downpour. Panic tightened his throat, each step felt heavy and leaden. Focused firmly on the wolverine, he slid to a stop before Geira, gripping his sword with both hands and raising it at the very moment the animal leaped, snarling, forelegs with deadly sharp claws extended toward them.

Kori slashed at the creature, the steel thrusting into the beast's chest with little resistance. He sliced down, blood spraying over him, mixing with the rain dripping down his face. The animal gave a snarling growl and fell to the ground at his feet. The wolverine writhed in the dirt, jaws snapping, trying to raise itself to attack once more. Twice Kori evaded the slicing claws, watching for his chance. It finally came and he hacked through the beast's neck, severing its head.

The skies chose that moment to release the full fury of the storm, a sheet of water that drenched Kori instantly. Chest heaving, he turned to Geira. The wind whipped her fair hair around her head, the bright blue eyes wide with fear. She trembled violently and he sheathed his sword, drawing her soaked and shivering body against him. He guided her toward the shelter. Hradi met them halfway.

"Get the wolverine!" Kori ordered and eased Geira under the canopy of pine branches. She quivered wildly, clearly still held in fear's tenacious grip. He reached for her hand, her fingers tight around the twigs she held. She jerked away then quieted, releasing her hold and the branches fell to the ground. Her gaze sought his. Though she tried to hide it, a glimpse of gratitude and affection lurked in her eyes. Yet, wariness shadowed her face. He resisted the urge to reassure her, to haul her against him and reassure *himself* she was safe.

Hradi returned, dumping the animal carcass to the side. Kori rummaged through one of the sacks and found a blanket, quickly wrapping it around Geira's shoulders. He slid an arm about her, pleased, yet still surprised when she leaned into him. Her wet hair clung to his arm. While the downpour made the ground a sodden, muddy mess, the lean-tos kept the muck to a minimum.

The fury of the storm surrounded them, the cloud-darkened sky alight with flashes of lightning. The earth shook with the roar of thunder. As if mimicking the continued pounding of Thor's hammer, Geira's body shook in fear, each movement driving her to burrow further into Kori. He tightened his embrace, lifting her chin so she stared into his eyes.

"Thank you."

He almost didn't hear her whisper. Half a thought rose to again remind her of her place, but he held it back.

"I will make you a cloak, with a hood from the beast's pelt."

The shock in her eyes surely matched his own. Why in Odin's name had he said that? His men would assuredly think him mad to gift her this way. Such finery was not worn by slaves. Thankfully, none but Hradi gathered with them in this shelter. He glanced at his brother, who gave him a knowing grin.

"What?" Kori scowled at his brother before returning his attention to his *ambátt*. Eyes still wide, she stared at him and a shiver that had nothing to do with the storm slid along his spine.

"Why?"

He wasn't sure he understood her question. Hell, he

barely understood the thoughts running through his head at the moment. All he could see in his thoughts was the wolverine staring Geira down, ready to leap. Admiration for her strength in the midst of terror deepened. She'd held herself completely still, watching the creature carefully. She'd not panicked, screamed or fled, which would have spurred the animal to attack much more quickly, and likely before he would have had a chance to reach her. He lifted his eyes heavenward, silently thanking Odin for giving him the strength and speed to prevent her from being mauled by the beast. His gaze fell on the carcass. The animal would harm no one again, and its pelt would make a fine hood. He already envisioned his *ambátt*'s face framed by the fur keeping her warm against winter's cold.

"You showed great courage today."

Her brow furrowed, her gaze wary, but she said nothing more. "I… I came upon it while I was gathering the wood. I didn't see it hiding in the brush."

A shudder ran over her and he stroked her cheek. She settled once more.

"I was afraid to move, or even to call for you. I'd already startled it. I didn't want to make it angrier. But then… you were there."

Another tremor shook her. She closed her eyes briefly, then turned away, staring at the torrents of rain still falling from the sky. More rumbles of thunder echoed throughout the forest, but they had grown less powerful. The lightning faded, the rain finally tapering to a steady but tolerable drizzle.

"You were very brave and did the right thing by not running."

She said nothing and he chose to let the matter drop. No sense in continuing to act like an untrained lad worshipping his first woman.

"Might as well stay the night."

Hradi's voice cut into Kori's still-racing thoughts. He nodded.

"The trail will be treacherous after such a storm. It's late, and we won't make much more progress before nightfall. When the sun rises, we will continue."

"Glad I'll be to get home."

"All of us, brother," Kori remarked, sliding his fingers through Geira's damp locks. He gazed beyond their small shelter, glad to see all of his men safe around him, protected from the gods' anger. While inconvenient, the storm reminded him of how easy it was to anger Thor. The terror of the wolverine encounter tested his ability to keep a rational head and had also proven his strength. Kori knew he still held the gods' favor.

However, he suspected the coming night might be more of a tribulation than he could endure.

***

Exhaustion thwarted Geira's intentions to keep her captor away. Fear of the wolverine still quivered through her limbs, but Kori's arm around her, his fingers sliding through her damp hair, stirred a feeling of safety she shouldn't have, much less savor. The fury lining his face when he'd run toward her and the beast seared into her memory, rushing through her thoughts. Over and over, never stopping. Shivers of panic cascaded along her spine, even now, when she knew she was safe. There'd been a desperation in the way he ran, his rage-filled war cry making the animal hesitate for merely half a breath, just enough time for Kori to save her.

Save her. He'd subjected her to cruelty since he'd taken her captive, yet she'd never been so grateful to see him racing to her, terror etched into his expression. The realization had struck in the moment, but until now, had remained buried beneath her own fright. Full recollection returned, and with it, some wisp of an emotion she couldn't quite grasp, or name. Appreciation for his ability to protect her warred with her obligation to resent him. Especially when he appeared to show real concern.

Now, the warmth of his body soothed her and slowly, the tightness of her body eased. Her head drooped, falling against his shoulder. His fingers stroked her cheek and she let herself melt against him, seeking the comfort he offered. Odd that she sought solace from him, but her thoughts blurred and she yawned.

Kori's deep chuckle rumbled under her hands. His embrace strengthened and she snuggled closer.

"Sleep, *ambátt*."

She said nothing, longing to do just that. But slumber taunted her, hanging just out of reach. Her fogged mind was barely aware of Kori speaking with his brother, their voices an obscure hum that soon soothed her frayed senses.

The rain continued to fall, though the wild winds and vicious rumble of Thor's hammer had ceased. Flashes of lightning still sporadically lit the sky, but the black rolling clouds had passed, leaving a pale gray sky in their wake.

She forced her heavy-lidded gaze toward Hradi. Kori's brother watched her while he spoke. Desire sparked in his eyes; he made no attempt to conceal it. She should look away, but the sensation of Kori's fingers stroking along her arm, combined with his brother's intense stare, stirred a heat she now well-recognized. His lips moved, but she barely heard his words, too tired to attempt deciphering them. If only she wasn't so tired and hungry. At that moment, her stomach grumbled, loud enough to stop the men's conversation.

"Why didn't you tell me you were hungry?"

Kori slid his arm from her shoulders, leaving a sharp chill in its absence. She rubbed her arms, once more catching Hradi's gaze. For several moments, he said nothing, merely smiled. Finally, he spoke.

"Kori, are you sure your slave is worth the beast's pelt? Fur like that will fetch a fine price."

Geira pressed her lips together, forcing herself to

silence knowing he deliberately taunted her. His smile widened and he winked. Her heart rushed into her throat, a strange excitement sparking. Just as quickly, the racing heartbeat fell back to settle like lead in her belly. When Kori turned to face her, his stare intense and studious, she thought she might succumb to the darkness hovering at the edges of her awareness. Yet, even that blessed oblivion didn't oblige, forcing her to face the realization that she felt desire for both men. Surely, her abduction and the journey had driven her to such madness.

She ignored Kori's offer of meat and turned away from them both, curling up on the blankets keeping the rain from soaking the shelter. Her hunger had fled, and all she wanted was to be left alone, if only for a little while. Thankfully, neither of them tried to speak with her, they simply let her be.

The rain stopping woke Geira. She hadn't even realized she'd slept, but when she jerked awake, she realized the sky had grown dark. Long ago, judging from Máni's position in the sky. Beyond the edge of the shelter, she could see the now-clear night, hundreds of stars twinkling above. She looked over to find both Kori and his brother asleep. Thoughts still fogged by sleep, she remained still, studying the men. Her senses slowly returned, awareness sharpening. This was the chance she'd hoped for! Slowly, she eased herself from her curled position, biting her lip at the pang of tenderness when her tight and aching muscles stretched. Her heart pounded, forcing her to take several slow, deep breaths or risk the calm she needed to succeed.

She closed her eyes. Another sharp breath. Sliding out of the shelter seemed her only likely choice. Each movement slow and careful, she turned to her back. Her fingers curled in the blanket beneath her while debating her options.

She dared another glance toward Kori. Hope shattered, her heart sinking. He was awake, watching her as always, an eyebrow arched in question. Did he know the thoughts racing in her head? Her gut churned, accompanying the bitter taste on her tongue. Tears of disappointment pricked her eyes but she refused to let them form completely. She'd show no weakness.

He leaned up on one elbow, a hint of a smile hovering on his lips. Why?

"Are you hungry?"

His low whisper hovered in the air, the kindness in his voice calming the frustration at freedom thwarted once again. She nodded, her hunger rising with such force, her belly hurt. Kori sat up and rummaged in one of the packs, pulling out some dried meat and a piece of stale bread. He held it to her, waiting patiently as she raised herself up to rest on her knees. She took his offering, biting into the hardened meat. She chewed carefully, not wanting her stomach to repel the meager food by eating too fast. Still, the bread tasted sweet as any tart and she took another bite.

Kori handed her the waterskin and she drank deeply, soothing her parched throat. He handed her more bits of meat and bread until she finally felt sated, her muscles relaxing. After handing him back the waterskin, she gazed out of the shelter. The sky pinkened on the horizon. Nearly dawn. Was it really only a day since she'd almost been killed by the wolverine? She sat silently as the sky brightened, thoughts racing with all that had happened in the last several days.

She glanced over at Kori, not surprised to find him studying her. She held his stare, again wondering at the worry she found in his dark eyes. He moved closer and her heart quickened.

Her fingers curled against her dress, her only movement when he leaned in close, his breath warm against her cheek.

"Mine."

The whispered word barely registered before his lips closed over hers, his hands coming up to hold her head still as he ravished her mouth with his. The suddenness of the fire sparking in her core shocked her, even as she responded, her own tongue dueling with his.

A low rumble sounded from deep within him and the sound roused the realization that he felt this passion as much as she did. The thought spurred her excitement and she found herself gripping his arms, holding on as the earth tilted beneath her.

Without taking his mouth from hers, he crushed her against him, rolling her to her back. His hands seemed to be all over her body at once, caressing, pinching, stroking. He took his time toying with her breath and she found herself whimpering under the onslaught. Her own hands roamed his shoulders, hating the tunic preventing her from touching his skin. One of his knees shoved her legs apart and he lifted her dress. The heat of his hand against her sex drew a keening cry, muffled by his mouth still claiming her.

His fingers slid into her cleft, circling her sensitive clit, drawing shudders of excitement, Thought eradicated, she merely felt each sensation he drew from her. He paused for a moment, finally pulling his mouth from hers, panting heavily. The urge to beg him to continue danced on her tongue but she held it back.

He moved over her, his now free cock brushing against her leg. Hot. Hard. *Oh Freyja, yes!* She arched toward him, offering herself, not caring about anything but reaching the pleasure his touch promised.

Kori hesitated a few seconds. Had he changed his mind? Then she felt his tip rubbing against her sex and the excitement flared hotter than ever. He eased himself into her slowly, despite her tugging at him, urging him to hurry. Each shift deeper roused a maelstrom of sensation radiating outward from her core to suffuse each part of her. Once seated inside her, he remained still, a half smile curving his lips.

"Your eyes tell me so much when I fill you. I like that."

Heat raced up her cheeks, but the embarrassment

was softened by the notion he was pleased with her. Then he began to slide within her and any hint of a response was lost in the passion roaring back to life.

She wrapped her legs around him, hips rising to meet each thrust. He braced himself on one arm, his free hand falling to her sex and teasing the bundle of nerves that seemed to be her very essence. A primal scream broke the quiet morning and she realized it was hers. She didn't care, only cared that he continued to stroke deeper into her, his fingers dancing along her clit until the world seemed to explode in a fireball, searing and scorching, her body rocking with waves of bliss.

His rough thrusts continued and she rode crest after crest, her senses muted and heightened at the same, until finally, a hoarse shout surrounded her and Kori's hot seed bathed her sex. He stilled, breathing heavily before easing to his side, tucking her against him. She snuggled into him, his heart racing beneath her hand.

After several moments of sated drowsiness, Geira's wits finally returned. She took a deep breath, again astounded by the force of the passion that swept her away every time he touched her. She forced her heavy lids to open. She gasped.

Her gaze settled on Hradi, who grinned as he rubbed his groin. He'd watched them? She hadn't given his presence a second thought once Kori kissed her, but now… A strange combination of embarrassment and excitement taunted her. She looked at Kori. His grin matched his brother's.

"I think he likes what he saw, *ambátt*."

"Most certainly, brother!" Hradi laughed, again squeezing his crotch. Geira's eyes widened and she buried her face in Kori's chest. His rumble of laughter, the feel of his fingers tangling into her hair, raised all sorts of wanton sensations she had no desire to think on.

After a few minutes, Kori sat up, setting her away. "Come, we prepare to depart."

The fog of desire faded, replaced with the

apprehension that had dogged her these last days.

"How much longer do we travel?"

Kori stood, adjusting his tunic and trousers. "Today we will meet with more men, who have carts to carry our goods. If the weather holds, we will reach my village tomorrow."

Geira straightened her dress, pleased that despite yesterday's downpour, the clothing had dried. Appreciation grew for Kori's capability in keeping them sheltered and dry grew stronger. Thor's blood, she shouldn't feel so many kind emotions toward him! Keeping her eyes averted, she helped gather the bedding, heat scorching her face when she recalled his passion of moments ago. Odin's teeth, she wanted to feel it again.

In a short time, the camp had been cleared. Kori's men continued lugging their goods further up the mountain. Kori approached Geira, rope in hand. She shook her head, backing away. Her wrists bore the marks of her bondage and the thought of being tied once more made the soreness grow.

"I will not run!"

His grim expression set her heart to a panicked rhythm. "You'll not have the chance."

He advanced on her, but before she could flee, he'd caught her arm, quickly securing her wrists and tying the rope around them.

"Damn you!"

He said nothing, merely turned, tugging her rope so she fell into step behind him. Having no choice but to follow, Geira imagined all sorts of gruesome ways to kill him.

CHAPTER EIGHT

After several hours, Geira's feet ached, her legs grew weaker and she worried she might collapse. Sheer will kept her upright, following behind Kori and Hradi. She longed for a chance to rest but didn't ask. She'd not beg him for anything.

All around her, the men continued to speak of the raid. Clearly, these warriors had enjoyed the attack and she kept her eyes lowered to prevent anyone from seeing her angry expression.

One of the men described raping a woman. She dared a look at him and shuddered, feeling for the poor woman who'd suffered under him. His stocky build revealed his strength and his hands, large as horse's hooves, looked as though he'd beaten his victim, judging from the marks on his knuckles. His small, cold eyes alit with laughter that grated on her ears. She wished for a weapon with which to cut out his black heart.

He continued to talk about the woman and Geira's heart seemed to stop. He spoke of Dota! Tears burned her eyes to learn what her friend had suffered. Geira dared glances his way, her heart aching at the thought of Dota's agony. She nearly stumbled at his last words.

"I took her as a slave. She is with the others."

Others? There were more from Einnar's clan who had been taken? Her legs trembled. Could it truly be? It meant she would not be alone in Kori's village. Her thoughts grew frantic as she pondered the possibilities.

Kori's tug on her arms drew her out of the whirlwind. "Only three other slaves, *ambátt*. They probably won't be with us for long. Bjorn and Hersir will likely sell them."

She said nothing, the hope fading at hearing those words. Who were the slaves besides Dota? She desperately wanted to see her friend.

"I think one of them may be... I'd like to speak with her."

Kori studied her then shook his head. "No."

"Why not? What purpose is there in keeping me from seeing how my friend has fared?"

"Muli has claimed her for the time being. You need not concern yourself."

"But –"

"Silence. Remember your place."

He turned his attention to the trail, once more conversing with his brother about the distribution of goods. Odin's teeth, she wanted to hit him. She *would* find a way to see Dota, and hopefully, between the two of them, a plan to escape their captors would be easier to accomplish.

***

Over and over, Kori's gaze moved back to his slave while he walked beside Hradi. Her reaction to Muli's tale of taking a slave indicated Geira spoke the truth about knowing the woman. Did she know the others as well? Had his brother and Muli made a wise decision claiming additional thralls? Hradi admitted his own uncertainty at the whim of the action, and made a strong argument that the men who'd claimed them should sell them to another clan, and soon. Only Muli refused, he wanted to keep his.

If the girl was indeed a friend of Kori's *ambátt*, her presence among his people could raise problems he couldn't afford to deal with. Part of driving Geira to depend upon and be loyal to him required her isolation from everyone, most importantly, anything or anyone from her home and family. With possible friends in his village, his efforts at binding Geira to him might take much longer. Selling the two was the best course of action. And knowing Muli and the way he hurt women, the girl likely wouldn't last long anyway. That idea raised more worries about Geira. If her friend died, would she blame him? Resist him?

The climb up the mountain took longer than he'd anticipated, the men tiring from the longer route home and the weight of their spoils. Yesterday's storm had compounded the sluggish rate of their travel. He'd deliberately chosen this backward route into his village, instead of sailing directly up the river. If by some small chance they'd been followed, this would ensure any of his enemies' attempts to find them were made near impossible. Still, he didn't like how their pace slowed.

He reminded himself each step brought them closer to the rendezvous point, before the final leg of their return. No wives would be left without a husband, and the few injuries his men had suffered were almost inconsequential. He was pleased all his men had survived the battle, once again in awe of the speed with which they'd vanquished their enemies.

"They were not ready at all for us." He directed the words to his brother, but knew his *ambátt* listened.

"The celebration kept them preoccupied. It was easy, most were in the longhouse when we arrived."

Kori kept a watchful gaze on Geira. She stiffened, but showed no other emotion, and kept her pace, one step behind him. Her wedding had been the reason the village had been blind and deaf to the signs of attack, until it was too late. Would she feel guilt over that?

He recalled the fiery way she'd responded to him upon awakening. Just the recollection was enough to make him half hard again. How long would it take before this constant desire for her ebbed? No matter, he had plenty of time to sate himself on her. Knowing he could bring her to heights of passion he himself shared roused his eagerness. Soon, once they met with Galinn and settled for the night, maybe he would take her again then, reminding her of her place. A hint of regret at being so harsh poked him. He forced it aside.

"Hradi, you are sure there were no other survivors?"

His brother shook his head. "We burned everything. Muli took some men into the woods. It was where he found his slave. The others who'd fled with her, they killed."

This time, his *ambátt*'s slave's head snapped up. She met his gaze, fury and anguish mingling in her eyes. Her lips pressed together, as if she struggled to hold back a response. Likely a threat, or a curse. Always fire with this one. He liked that. Holding back a pleased smile, he tugged on her rope, pulling her closer.

"There is no one to save you, now. You will soon get used to your new life."

A sharp intake of breath, but still silence. He arched an eyebrow.

"Nothing to say, *ambátt*?"

"What is there to say? There is no one left alive in the village. No one from my village knows I am here."

"I am your only protection."

"Who will protect me from you?"

"I will."

Hradi spoke up, startling Kori. The eagerness in his brother's eyes revealed more than Kori expected. He grinned.

"You fancy her, then?"

"Aye. She's a pretty thing. Her fire intrigues me."

"Careful you don't get burned." He laughed and looked at Geira.

She gaped at Hradi, but Kori again recognized an attraction in her eyes, confirming his suspicions. His slave and his brother both had interest in each other. He'd shared women with his brother before, prior to his marriage. The idea of returning to their youthful exploits excited him.

"Very well, Hradi. Tonight, when we make camp, you may have a taste."

A sound escaped Geira, outrage clear, though her unintelligible words eluded his understanding. Fire sparked in her eyes now, darkening them to the color of a stormy sea.

"You will show my brother respect tonight, slave, or you will suffer for it."

She still said nothing, merely glared at him before looking away. He held back a grin. Hradi was right, her fire *was* pleasing, in many ways. He wondered just how far he would let his brother take Geira, excitement growing at the thought of watching Hradi seduce the *ambátt*.

Yet, a healthy dose of envy mingled with his eagerness. How had he become so possessive of a mere slave in a few short days? Worry she might prove more trouble than her worth taunted him. He reminded himself she was only a symbol of his vengeance, to be used accordingly for his needs and those of his daughter's.

But he would still enjoy her spirit.

The sun had risen high in the sky when they finally reached the meeting point. Kori was pleased to find Galinn waiting with enough men and horse-carts to carry the bounty the rest of the journey. While his men loaded their bulging sacks onto the carts, Kori issued orders for the rest of the day's travel. He kept a careful study of Geira, noting how she studied everything and everyone around her. Did she watch for a chance to flee again? As he expected, she made a move toward the edge of the group. Yet, when he made his way toward her, realization became clearer.

She had seen the other slaves, and clearly recognized the one Muli had claimed for his own. If the two *ambátts* had the opportunity to discuss their situation, it could spell trouble, trouble he didn't want to have to handle at the moment. Before she reached the other woman, Kori grabbed her arm and spun her about, giving a sharp tug on the rope binding her.

"If you insist on disobeying, your life will be very difficult."

She tried to jerk free, but he merely drew her closer.

"Disobey? I merely wanted to see my friend and how she fares. She's been treated far worse than I, from the looks of her."

Kori glanced over at the dark-haired slave. Indeed, she looked as if she'd given Muli quite a fight. Her lower lip was split and swollen, and one eye had been blackened. Her hair resembled a bird's nest, and Kori didn't like the ashen color of her face.

He usually didn't bother with his clansmen's handling of their property, but he also hated when slaves were abused and neglected, treated little better than the goats and pigs on the farms. He met Geira's angry stare, and recognized a hint of hope in her eyes as well.

"Very well, you may see to your friend. She needs food and drink." He pulled out his dagger and sliced through her rope, noting the way she rubbed her raw and reddened wrists. He resisted the urge to soothe them for her.

"She needs more than that. Your clansman has beaten her. Her wounds need tending."

"I will speak to Muli and advise him to let her ride in one of the carts."

"I want to ride with her."

He shook his head and grabbed her arm once more. "You stay by my side. Come."

Never relinquishing his grip, he reached for his pack and removed some bread and a small waterskin. He escorted Geira back to her friend. The woman shrank away at his nearness, but accepted Geira's offer of food with gratitude.

"What are you doing?"

Muli's demand rang out around them. The other slave cowered even further away. But Geira straightened, trying once more to shake off his hold.

"Bastard! What have you done to her?" She tried to confront the larger man, but Kori grabbed her arm.

"She's my slave. As a slave yourself, you should know better than to defy me!" He folded his arms and grinned. "Tell her, Kori."

"The woman is weak and can barely walk. She rides in the cart and when we return to the village, I want the healer to see her."

Muli's smile faded. "Kori, you care what happens to a slave, one of our enemies?"

"If you keep her, you are responsible for her well-being. I'll not have your treatment of your slave causing trouble with mine. Then I will hold you accountable."

"She's nothing more than –"

After several attempts, Geira managed to jerk her free. She leapt at Muli, landing a solid punch to his chin before the man could react. A moment later, Geira landed at Kori's feet, after Muli delivered a vicious blow to her head.

When the man moved to kick at the fallen woman, Kori stepped in front of Geira, curled on the ground.

"Hold!"

"She struck me! A slave! I have the right to retaliate."

"I will see to her punishment. You will stay away from her and from your slave until my father can hear your argument. He will determine what is to be done."

Muli panted heavily, fists clenching at his sides. Kori's hand moved to the hilt of his sword. With a sneer, Muli spat on the ground beside Geira then strode away, grumbling. Kori looked at the others who had gathered to watch.

"Prepare to continue our journey!" He turned, his attention on the woman at his feet. She stood, rubbing her cheek. Already a bruise formed. He pushed aside the concern.

"So will you kill us both now?"

"It is not my decision. My father, as chieftain, will determine who is in the right and who should be punished."

"I will defend myself against any accusation."

"You haven't the right to defend yourself. You are a slave. I will speak on your behalf if I deem it necessary."

"Of course it's necessary! His vile lies will have me gutted like a pig!"

The idea sent a chill along Kori's spine. Slave she might be, but she didn't deserve that. Just as the other slave didn't deserve the abuse she'd endured. Speaking on Geira's behalf was no longer a choice.

"Don't fear, *ambátt*. You will be treated justly."

She folded her arms, that ferocious glare still fixed on him. "I've already seen your justice."

"My father is a wise and fair man. He will hear what Muli says, and he will hear what I say on your behalf."

"You must speak for Dota, as well. She doesn't deserve to be treated so poorly." She grabbed his hand, the anger now replaced with earnest hope.

He hesitated.

"Please. If you do this, I will submit willingly to you."

He studied her. This could be the biggest mistake of his life. If she tried to deceive him, he would know soon enough.

"You will obey every order I give?"

CHAPTER NINE

Geira held her breath, her thoughts frantic with the things he might ask of her. He had already ordered her to give in to whatever his brother had planned for later tonight. How much worse could he demand?

"Yes."

"Even if I ask you to do something you truly don't wish to do?"

She swallowed, the lump in her throat sharp, like the point of a dagger. What choice did she have? She couldn't let Dota remain with that brute, unprotected and in danger. She nodded.

"I will try my best."

Did the corner of his mouth just lift? He thought this funny? Before she could ask, he cupped her face with one hand.

"Your loyalty is admirable. Very well. I will speak on her behalf."

The first moment of real joy since she'd left her own village left her breathless. She threw herself at Kori, hugging him tight.

"Thank you!"

When his arms came around her, she found herself comfortable, even delighted in the embrace. How could she forget her plan? She had agreed to submit to him as her master. Since this fell into place with her plans, her gratitude could only help. Everything she did must convince him she wanted to stay with him. Only then would he let down his guard and her chance to free herself would come.

"Help her into the cart, then return to my side."

She turned toward Dota, but Kori's hand on her arm halted her.

"I will be watching you."

She expected nothing less. Lifting her chin, she held his stare for several moments. When he finally released her, she turned, heaving a sigh of relief. She approached Dota. Silently, she cursed the monster who had done this to her friend.

"Come, you may ride in the cart."

"You belong to their leader, don't you?" Dota leaned into her while they slowly walked to the cart.

"He's taken me, it's true. But I belong to no one."

"You hugged him. Do you… did you plan this with them?"

Geira gaped at her friend. "Of course not! How could you think such a thing?"

"You seem to prefer him to your husband, and he is the enemy."

Geira hesitated, not sure what to say. She'd never shared her suspicions about Einnar. Would Dota believe her? She kept her voice low.

"I've learned something about Einnar and it troubles me."

Dota fixed a hard stare on her. "What did you hear?"

"That he killed Kori's wife after raping her, and was about to do the same to his daughter."

Dota shook her head. "He wouldn't."

"I am not so sure."

"I am. Einnar was a good man. You were lucky to have him."

Why did Dota defend Einnar so vehemently? A hint of suspicion rose, adding to the doubts she already held about her husband. She placed a comforting arm around her friend's shoulders.

"Dota, Einnar was not what he seemed. I've seen things… I wondered about them and now… "

"Your husband was an honorable man!"

"Was he? Listen, Dota, I am not saying Kori is an ally, but he's shown some moments of kindness, and he agrees to speak on your behalf. Perhaps you will be free of the one who took you."

"You are in league with them."

"No, I'm not. I am merely doing my best to survive until I have the chance to escape."

They reached the cart and Geira helped her friend into it. She clasped Dota's hands.

"I don't care what has passed before. You are my friend Dota, and together, we can survive this."

Tears glistened in the other woman's eyes, and burned Geira's as well. The sensation of being watched drew her gaze to where Kori stood a few feet away, leaning against a tree, arms folded. Damn the bastard, why did he have to look so appealing? Her traitorous body, as always, responded to the intensity of his stare, hot and eager, swelling in anticipation.

"I must return to him. But we will speak again. Soon."

The slump of her friend's shoulders tugged at Geira's heart. How could she leave Dota? But she had to, lest her captor decide to punish her. Her legs leaden, she walked toward Kori. When he wrapped a rope around her wrists, she tried to pull away.

"I said I would submit to you!"

"You did, but you are still a slave."

"And you are cruel!"

He said nothing, merely trudged along the trail, leading the way up the mountain.

***

Kori tried not to think of the hurt in Geira's eyes when he'd bound her once again. Instead, he focused on her anger, knowing how easily he would turn that to passion. The thought of watching his brother take Geira tonight spurred his own eager lust. As the sun traversed the sky, his thoughts remained filled with anticipation of the coming night.

With the carts to carry the goods, the men had quickened their pace and by the time the sun had traversed across the sky, Kori and his men had already begun the descent down the other side of the mountain. Tomorrow, he would sleep in his own bed. With Geira. The thought of her in the fur-piled bed, naked, her skin glistening in the light of the fire, stirred his cock. He shifted in an attempt to ease the discomfort, and forced his thoughts elsewhere. To Muli and the slave he'd taken. That man always caused trouble, and this journey had proven no exception. Several ideas about how to handle the situation arose. He needed to speak with his father. A wise and fair man, Thorfinn would know the best way to resolve the matter.

The sun began to fade into the distance, Sól's chariot nearing the end of the day's journey. Kori called his men to a halt and advised them to make camp, before the remaining light faded. He set Geira near a tree.

"Stay here."

"But –"

"I may allow you to see her. Later. But not if you disobey."

Her lips pressed together, no doubt to hold back her argument. He held back his own smile and turned to help his men prepare for tonight's meal. Galinn had brought extra bedding and supplies, ensuring a more restful evening.

A large fire soon burned, creating the center of the camp. Kori sent several of the men deeper into the forest for game and fowl. Hradi excused himself from the group of hunters, urging Kori to the side.

"Shall I build a shelter? Away from the main camp, perhaps?"

The knowing glint in his brother's eyes drew a laugh. Kori nodded, glancing about to ensure none of the men overheard. "Do it. I'll be along to help soon."

"Do you think she'll fight?"

Kori shrugged. "I don't know. She vowed to submit to all I demand of her, but she's rebellious."

Admitting he liked that part of her, didn't want to break it, only half-surprised him. He sought to savor that wild quality and take pleasure from it. Turn the pleasure back into her, so she would crave it as well. Crave him.

A voice warned Kori forcing her too far might work against his plans, but anticipation at watching

Hradi make love to Geira had taken hold in his imagination. He couldn't let it go.

He shook his head and strode back to where he'd left her, pleased to find her waiting, although judging from her scowl, somewhat impatiently. She rose when he neared.

"I want to see Dota. Now."

He chuckled. "You do not give me orders, *ambátt*." He folded his arms, staring intently at her.

She glared, but quickly contained her ire, lowering her head. He suspected anger still shone in her eyes.

"Very well. May I please see my friend?"

A hint of annoyance laced her otherwise respectful tone. He found himself taking delight in the tiny show of frustration, but not for any malicious intentions. He simply liked watching the fiery reflection of her determination.

"Not yet."

"But –"

"I want to speak with you first."

He sensed her desperate need to ask for more, but she remained silent, merely following when he pulled her a little further from the camp. He stopped when he felt none would overhear. He turned. Unable to resist, he caught her chin to hold her still, taking her mouth with a hunger that startled him. Her response sent a thrill surging through him and he cupped her ass, forcing her against his achingly hard cock. Her soft moan shivered through his bones. He set her away, his breath unsteady, hating the weakness this might appear to any who watched.

"Hradi is building us a shelter for tonight. He will be joining us."

His growled the words out, knowing the coming hours would seem interminable. Her eyes widened, but more than a hint of excitement lurked in her deep blue gaze. Good. It would make things so much more enjoyable.

"I know you find Hradi pleasing to the eye. Many

women do. But you are mine and will remain that way."

She gulped and nodded, and something else rose in her gaze. He had no name for what he saw, but whatever it was, it made the burn in his veins hotter.

"Come, you may see your friend."

The happiness in her gaze sparked a need to do whatever he must to keep that expression on her face. Scowling, he looked away. He was not supposed to care about her feelings. Then why did he?

He tugged at her rope, perhaps a little too harshly, judging from her pained cry. Forcing himself to calmness, he turned and sliced the rope binding her. The red marks around her wrists looked worse than ever. Guilt at his callousness left his gut in knots. When she finished visiting her friend, he would see to the wounds.

He led her to the cart where Dota still rested. She eyed them both warily. Kori narrowed his eyes. He particularly didn't like the way Dota glared at Geira. The woman should be pleased to still live, not asking for punishment. Kori knew his annoyance sprang more from the way Dota seemed to resent Geira.

"You may visit for a little while. I will be back to fetch you."

Geira nodded. Unable to stop himself, he leaned over and pressed a kiss to her lips before turning away. Hradi likely needed help assistance building their shelter.

"Kori!"

He turned to find Leif hurrying toward him.

"What's wrong?"

"Muli is threatening to steal his slave back tonight."

Kori uttered a series of oaths. "He only wants to cause trouble."

"He said he won't let anyone stop him."

Kori gave the orange haired warrior a grim smile. "Really? Do you think he means to go against me?"

Leif's bitter chuckle echoed in the trees. "He's

never been very smart."

A plan formulated in Kori's thoughts. He grasped Leif's shoulder. "Don't let him know I'm aware of his plan. He will be very surprised to find his slave not where he thinks she'll be. Tell a few of the men I need to speak with them."

"Will do, Kori! Muli has been angering the clan for years, he has few allies these days. Just about everyone will be willing to help. You know, you would do well to banish him."

"I'll leave that to my father upon our return. I must find Hradi now. I'll be back to tell you of my plan."

He turned, setting into a slow run toward the shelter Hradi was building. While this turn of events would change their plans for tonight, there was no hope for it. Carrying out this adjustment left him with the bitter taste of disappointment coating his tongue. The slave girl needed to be hidden. He had only one choice, and getting her here without notice would be difficult. He'd need Geira's aid as well.

He reached Hradi and explained the situation. His brother frowned.

"The cretin is relentless. If we keep her with us tonight…"

"I know. I'm sorry, but there's no choice. If he ends up killing her, Geira will be…" He ran a hand through his hair. Was his concern more for his own slave or the matter of being seen as a fair and just leader? Allowing Muli to defy his instructions was not an option.

"There will be another time. You can't let him kill her."

Kori nodded. "When you're finished, meet me and Leif. He'll bring the men we can trust to help."

He headed back to the main camp, the laughter and shouts growing louder. Most of the men had already taken their places around the large fire pit. Already, a considerable pile of kindling filled the hole. He ordered several of the men to the carts, directing them to place them in secure positions surrounding the camp. He walked over to the cart where the slave girl sat with Geira. He looked around the forest, visualizing his plan. His *ambátt*'s bright blue eyes held a question.

"We must secure the carts. Tonight's plans have changed."

"What do you mean?"

"I will explain later. You must remain here until I come for you."

She nodded. Kori glanced at the other slave. The fury in her dark eyes didn't surprise him, but seeing her also direct her anger toward Geira unnerved him. Doubt about his plan sparked but he ignored it. It wasn't about the girl, it was about Muli's defiance. This girl was less of a threat, and easily managed. Muli possessed the potential to shame him. Kori wouldn't tolerate it.

CHAPTER TEN

Geira waited until Kori was out of earshot before turning back to Dota.

"Something is wrong," she commented.

"Yes, we are still captive." Dota sneered. She continued to run her fingers through her tangled dark locks. "Not even a comb to be found."

Geira imagined she must look much the same. She wanted a bath, to be clean of the dirt of the journey. She longed for a comfortable bed and a fire where she could sleep restfully, instead of dropping from sheer exhaustion at the end of the day, waking with aches in her muscles.

She glanced over at her friend. Some of her injuries healed, but her eye seemed to have swollen more. She grabbed the waterskin and ripped a strip from her dress. Pouring some of the water onto the cloth, she reached over and helped Dota press it against her eye.

"I wish I had some herbs to help heal you."

"I'll be fine."

"Kori mentioned a healer in his village. Maybe you should —"

"I said I'm fine!"

Geira leaned back. "Are you angry with me?"

Dota shook her head but refused to meet Geira's gaze. "I just want to be free of these monsters."

"He won't get near you again."

"What about the others?"

Geira held back the defense of Kori that hung on her tongue. Why did she so quickly think to support him? She should be agreeing with Dota.

"I think you will be safe. Kori has already protected you from him."

Dota's head snapped up, her one good eye wide and filled with anger. "You defend the one who enslaved you?"

Geira didn't know how to respond. Despite the situation, she found herself oddly unwilling to revile the man who'd taken her captive. He'd protected her more than once. Saved her from death at the hands of a vicious beast. Gave her the most incredible pleasure. Passion. The very thing she'd prayed for on the night she'd been wed.

"He has... moments of kindness." She chewed on her lower lip. "Dota, you know I was not happy about marrying Einnar."

"Your husband was a fine warrior. Any woman would be lucky to be his bride."

"He scared me."

"More than his murderer?" Dota spat.

Geira's thoughts immediately turned to Hradi's tale. "Kori has reasons for what he's done."

Dota's mouth fell open. "Geira, how can you say such things? Look at us! We're prisoners, taken as slaves!"

"I don't know what to think anymore, Dota! I just..."

"Just what? Are you glad you're now a lowly thrall, not the chieftain's wife? A plaything for another?"

Geira reached over and took Dota's hand. "We will be free, I promise you. I don't yet know when or how, but trust me. I am planning every moment, and will watch for the right time."

Dota gave a skeptical frown then nodded. "I will hold you to your word, Geira."

Geira sensed his approach before she heard him. She turned. Kori strode toward the cart, his brother a few steps behind. Geira met Kori's gaze, the air around her suddenly thick when she recognized the desire in his eyes. The intensity drew a shiver, and from the way his lips quirked, he'd noticed, too.

By the time he stood before her, she'd managed to regain clarity. "You needed something?"

"This cart must be moved. You and Dota will come

with us."

Kori offered his hand, helping her down while Hradi tended to Dota. When Kori moved to cover her with a dark cloak, she froze.

"What are you doing?"

"Come with us, but don't speak to anyone."

He covered them both with the cloak, an arm tight around her waist to hold her against him. They made their way through the trees until they came upon a small lean-to. The shelter where she and Kori... and she and Hradi... Her thoughts whirled. But why was Dota here, too?

When Kori removed the cloak, he pointed to the farthest corner. She hesitated a moment before obeying. He arranged a few blankets then reached for her wrists. She drew back when she saw the rope he held.

"No! There's no need to bind me!"

He gave her a grim stare. "I have trouble to attend to and must ensure you'll remain here." He grabbed her wrists despite her attempts to evade him and soon bound her to the pole supporting the shelter.

She'd barely had a chance to register his words before she was once again rendered helpless and caught. "You're leaving?"

"For a little while. And I know you vowed to serve me, but I am not willing to risk you fleeing."

"I am not so foolish to run into the forest without a weapon."

He shrugged. "Perhaps."

"Get away! No, don't!"

Dota's shout drew Geira's attention. Hradi gripped her friend's chin.

"Quiet, or I will gag you," he growled. Dota fell still.

Geira faced Kori once more. "Must you be so cruel?"

"Muli wanted to steal her from the cart. She is safer here."

Surprise rendered Geira mute. He did this to

protect Dota? Why? Would she ever understand this man's motives?

"Unfortunately this also means we will not be able to share... Dota will remain with us tonight."

So many conflicting emotions tangled in her thoughts, but Geira couldn't focus on a single one. She merely stared at Kori when he rose and walked back to camp.

***

Kori hunched beside Hradi in the trees. Several of his men were scattered through the area, forming a wide circle around the cart. Leif had done a fine job of distracting Muli while Kori had led Geira and Dota to the hidden lean-to. Now they waited.

A rustle of brush alerted him to someone approaching. Muli's broad-shouldered silhouette appeared in the path. He approached with stealth, not realizing that while he neared the cart, the men closed in behind him until he was completely surrounded.

Muli hesitated and looked around, but the men remained hidden from his view. Kori's fingers tightened on the hilt of his sword. Muli crept closer, withdrawing his own sword. He neared the cart, moving cautiously, and rounded the end.

"What in Odin's name...?"

Muli's shout spurred Kori to give the bird call. He stepped from his hiding place, sword ready. Muli spun about.

"Son of a whore! What have you done with her?"

"She's where you can't harm her."

Kori stepped closer and his men stepped into view. Muli looked around, eyes wide with anger and surprise, finding himself encircled by the warriors.

"You'd protect a worthless slave over me? One of your valued men?"

"I gave you orders to stay away from her. You go against my command, you face retribution."

Muli spat on the ground. "You're weak and foolish! That slave of yours has rattled your wits!"

"She has nothing to do with this! You defied my orders! You risked the entire quest not once, but twice. I'll not let you do it a third time."

Muli stalked closer but Kori held his ground, sword raised. The shorter man was forced to look up to meet Kori's gaze.

"I will bring this to your father."

"No doubt. As will I."

"You'll not get away with stealing my slave!" Muli's shout echoed in the still forest.

"Until the bounty is divided when we return, she belongs to me!"

"I took her for mine!"

Kori narrowed his eyes. "I am the leader. My word is law."

The pronouncement hung between them, seconds creeping by, Finally, Muli sneered and turned, looking among the men surrounding him. "Do none of you see the crime? I am being wronged!"

No one responded. Muli grunted in disgust and stalked back to his bedroll. Kori released a heavy breath. He'd feared the angry man might force a fight. That was the last thing he needed. He lowered his sword.

"Find your beds. We break camp at dawn."

He turned toward the waiting shelter, Hradi falling into step beside him,

"I thought he might strike," Hradi remarked.

"So did I. He's smarter than I credited him."

His thoughts racing, he quickened his pace, suddenly worried Muli might decide to wander and find the lean-to. Geira and Dota were helpless, bound as they were. A brief recollection of the wolverine spurred him into a jog.

Approaching the shelter, he slowed his pace. Geira and Dota were as they'd left them. He said nothing as he bent down and sliced Geira's bonds. He looked around, disappointed the shelter would not be used as originally intended. He assisted Geira to her feet.

"We will eat and camp with the others tonight. It will be safer. The men have prepared a meal."

Geira still rubbed her wrists, saying nothing, but she nodded. He grabbed her arm and guided her back toward camp. While he might not be able to sample her passion tonight, he looked forward to holding her while they slept. Weary from the journey and the tension of confronting Muli, Kori found himself longing for slumber. He glanced down at the woman beside him then raised his eyes to the heavens. He needed the strength of the gods tonight.

CHAPTER ELEVEN

"When we enter the village, all will know exactly who, and what, you are. You will do nothing to disgrace me."

Exhausted and confused by Kori's strange coldness since they woke this morning, Geira scowled. "You are truly pitiless. I have already vowed to obey you, why must you humiliate me so?"

"I am the son of the jarl. I'd have none question me. That especially means you."

He tugged on the rope. At least he had wrapped cloth around her wrists before binding her again. Once again, his words conflicted with his actions, leaving her thoughts dazed while he pulled her along on the path behind him.

They hadn't walked far when the smell of fires, those of hearth and smith, filled the air. The men's voices grew excited and Geira guessed they must be near the village. At the top of the hill, Kori stopped. Geira stepped up beside him.

Nestled in the lush green valley below was a village much larger than she'd expected. Well more than a handful of buildings gathered near the center, many others surrounding those. Still more buildings lined the shore, with substantial docks. Kori was clearly much wealthier than her father and even Einnar. People bustled everywhere, tending chores, visiting with each other, or sampling the wares of the fishermen and tradesmen. Beyond the village lay several fields, dotted with cows and sheep. Even if her father and brother had managed to escape the attack, they didn't have the men or means to rescue her. They would easily be outnumbered. Murdered for sure.

The tug on her arms compelled her to follow Kori down the hill. The hope she'd held of being found and rescued sank deeper into the abyss. She paid no mind to his conversation with his brother and some of the other men. All she could think on was how much riskier her plan had become. She would need a lot of time to learn all of the ways to flee the village.

With half her attention on the path before her, the other half remained focused on the day she would be free. Where did the river lead? She must learn that, along with so much more. And protect Dota in the meantime, until the day they could both walk away. Where had her friend gone? She no longer rode in the cart and Geira feared Muli had reclaimed her. She craned her neck, tears of relief burning her eyes to see Dota walking behind Leif. Though her hands were bound, Geira knew her friend was still safe. Another worry rose swift.

"You have given her away?"

He shook his head, not even looking at her. "No, but we are almost home. I can no longer claim her once we enter the village and Leif will see no one else disturbs her until my father can decide. All the goods taken belong to him until the spoils are divided."

"But that's not fair! Does that mean I also belong to him?"

He shook his head. "No. You are mine. Only mine. I already told you that."

Geira fell silent. Arguing with him now would gain nothing and besides, she needed all her concentration to keep from stumbling and falling down the mountain. While the first part of the journey up the mountain had been difficult, maintaining her balance now grew trickier. She watched the trail carefully, avoiding rocks and branches that might cause her to trip.

She dared another glance at Kori. He now appeared to ignore her, but she had the sense he was aware of her presence at every moment. Sure enough, his gaze flicked toward her, a little smile curving his mouth. Why did he always take humor in her predicament? She looked away, once more focusing on where she walked.

The unfamiliar lands weren't so different from her own. Where were they, exactly? She had little navigation skills, but suspected the journey through the mountains had taken them north. How far? So many questions needed answers. Getting them would be tricky.

As they entered the village, shouts and cheers sounded throughout. People rushed at them from all sides, women and children laughing and throwing themselves into the arms of their returning heroes. Geira moved closer to Kori, suddenly afraid what the mob might say when they saw her. His hand on her arm oddly soothed her.

He guided her through the throng. She kept her face turned to him, trusting he would keep her from stumbling. Finally, the crowd parted and she looked up.

"Father!"

A girl, a young woman really, of perhaps fourteen winters, ran toward them. She was quite lovely, with dark hair and eyes that seemed familiar. Geira realized this was Kori's daughter. Kori released his grip on the rope and opened his arms as the girl ran into them. He swung her around, laughing.

"You were successful?" the girl asked when Kori lowered her to the ground.

He nodded. "He is no more. And we have our vengeance."

The girl smiled, and again Geira found herself struck by her beauty. But the joy in her eyes faded as she turned her gaze toward Geira.

"And who is this?"

"His wife. She belongs to me now."

The girl's eyes narrowed and she stepped close to Geira, appraising her with a cold stare.

"I hope she knows what is expected of her."

"She will, once we are home."

Geira stiffened, annoyance taking over her apprehension. How dare they speak of her as though she were no more than a pack animal!

"My name is Geira."

The girl snorted. "You're whatever I call you."

"Thora!"

The sharp tone in her father's voice drew a sudden redness to Thora's cheeks. She turned to her father, eyes wide.

"You scold me?"

"She was not part of her husband's crimes."

"She is still nothing more than a slave." Thora folded her arms and once again sneered at Geira.

Geira tried to ignore the girl and focused instead on Kori. His gaze remained fixated on his daughter.

"We will discuss this at home. However, I have matters to go over with your grandfather before you may return."

"You will claim her before the clan then?"

Kori nodded. Geira didn't know what to make of his aloof manner. She sensed his annoyance, but was it directed at her or his daughter? In light of Thora's obvious dislike, Geira hoped Kori wouldn't change his treatment of her. Her only hope was to befriend the girl, but she wondered if that was even possible.

A tug on the rope around her wrists drew her attention. She looked into Kori's concerned face. Somehow, she doubted the concern was for her.

The excited murmurings of the crowd grew louder. Once more, the people surrounding them backed away. A man taller than Kori, with flowing white hair and an impressive beard, approached.

He grinned as he neared, and Kori did the same. The two men embraced.

"A successful raid?"

"Very!" Kori agreed. "We've brought many valuables and a few other goods as well."

The white haired man turned his attention to Geira. She sidled closer to Kori once more, dark eyes again boring into her.

"She's lovely. Was she already wed?"

Kori nodded. "But I arrived before it was

consummated."

The other man laughed. "So you stole many things from Einnar. How long do you plan to keep her?"

Kori shrugged. Geira held back her indignant protest.

"At least until Thora is wed. She will tend the farm and household. And whatever else I demand of her."

He fixed a piercing gaze on her, reminding her of her promise. She lifted her chin. Without looking away, Kori continued his conversation.

"I have some matters to discuss."

"The bounty will be divided fairly, as always."

"Not that. Muli took a slave of his own."

"Has he killed her?"

"Not yet. We had a… disagreement last night about her."

"How badly did he beat her?"

Based on those words, Geira realized the men knew the threat Muli posed and gave another moment of thanks Kori had protected her friend last night. She grabbed Kori's arm.

"Please, you must still keep her safe!"

Kori's expression tightened into anger, his mouth twisted in a scowl. "Show respect to your betters. I am speaking with Jarl Thorfinn!"

"Kori, no need for anger. She worries for her friend. Rightly so."

Geira met the older man's eyes. Jarl? This must be Kori's father. The kind expression he bestowed on her soothed her jumpy stomach.

"Come, let's get settled. We have a feast prepared to celebrate your success. Then we will hear what matters need to be addressed."

Aware of the older man still studying her, Geira averted her gaze, unsettled by the frank appraisal in his stare.

A tug on her wrists drew her into step behind Kori. She tried to look around the village but the people surrounding them blocked her view. A fierce fatigue swept over her, and she longed to sit, to rest. Her belly gave a growl, loud enough to draw Kori's attention.

"We will eat soon," he said, before returning his attention to his father. She could barely make out their words, muddled by the chatter of the villagers. As they neared the longhouse, she watched the river. Again she wondered where it led. She sighed, knowing she wouldn't now find the answers she sought. First, she had to endure the upcoming meeting, where hopefully, Kori would be able to keep Dota free from Muli. What sort of debt would the jarl ask of Kori if he granted the request?

"I am looking forward to this evening."

The voice at her ear drew her from her thoughts. She stared at Hradi. She'd nearly forgotten Kori's promise to his brother. A shiver, a combination of unease and anticipation, tingled along her spine.

"Patience, brother. We have many hours before I return to my home."

Hradi chuckled. "I can't help my eagerness."

"You may find yourself too busy to visit with me tonight."

Kori said no more as they entered the longhouse. Geira looked around. The smell of cooking meat filled the air. She inhaled deeply of the savory aroma. Kori gave her a knowing grin. Heat flooded her cheeks.

"We will eat well now, girl. Then once matters are settled, we'll return to my home."

"There is much to be done, slave. You'll need to clear the ashes from the fires." Thora's voice cut through the murmur of voices.

Geira turned, once again unnerved by the animosity in the girl's eyes. Was the threat of one of the filthiest of chores meant as a humiliation? Probably. Still, she refused to cower.

"I am to give the orders, Thora."

Kori's rebuke was gentle, but seemed to anger his daughter further, whose voice grew sharper.

"You said we need her to keep the house. She

doesn't know how we do things. I'll have to show her. She's only a stupid slave."

Geira's fingers clenched. Kori's hand on hers told her he'd noticed.

"Thora, you do not decide her tasks. I do. And *you* will do as *you're* told as well."

Thora gave her father a sulking glare and turned away to take a seat near her grandfather's chair. The ornate throne-like structure was decorated with the antlers of a huge stag, jewels positioned amid the jutting horns. Geira had never seen a throne so fine.

She swallowed the lump choking her. Being chieftain had afforded her father and her family many luxuries, but not such as this. For a moment, she truly did feel like a lowly slave.

It didn't help when Kori, still holding her hand, led her to a table adjacent to the throne. He sat and directed Geira to kneel at his feet. She pressed her lips together to hold back her protest, then gracefully lowered to her knees. Aware Kori still held her hand, she looked up at him.

He slowly pried her still-clenched fingers open. "You are angry. Because of me or my daughter?"

She didn't dare answer, suspecting a trap. His knowing grin sent a shiver through her veins, one of both dread and anticipation.

"No answer? Perhaps a little of both, then."

She despised how he seemed to know her every thought. "Your daughter clearly hates me. More than you do."

He chuckled and leaned close. "I don't hate you, *ambátt.*"

The warmth of his lips against her ear drew another wispy quiver. The tenacious haze of desire poked her, but she forced it back.

"You make me kneel at your feet like a dog."

"You are a slave. It's where you belong."

The roar of cheers drowned any response she might make. Several women entered the hall, carrying heaping platters of food and placed them on the tables before the men. Geira's stomach again rumbled at the tantalizing aroma of meat and fish, hearty vegetables and bread. Kori had said they would eat well, but would he make her eat from the floor?

The cheers quieted when Kori's father took a stance before his ornate chair. He grinned as he looked out over the crowd.

"We celebrate a successful raid and the restoration of my son's honor."

More cheers and applause filled the air. Geira found herself under the studious stare of Jarl Thorfinn.

"We have much bounty, which we can use in trade at Hedeby or keep for ourselves. I will see each of you gets a fair portion."

Cheers and laughter again. Geira watched the crowd, the excitement in all the faces almost making her smile. She recalled many nights such as these with her family and clan. For a moment, the bitterness at not knowing their fate singed her tongue. She resolutely pushed it aside. Dwelling on what she couldn't change only made her more vulnerable to her captor.

"We feast now. My son tells me there are matters to discuss, but I find it easier to make decisions on a full belly. Thank Odin for our blessings!"

Thorfinn stepped over to the table and sat beside Kori. He leaned back as one of the women handed him a horn of ale and placed a full trencher of food before him. Another did the same for Kori.

The two men began to talk, though Geira couldn't hear very well in the din. A large yellow dog trotted over, tail wagging furiously as he sniffed at Geira's hair. The idea Kori thought her no better than a lowly animal rose again. But when the dog continued his playful inspection, she giggled and patted him, and was rewarded with a lick. It wasn't the canine's fault she'd been lowered to his status.

"Shoo, dog," Kori pushed the whining animal away.

"He does not bother me." Geira bit her lip at Kori's arched eyebrow. Had she angered him again? She wondered if she would ever fully gauge his moods.

"He's a nuisance."

He shoved another bite of meat into his mouth. The sight reminded her once again how hungry she was after the long journey today. Despite his earlier words, Geira suspected her captor had no intentions of allowing her to eat. Her anger simmered again and she closed her eyes to subdue it.

"Here."

The aroma of the meat and bread filled her senses, making her stomach protest its deprivation yet again. She opened her eyes to find morsels of both before her, held in Kori's hand. When she reached for the food, he pulled it away, shaking his head. Realization sparked and with it another surge of annoyance.

She briefly narrowed her eyes, but was too hungry to fight. She leaned forward, catching the bite in her lips, brushing against Kori's fingers. She felt, rather than heard, his intake of breath. His plan to humiliate her had come back to taunt him. She took satisfaction in the knowledge.

His dark stare held hers. When she finished chewing, he scooped up another bite and held it to her lips. The heat in his eyes grew as hot as the flames in the hearth.

Again and again, he fed her from his hand, holding her gaze captive the entire time. Each time she accepted the offered food, he stroked her lip. Hunger remained strong, but no longer only hunger for food. Humiliation lay forgotten in the tempest of emotions, his touches not demeaning but passionate, his stare burning as hot as the fires in the hearth. She clenched her fingers, desperate to hide the effects of the rising desire.

After the last bite, he wiped his fingers and reached for a horn. Hesitating a moment to run his knuckles across her cheek, he offered the horn, allowing her to take it in her own hand.

She tried not to gulp all the ale down in one swallow, but once the brew touched her tongue, she realized how very thirsty she'd become. She stopped, took a deep breath and looked up at Kori's grinning face.

"You've quite an appetite."

The husk in his voice revealed the hidden meaning in the words. Heat rose in her cheeks, but she didn't look away. He awakened the yearning again, with just a few words and a knowing stare.

She returned the empty horn to him, still saying nothing. A glance at the holes in the ceiling above the fires in the hall revealed the sun still shone, though dusk drew near. Suddenly fatigued, Geira's eyelids drooped and she leaned into Kori's leg. His hand stroking her hair added to her weariness. She fought to remain awake, but every second staying alert grew more difficult. She rested her head on his thigh while the men spoke.

"Muli nearly killed the girl the night he took her."

"Better he had than I have to deal with this."

At the mention of the man who had enslaved Dota, Geira's exhaustion evaporated. She sat up, earning Kori's attention, as well as that of his father. The older man pierced her with a stare very similar to Kori's.

"Your *ambátt* knows the one you speak of."

"They are friends."

Both men watched her. Was she permitted to speak? It seemed so but she nodded first.

"I knew Dota from my home village."

"So she is not one of Einnar's clan?" Kori asked.

"No, she came with me from my village. To attend me at my wedding."

Kori leaned close to his father, whispering. Geira couldn't make out the words, though she tried. The noise in the hall stifled everything not shouted out clearly for all to hear.

Hradi approached, taking a seat across from his brother. He gulped down a horn of ale, then asked a passing serving girl for more. Despite her intention to ignore him, she couldn't help but be drawn to him. He resembled Kori in many ways, the eyes, the line of his jaw, the strong chin. But something about Hradi appealed in a different way. Was that why she'd been disappointed last night's intended plans had changed? Kori had done it to save Dota from Muli, but where was her friend now? She looked around, but didn't see her.

"Odin smiled upon us," Hradi said, biting into a piece of mutton. His gaze hovered on her for several tense moments before he turned his attention to his father and brother.

Geira sat quietly as the men talked about the success of the raid. Einnar's clan possessed much gold and jewels and Kori's men had apparently found all of it before setting the village ablaze. Geira thought of her father and brother once more. She'd prayed to the gods several times to give her a hint that her family escaped the carnage. If only there were some way to find out. Did her father know she'd been abducted? How she wished she could feel his strong hugs one more time.

So deep in her worry and sadness, she nearly missed Dota's name. Pushing aside her sorrow, she focused on the men's discussion.

"If I let him keep her, he will surely kill her before long." Kori's casual tone contained a hint of concern. "So far, I've kept him away from her, but what more can I do? He claimed her, as was his right. I declared her mine for the journey, but now…"

Thorfinn contemplated silently for a few moments, every now and again his gaze darting to Hradi. Geira tugged on Kori's leg.

"What is it?"

"May I ask a favor? Please?"

She hoped her submissive demeanor would sway him. His lips curled in a half-smile, as if he understood her manner.

"You wish to see your friend saved from Muli."

She nodded. "I will do anything you ask if you free

her from him."

The gentle caress of her cheek drew the burn of tears. The tender gesture seemed more dangerous than any brutality he might visit upon her.

"You already promised me that on the journey here."

Despair rose. She had nothing left to offer in exchange for helping Dota. His hand slid into her hair, tilting her head back.

"Fear not, *ambátt*, your friend will be free from Muli. It will be costly though."

What did he mean? Releasing her, he turned back to his father.

"I doubt it will be easy to convince him. Even before we stopped him from taking the woman back, he was angry. My slave attacked him during the trek here."

"Will he demand retribution?" Thorfinn asked.

Kori shrugged. "Most likely. I stood against him twice, in defense of slaves. I will offer him my share of the bounty."

"As will I." This from Hradi. Geira focused her wide eyes on Kori's brother. "Don't fear, girl, he won't touch you. Or her."

"Thank you, brother." Kori and Hradi shared a knowing look before resuming their conversation, once more seeming to ignore Geira.

Thorfinn nodded. "It might be enough. I will spare a portion of my share. He's buried three wives and two slaves already. He costs us too many good women."

Kori and his brother laughed, though Geira didn't find any shred of humor in Jarl Thorfinn's words.

"The meal is nearly finished. We will attend this matter now." Thorfinn stood and returned to a position before his throne.

"Now that we have celebrated, it's time to share the spoils!"

Raucous cheers filled the air.

"Wait!"

Geira's heart sank.

***

As expected, Muli's voice rang out in the ensuing silence. He strode to stand before Thorfinn. Kori saw the anger in the man's eyes when he turned to look over at him. And Geira.

At his feet, his slave inched still closer, as if she could hide within his legs. He gave her hair another stroke, savoring the way her body softened against him. He fought the urge to pull her into his lap.

"Kori's slave attacked me! Not only that, he deliberately took my slave. I claim reparation!"

"Yes, Kori has explained."

"She must be whipped for daring to strike me! And Kori must repay me for keeping me from my thrall."

Kori's slave went tight as a bowstring.

"Ease, *ambátt*. You will not be whipped." He stared into her blue eyes. "Not today, anyway."

Her eyes widened again, that alluring flush creeping into her cheeks. He turned his attention back to his father and Muli, unable to completely ignore the longing to possess her.

"You must ask him." His father's voice rang through the now-silent hall.

Kori stood. "Sit near Hradi."

He strode toward the front of the hall, looking back to see Geira now seated between Hradi's legs. Safe.

"You will not whip my slave, Muli."

The other man spat on the ground beside Kori's boot. "Then you do it."

Kori nodded. "I will see to her punishment, don't worry. I will also give you my share of the spoils. As will Hradi."

Muli hesitated but clearly the mention of all the wealth he would obtain pleased him, his greedy eyes darkening with pleasure.

"But I claim the slave permanently."

"What?" Muli's outraged shriek rang out over the startled murmuring in the hall. "I want her back!"

"She'll be dead in a week with you. I have need of

her."

"You already have a slave."

Kori nodded, keeping calm. Let Muli grow more agitated. His father would step in and order the man to give up trying to regain possession of Dota. But the slave wouldn't be awarded to Kori.

"And she will serve a purpose. Dota is for Hradi."

Muli sputtered, his crazed eyes darting frantically. He stalked over to Hradi before Kori could stop him. Hradi never flinched, but Geira shrank away, eyes wide with fear.

Kori clenched his fists but remained where he was. She was a slave, and he could not rush to her side and defend her, protect her, as if she were his wife.

"Why do you want her? She's nothing but a useless, stupid slave!"

Kori held back a grin at Geira's sharp gasp. She squirmed under Hradi's restraining hands. In just the brief glance he gave her, outrage glowed in her eyes. If Hradi released her, she would likely strike Muli again. He almost wished to witness that.

"I'll get more use out of her for much longer than you." Hradi spoke calmly, as if discussing the output of the season's crops.

Muli spun around, stalking close to Kori and poking a finger into his chest.

"Your *ambátt* has made you cloud-headed. Who's really the slave?"

Kori slapped the man's hand away. "I don't need to rape my women."

The insinuation had the desired effect. Muli pulled his sword. Thorfinn's voice bellowed through the hall.

"Enough! Muli, you will accept three additional shares of the goods from the raid and you will relinquish your claim to the slave. I'll not have you killing a woman every other month."

"But his slave struck me!"

"In defense of her friend. And seeing the condition you've left the girl in, I might do the same. I will not tolerate this anymore."

Muli lowered his weapon, silent. His eyes still burned with fury and Kori knew he'd best be wary.

"Then give me the others."

"You may have one of them."

Thorfinn's decree set a murmuring about the hall that quickly grew louder. Muli stared at the jarl, not happy about the offer, but clearly, the resignation in his face revealed the man knew he had no choice. He gave a curt nod. From the back of the room, a shrill scream echoed, sending the hall into silence once again. Leif dragged one of the other women taken in the raid to the front of the hall and pushed her to the ground before Muli.

"Take her. She has a vicious tongue. I expect you'll cure her of that quick enough." Leif bowed to Thorfinn before returning to his seat.

Kori remained silent when Muli strode to where Dota knelt on the floor. He spit on the floor before her. Dota kept her head down. When Muli yanked her to her feet, Kori took a step toward them, but his father's hand on his arm held him back.

"Whore! Not worth my trouble." Muli's words hung heavily in the quiet hall. He sneered when Dota pulled her arm free. She had spirit, that one. Hradi would have his hands full. Muli took the rope of his new slave and pulled her out of the longhouse.

At a small push from Leif, Dota walked toward Hradi, slowly, as if unable to hold herself up. Kori nodded to his brother, who released his hold on Geira, slicing the rope to separate her wrists. She rose and rushed to her friend, placing an arm about her shoulders and guiding her to Hradi. Both women sank to the floor. Geira held her friend close. Judging from the tight grip, she had no intention of letting go anytime soon.

He heaved a resigned breath. The remaining celebration stretched endlessly before him.

CHAPTER TWELVE

After the spoils were divided, the hall quieted as the weary raiders resumed their feast. The boisterous mood of earlier had grown muted, though not quite peaceful. Laughter rang out among insults and dares, though no one acted on the threats of retribution.

Geira continued to shield Dota from the curious stares. She knew what they wondered, would any dare voice the questions still unspoken? Who would be the first to question Kori's motives?

She wished someone would, so she knew the answer as well. Despite the dire nature of her situation, Kori made decisions that continued to surprise her. In saving Dota, he had proven he was a man of at least some honor. More and more, she began to think him truly justified in his actions. Surely she'd gone mad!

She knew full well that as slaves, both she and Dota could be subjected to brutal cruelty, possibly torture, should her captors so desire it. Her father and brothers had kept slaves, and while keeping them healthy was always a consideration, as their ability to perform their labors were very important, thralls *had* been subjected to abuse and punishment. The reasons varied, but were often due to failure at their assigned tasks. Yet, oftentimes they were subjected to suffering without justification. Until now, she'd never given thought to the unfairness and cruelty of a slave's life.

Kori had spanked her, yes, but something about his punishment seemed different, as though he were personally hurt by the offense of her attempted flight. Why? The man was one contradiction on top of another. The way he'd saved her from the wolverine, protected her around his men, left her bewildered. Rescuing Dota had been the actions of a fair and just man. Recognizing that threatened the very foundation of her plan.

Geira wondered if she would ever understand him. Why did she want to? She had a role to play, a vow to keep. Viewing her captor with anything akin to affection could be deadly. Somehow, her goals seemed further out of reach than ever before.

It was the desire he provoked that addled her wits. Made her think there was more between them than just the station of master and slave. Made her believe he was an honorable man.

He is, the tiny voice in her head taunted, raising even more questions she feared to answer. Still, one idea loomed larger in her thoughts. Had Kori saved her by taking her captive?

Hradi leaned over, cutting into her thoughts when he handed her a chicken leg. "Give this to her. She will need her strength tonight."

Dota stiffened under Geira's hold. Still, she took the offered food, devouring it quickly. As Hradi continued to pass morsels down, Geira gave them to Dota, recalling the way Kori had fed her earlier. The now-familiar heat in her belly grew stronger, spreading outward. There had been something intimate about his act of feeding her. Recalling the glimmer of lust in his eyes affirmed he'd felt the same. She looked up to find him watching her.

He said nothing, but he didn't need to, the familiar wanting in his stare saying more than a thousand words. Freya's blood, her longing matched. Her sex swelled and she pressed her legs tighter together to ease the intense yearning. In the week since he'd taken her, her life before seemed a distant dream. Now, all she wanted was to answer the call of passion he silently sent.

She forced her attention back to Dota, offering some ale. Her friend had stopped shivering a while ago, and after having eaten, looked refreshed.

"You're truly safe from him now, Dota." She whispered the words, not wanting any to hear.

"But I've been given to another. Nothing will

change."

"Yes, it will. You'll see. I believe Hradi is different than Muli. You will not be so terribly abused."

"I am still a thrall. As are you."

Anger flashed in her friend's eyes. Geira couldn't blame her friend. She'd been taken violently and viciously. While Kori *had* stolen Geira's innocence, she had to be honest with herself and admit he had not once brutalized her. She enjoyed the carnal pleasure he roused, and wanted it again.

"Yes, for now. We will find a way to free ourselves. This I promise."

Dota didn't respond, but her shoulders drooped. Geira pulled her closer, settling her friend's head against her shoulder.

She didn't know how long they stayed there, Dota accepting her comfort. The tug drew Geira from her reverie. She'd nearly forgotten the rope remaining on one wrist. Slowly, she eased her friend from her embrace. The pull continued, urging her to her feet. How she hated to let go, but resisting would only cause trouble. She'd offered her submission to Kori and would honor her word. She faced her captor, a thrill skittering along her spine at the heat in his gaze.

"Come, we go to my home now."

"But Dota ..." She cut the protest off. With a silent curse, she reminded herself of her vow.

"Hradi will bring her and they will accompany us."

She nodded, hoping she hadn't angered him. Her bottom tingled at the recollection of the spanking. Yet, a strange part of her wanted him to strike her again. The pain of the punishment had been real and fiery, but it had stirred other yearnings. Making sense of that eluded her still.

With quick movements, her hands were once more secured together. She followed Kori as he led her out of the hall. The fast approaching darkness revealed the feast had gone on for much longer than she'd thought. Many still lingered inside, and likely would continue to celebrate until late into the night. She followed her captor to two horses tethered nearby. Before she could voice her question, he scooped her up and settled her atop one of the animals, quickly climbing up behind her. Thankfully, his strong grip around her waist kept her from sliding out of the saddle.

His arms around her, the warmth of his body at her back, soon had her forgetting all but her weariness. She longed to rest, but doubted he would give her that chance. She peered around him to see Hradi secure Dota in a similar fashion. Except her friend struggled against the mad holding her, terror in her eyes sending Geira's heart lurching. Hradi whispered something to the woman, who seemed to calm.

Kori's brother caught her stare and winked, a knowing smile curving his lips. Heat flooded her face and she turned away. The rumble of Kori's laughter vibrated through her.

"My brother still desires you. Should I let him have his taste tonight?"

She twisted around, hoping her excitement didn't show in her eyes. In the chaos of the day, she'd forgotten her disappointment about last night. Hradi held a strange fascination. Did that make her a whore?

"I know the idea intrigues you. I want to watch him take you, make you scream as you come."

"You are wicked."

"Perhaps your friend will be amenable to participating."

Her mouth fell open. He wasn't serious, was he? His hearty laughter rang through the village, quiet but for the sounds of the feast drifting from the longhouse.

"Easy, *ambátt*. I've no desire to take a skittish hellcat, and Dota has been brutalized enough. Hradi will be busy proving he is not like Muli."

"For her sake, I hope you are right."

"Muli is dangerous because he cares nothing for anyone but himself. My brother is a better man. Honorable. If Muli was not such a mighty warrior, my father would have banished him long ago."

"But Hradi will take her whether she wishes it or not."

"Have you not found enjoyment in my taking of you?"

His lowered voice, deepened with a lustful husk, shivered through her. Unable to force herself to speak, she nodded.

"It will be the same with Hradi. While we will take you if and when *we* wish, we'd prefer you enjoyed it. It makes everything so much more fun."

Why did he have to be so reasonable? How would she maintain the tenuous hold she held over her ever-crumbling resentment? With each passing moment, she felt more comfortable with him than she had for the week spent in Einnar's village. How could that be? No doubt, Kori had proven himself a brutal and formidable man. Yet, her fear of him was different than her dread of her husband. She didn't possess the revulsion that always seemed to accompany her thoughts of Einnar. Now that she'd experienced Kori's prowess in the art of pleasure, she knew the uneasiness she'd felt those few intimate moments with her husband had actually been disgust.

From the little she'd seen of his clan, Kori's family treated everyone equally and honestly. Jarl Thorfinn reminded her of her own father. Soren Sturlassson was a fair and just man, ensuring every member of the clan was cared for as needed. He had been respected by all those he ruled and they valued his guidance and leadership.

She suppressed a shudder, recalling the crude way Einnar's father had acted, his lack of concern for his people, even for his wife. The way he'd taken the slave right on the table before everyone showed nothing but callousness. His wife said nothing, but Geira had seen the resigned sorrow in the woman's eyes. The fear she would end up as her mother-in-law, sad and broken, with nothing but despair for the future, had added to the foreboding feelings toward Einnar.

"What has your attention, *ambátt*?"

Kori's words, rumbled in her hair, roused those shivery sensations once more. He guided the animal out of the village proper, toward the river. She should probably pay attention, but dusk had given way to early evening, creating shadows that blurred landmarks. Exhaustion contributed to her lax concentration.

"I am thinking of my father. My brother. They were in the village before..."

She let the words trail off, as if giving voice to her fears made them real. An odd tension seeped into Kori, his arms and shoulders tensing around her. He said nothing.

The ride continued in silence, along the river. After what seemed to Geira to last an eternity, Kori guided his mount away from the water's edge. A narrow path wove through the sparse trees, revealing a farmhouse built into a gently sloping hill. There were several outbuildings, a sign of Kori's prosperity. She looked around, taking in the sheep in a pen beside a barn, cattle in the fields beyond the house.

Kori reined in his mount and quickly climbed down. Geira accepted his assistance when he lowered her to the ground. She found herself pressed tight against him, no room for her to move, for he kept her pinned between himself and the horse. Several moments of silence passed between them, but the light of the rising moon revealed the heat in his eyes. Her breasts tingled, nipples tightening into hard points, her pussy slickening in anticipation of his unspoken message.

"Come girl, let's go inside."

Hradi's voice carried in the quiet evening. Geira peered around Kori to see his brother leading Dota toward the house. Concern for what Hradi had planned for her friend briefly cooled her desire. But Kori's fingers on her jaw stoked the flames once more.

"Come, I will show you your new home."

Odd to think she should be settling into a new home as a bride, not a slave. Yet, a peace settled over her that gave her the strength to hold her head up as Kori tugged on her rope.

The house was cold and dark. Where was Kori's daughter? Hradi's low voice as he spoke with Dota carried through the home, but Geira couldn't make out the words. The flare of a candle brightened the room. Kori pointed to the floor beside the hearth.

With a resigned sigh, she lowered herself to her knees. Hradi appeared from the shadows. Remaining silent grew into a battle she nearly lost. She watched Kori's brother as he settled into a chair. Kori busied himself starting a fire. The tinder began to smolder, then erupted into flames, chasing the chill. For a few minutes he disappeared, then returned to stoke the fire until the blaze grew.

"Will you join us tonight Hradi?"

Kori's words jolted through Geira. She met his stare, the roaring in her ears nearly drowning Hradi's assent. Her heart pounded until she feared it would break free of her chest. At the same time, excitement suffused her body with wispy heat.

Kori's motion brought her to her feet and she stood before the two men. Both looked on her with hunger, spurring her own desire. Kori pulled on the rope, leading her to the sleeping room on the other side of the wall. A large bed piled high with furs glowed with the burnished light of the hearth, which joined the room with the common area.

Fingers at her nape quickly undid the laces of her dress. Both men worked together to strip her of the garment, Hradi slicing through her bonds so Kori was able to slide the dress down her arms. In mere moments, she stood naked before them.

"You've done well with this one, Kori."

The gruffness of Hradi's voice revealed his desire. A shiver swept over Geira in response. She savored it, refusing to permit shame to grow because she desired both men. Why shouldn't she enjoy some part of her captivity? None would blame her.

Her thoughts veered to Dota. Try as she did, maintaining focus on her friend became impossible. Under the hungry gazes of the two men, she cared for nothing but their irresistible and lustful allure.

Kori's gaze swept over her, returning to catch her stare. He winked. Her knees trembled. At that moment, Hradi reached for her, drawing her into his arms. Eyes still locked with Kori's, her breath quickened at the feel of Hradi's calloused hands rasping over her skin. He reached down to cup her bottom, giving a sharp pinch that drew a gasp. He tapped her chin, drawing her attention. His grin widened and he lowered his head, his mouth covering hers in a bruising kiss.

His hot lips and tongue sparked the familiar desire, yet there was something different, something brusque in his touch. His hands roamed her body, calloused fingers leaving a jagged fire in their wake, much as Kori had done. But the heat held a different pitch of sparks and spontaneity. Kori's touch drew a smoky and heady fire that consumed her from the inside out. As if she'd called him aloud, she felt his chest press against her back. Caught between them, she could only respond to Hradi's powerful kiss, as both men's hands slid over her flesh.

When Hradi released her mouth, her head fell back against Kori's shoulder. His mouth slid along her neck, and she cried out at the sensual and soothingly familiar feel of his lips. She gave a silent prayer of thanks they held her up, for surely she would have fallen otherwise. Against her bottom, Kori's shaft, hard and hot, pressed in close. Before her, brushing against her sex, was Hradi's cock. The dual sensations staggered her, her breath catching.

Long fingers slid into her cleft. Whose? She found she didn't care, she only wanted more. Hradi nuzzled her breasts and she realized the soft cries echoing in the room came from her. Her fingers clenched in Hradi's hair, but Kori caught her hands and drew them away, holding her still as Hradi took the tip of one breast into his mouth.

Her knees buckled at the first pull of his lips. Kori continued to slide his tongue along her neck, up to her ear. Flames licked at her spine.

"You like this, *ambátt*, don't you?"

Words of refusal evaded her. Kori's hot breath in her ear, the low rumble of his voice, sent sparks of delight skittering along her arms and legs.

"I want to watch him pleasure you. I want to see your face when he near sends you to the gates of Valhalla."

Her eyes snapped open. Hradi still tormented her breasts with his hands and mouth, keeping her thoughts scattered.

"Come."

Hradi stepped away at the order, allowing Kori to sweep her into his arms. Dizzy and chilled with the loss of their touch, she relished the feel of the furs beneath her as he laid her atop the bed. He stood for a moment, watching her, then turned to Hradi.

"She's your to enjoy, brother."

Geira's eyes widened. Wasn't he going to…? She sat up.

"Lay back, *ambátt*."

His use of the title stung, but she obeyed, watching him warily.

"I told you I want to watch him pleasure you. You will not hold back."

The heat in his eyes told her how badly he did want to watch her taken by Hradi. She looked at the other man, whose smile raised all sorts of sensations. But not fear. Her anxiety eased, though every nerve in her body seemed more sensitive than ever.

Hradi climbed on the bed, his gaze roaming over all the places he'd touched before.

"Lovely and responsive. Who could ask for more from a slave?"

She should be angry at the constant reminders of her station, but oddly, she sensed only affection in their words. She truly had gone mad. She bit her lip against a panicked giggle, her gaze settling on Kori. He sat upon a chair, one foot casually resting against the edge of the bed. Her eyes widened to see his cock, erect and hard, exposed by the spread of his legs. He slowly stroked himself.

He grinned. "See how much I am enjoying this." He leaned forward, his eyes alight in a way that sent a tremor of apprehension along her spine.

"Hradi, wait!"

Geira gaped. When Kori's brother ceased his attentions, she groaned. What in Helheim was he doing?

Kori gave her a leering grin. "I nearly forgot. She still needs to be punished. For striking Muli. I vowed to see to it."

"What? But… you can't! You said –"

"I can and I will."

Kori stood. Her gaze darted between his stern expression and his cock, his fingers still moving slowly over the tip. Mouth suddenly dry, Geira swallowed.

"Hradi, fetch the rope."

Geira shook her head. "No, I won't fight. I've promised to obey!"

Kori remained silent as his brother returned. Geira tried to slide away but was soon caught between them. Within moments, her hands were tied above her head, secured to the elk antlers making up the headboard. Kori stepped back to study her.

"You may continue, brother. But she is not to receive her pleasure."

"I don't understand!" she wailed, though her suspicions strengthened. A mixture of alarming excitement seized her heart.

"You'll see."

Kori's words echoed ominously.

***

Kori resumed his seat, his cock hard and aching to be inside her. He would wait. He hadn't lied when he'd told her he wanted to watch, but he'd never imagined how difficult a position he'd put himself in. Still, with his command to deny her pleasure, he could end her punishment at the right time to increase his own delight.

The sight of her fair body contrasted with Hradi's darker skin and sent another twinge of yearning along Kori's spine. He tightened his fingers at the base of his cock, holding his breath until the need to come passed.

He leaned forward when Hradi moved along Geira's belly and spread her thighs. She tugged against her bonds, but Kori caught a glimpse of her moist sheath, glistening with desire. The earthy scent of her arousal lingered in the room. He caught her gaze, read the need building in their pale depths. She was a delight.

He returned his attention to his brother, grinning as the other man lowered his head between Geira's legs. A little shriek escaped her, accompanied by a tensing of her body. Unable to resist, Kori leaned over, catching a breast in his hand and rolling the nipple between his fingers.

"Please!"

The frantic undulations told him Hradi drove her close to release. At the moment Kori realized he needed to render an order to stop, his brother pulled away. Geira groaned in protest, then squealed as Kori pinched her nipple hard.

"You are not to receive any pleasure until I determine you've been punished enough."

"You heartless... pig's ass!"

The break in her words and voice, the rasp of frustration when her pleasure was again denied brought a dark pleasure he hadn't felt in many seasons. He forced a grim smile, fighting to ignore the aching pulse in his cock. Another hard squeeze of his fingers drew a gasp, but she sealed her mouth against any further words or sounds. The fact she hid her response somehow displeased him.

"You are a slave. Such actions are forbidden. You dared anyway. My vow to see you punished must be honored. You should be grateful I didn't allow Muli to determine your fate."

Her eyes widened, but she remained silent. Did she understand she could be suffering so much worse at this moment? She would suffer, he would ensure that, but in ways far different than those she could endure at the hands of someone like Muli. Did she truly understand the misery she'd escaped? This suffering would ultimately lead to pleasure. Not that he intended to share his knowledge.

Bah! He'd gone soft for this girl he'd taken as slave. How else to explain the tender feelings? She was meant to be a hated symbol of his enemy, yet he found himself forgetting that far too often.

Failure tightened his throat. He leaned back, giving his brother a nod, allowing anger to ignite. Anger at what she made him feel, anger at making him feel at all. Since Borga died he'd sworn never to care for another, hating the way losing her made his heart ache. His *ambátt* must not be permitted to touch his heart in that way.

With a nod, he caught his brother's gaze. Hradi grinned and resumed, using his fingers and mouth to once more set Geira to squirming on the bed. Again, Hradi sensed when she grew near to release and ceased his attentions.

"No."

Her low moan hovered in the room. Kori studied her, eyes glazed with lust, cheeks flushed, lips parted to suck in air. Her pleading gaze settled on him, but he remained still, careful to hide his thoughts.

"I want her." Hradi's voice cut into the silence.

"Take her."

Kori's gaze never left Geira's face. He savored the way her eyes widened, noted how she tugged against her bonds. Her struggles inspired more lust, surging powerfully into his cock. He looked away for a moment, finding it difficult to watch his brother in the position he desperately wanted to be. Hradi spread her thighs wider.

With Kori's focus firmly on her face, he knew the exact moment his brother filled her. Her eyes widened then fluttered closed, her tongue sliding along her lower lip. Delight melted into her face. Her back arched, hips rising to meet Hradi's swift strokes.

Kori's mouth went dry as sand watching Geira take her pleasure in his brother's passion. His gaze drifted over their bodies, seeing the way Hradi's fingers tightened on her hips, the way her legs wrapped around his brother's waist. He stroked his cock once more, both soothing and stoking his lust. He wanted to be inside Geira, as his brother was. Not yet. He would take her, soon, but only when it was time to let her come.

As if Hradi sensed his thoughts, he slowed his pace. Kori leaned forward, hungry to watch his slave's reaction. Her eyes opened, but she looked only upon Hradi.

"Not yet, slave. Not until he gives permission."

A pitiful cry escaped, her hips frantically moving against Hradi. Kori nearly came then. How he held back, he would never know. Several heated moments passed, Geira's chaotic squirming calming. Hradi moved, slowly. Geira whined once more.

With a deep breath, Kori sat back, awaiting the moment of his brother's release. Mere seconds later, he was rewarded with a shout from Hradi, his body stiffening in climax. Geira gave a keening wail, filled with vexation. Clearly she recognized Hradi's completion as well, while her own still dangled out of reach.

Kori smiled, settling his gaze on his slave's frustration-laden expression. The sight was more beautiful than he'd imagined. His brother eased from her body, drawing a rippling quiver. Desire flamed in her eyes. Would she beg? He suddenly wanted to hear her plead. Lust tinged his vision red.

"She is a delight, brother. You are truly blessed by the gods."

The words drew him from the engulfing haze. He looked into Hradi's grinning face. He smiled in return.

"Odin has indeed smiled on me." He held Geira's gaze as he spoke, recognized the passion that held her. He would savor that desire, imagining her response when he finally took her. And she would come for him.

He waited as Hradi tended to her, still lashed to the bed. She would remain thus. Her position left all options up to Kori and he wanted her to know her place. She would learn to depend on him for everything. He would win her undying loyalty. He'd already accepted her oath of obedience.

Excitement rose, then dimmed. Tomorrow, after the claiming ceremony, would she forsake her vow? Didn't matter. If she chose to fight him, he would see her chastised for rebelling. He found himself hoping she dared to defy him.

Hradi leaned over her, turning her so he could place a passionate kiss on her lips. Kori licked his own to see her respond, opening her mouth to let his brother taste her. When Hradi drew away, Geira panted for breath.

"Please," she moaned.

The rasp of her voice combined with the sight of her heaving chest, breasts tipped with hardened nipples, nearly drove Kori mad with wanting. He rose, standing at the foot of the bed.

"Brother, step away."

Hradi laughed as he rolled off the bed. Kori's focus remained firmly on Geira. Her gaze darkened with hunger. She widened her legs in invitation, one he found himself unable to refuse.

He knelt between her legs, remaining silent while he studied her.

"Please."

The soft plea undid his control.

***

Geira held back a joyful shout when Kori spread himself atop her. She longed to wrap her arms around him and hold him close. A tug on her bonds reminded her she couldn't. Still the familiar feel of his fingers gliding along her skin soon had her near crazed with desire. While Hradi's taking had been thrilling, Kori's mastery of her left her breathless and desperate. Needy. Her pussy slickened even more, juices dripping and leaving her surprised at the depth of her passion. Surely they could smell her need. She didn't care, only wanted the delight she knew Kori could give her.

One look in his steely eyes and she wondered if he meant to deny her through the night. The idea nearly made her scream. Instead, she focused on making him lose control, forget the punishment. She arched her hips up, pressing her heated sex against his hard cock.

He groaned, then eased back. He used his knees against her thighs to keep her splayed open and immobile.

"Kori?"

"Silence!"

The admonishment was soft, quiet. Gentle. At that moment, his fingers slid along her sex, the touch sizzling throughout her. She bit her lip to hold back a cry, but a sharp squeeze of her nipple coaxed the shout from her lips. Her back bowed, seeking more contact, craving that moment of pleasure-pain. As if sensing what she wanted, Kori again pinched the tip of her breast and she thrashed her head. Need rose higher and higher, his fingers circling around her clit, driving her closer and closer…

He drew away and her eyes snapped open. Denied pleasure knifed through her, her body trembling in the throes.

"No, please. I want… I want…"

"What do you want, *ambátt*?"

Words eluded her. She whimpered, trying to convey the need with her eyes. Judging from the devilish gleam she found in his gaze, he knew exactly what she wanted.

"I… I don't know!" The words to tell him what she wanted refused to form, no matter how she tried. Heat scalded her cheeks. She wanted the incredible bliss he always drew from deep within her. She was so close she could taste the pleasure on her tongue.

He grinned and leaned over, his lips hovering over hers. "You want to come, don't you?"

She nodded, the motion bringing their mouths together. She continued, tempting him with the barest touches of her mouth. Her eyes fluttered closed when he finally kissed her, his lips warm and teasing, sparking the tempered flames back to life. He continued to stroke and tease her pussy until nothing existed but the feel of his body surrounding her, the warmth of his breath on her cheek, the feel of his hair on her shoulders. Her very existence narrowed to Kori alone.

He paused and she moaned in despair. He would kill her if he continued. When he positioned his cock against her, she nearly wept with joy. She held her breath as he filled her, tormenting her with the slow pace. She wanted him to thrust in hard, to take her as he had before. Wanted his passion unleashed. She squirmed against him, but he merely gripped her hips to hold her still.

"This is for me, *ambátt*."

The husk in his voice betrayed his desire, softened his cruelty. The heat in his eyes burned nearly as much as his hard shaft stroking inside her. The way he kept her immobile brought a new level of exasperation. She thought her body might explode if she didn't find release. She wanted to wrap herself around him, hold him deep within her.

"Kori, please!"

He stilled, eyes piercing. "What do you want?"

She knew the wicked words he wanted to hear. Though motionless, his cock filling her enflamed her senses. She clenched around him, trying to break his control, but succeeded only in drawing a low moan and another harsh pinch to her nipple. Her will shattered, she pleaded.

"I... I want to come. Please, please let me come."

He studied her in the ensuing silence. He gave a nod to Hradi. Geira had nearly forgotten Kori's brother and gave an excited cry when he reached up to free her from her bonds.

She instantly wrapped her arms around Kori's shoulders, fingers digging in to his hot skin when he moved within her once more. This time, he increased his pace, until he took her the way she'd wished moments ago, fast and hard. Her legs now free as well, she locked them around his waist, holding him inside her. He slowed, and she buried her face in his neck, unable to keep from biting the corded flesh. He gave a hoarse shout, one hand sliding between their bodies to catch her clit. She threw her head back, white-hot bliss blinding her, her body rocking in the cresting waves of exultation. She seemed to hover for hours, caught in a tempest that refused to release her. Only Kori's body reminded her she remained on Midgard and had not catapulted into the heavens above. The echoes of screams cut through the roaring in her ears. Her screams. She continued to shudder as rolling shadows of delight drifted over her. Kori's body on hers was a welcome weight, a sort of haven where she could recover her wits.

His harsh breath against her neck roused a shiver of longing. When he lifted his head, she barely had a moment to take a breath before he devoured her mouth with his. She responded eagerly. If the man could give her such astounding pleasure all the time, she'd be more than content to stay in his bed.

He rolled to the side, sliding free of her body. In the same motion, he tucked her against him. "Come."

What? Then the bed dipped behind her and Hradi's warm body snuggled close, pressing against her back. Sated and drowsy, she savored the feel of Kori's fingers sliding in her hair. The odd thought her plans for freedom faded further teased the edges of her awareness. She didn't care. At that moment, everything felt right.

CHAPTER THIRTEEN

Sunlight glinted though the holes in the ceiling. Geira burrowed deeper into the warmth surrounding her. Awareness slowly dawned, the feel of a hard chest beneath her head, another at her back. She kept her eyes closed, trying to determine which man was which. The cock hard and tight against her ass belonged to Hradi. Kori's arm around her waist kept her securely nestled against him. If she were honest with herself, she would admit she liked waking like this.

A stroke of her hair roused her from the in-between world of slumber and wakefulness. She opened her eyes to find Kori studying her.

"Did you sleep well, *ambátt?*"

His voice, heavy with sleep, rumbled through her. She nodded, though she hadn't slept as deeply as she'd expected considering the games they'd played with her until the wee hours of the morning. When she had finally dozed, her dreams were filled with wicked fantasies of the brothers.

Kori gave her a lazy smile and pressed a kiss to her forehead. Another tender gesture that boded badly for her heart. She'd admitted last night that she'd come to care for him already, despite her situation. If only he saw her as more than a slave, vengeance to be taken without any regard for her choices or feelings. The moments of kindness, caring and passion made her forget his cruelty. She must remember her vow. And find a way to keep him from shattering her ability to focus.

"Come, we have a busy day. Hradi, wake up!"

Behind her, Kori's brother stirred, the cock moving against her more intimately.

"Not yet, brother. I need tending."

Kori chuckled. "Very well. I'll admit I do as well."

As much as she wanted to protest their intentions, she had no strength to resist when they turned her so she lay stretched beneath them. Surrounded by the large men gazing at her with hunger made her feel small and helpless. At the same time, eagerness to experience their attentions again now left her squirming with anticipation.

They seemed to move at once – Kori's mouth lowered to her breast as Hradi's fingers slid along her belly, seeking her pussy. Her hands remained free. She slid one into Kori's hair, holding him against her breast as she offered her mouth to Hradi's kisses.

She arched against their seeking hands, panting with excitement. Kori lifted his head and she met his stare. Intense as always, as if piercing her thoughts. He ran a finger along her swollen lips. The touch sizzled.

His mouth crashed onto hers, tongue driving deep inside. Hradi drove two fingers into her sex. Kori's mouth muffled her delighted cry. If only she could capture this moment of near perfect pleasure in some way, for she feared she might never feel this way again.

Both men drew away and she groaned, afraid they intended to torment her as they had last night. She didn't think she could survive more of that. Her hand slid from Kori's hair, and he caught her wrist, placing a kiss there. She sucked in a breath. At moments like this, she truly forgot how she'd ended up here with him.

He gave her a curious smile. She tried to raise to her elbows, but Kori pressed her back into the bed, kneeling up and straddling her shoulders. His cock stood out hard and straight, inches from her face. She held his stare, knowing what he silently commanded. She felt Hradi between her legs again, distracting her with his knowing caresses. Kori snapped his fingers.

"*Ambátt*, you know what I expect."

A thrill passed over her. She reached for his shaft, her fingers closing around the hot flesh. Beneath her hand, he throbbed, strangely soft for all his hardness. A harsh breath hissed through his lips and she lifted her gaze to his face. Another shiver of excitement skittered along her spine at the pleasure melding into his expression. She'd done that, she'd pleased him. Her own desire spiked, aided by Hradi's continued torment of her pussy. The feel of his cock sliding in her folds drew a sharp gasp.

"Geira, now!"

Kori's demand, husked and thick with lust, reminded her of his earlier order. She barely had a chance to part her lips when he thrust his cock toward her. At the first feel of his hardness invading her mouth, Hradi drove his cock deep into her body.

Suddenly filled in a way she'd never imagined, Geira could only brace herself. Hradi set a steady pace, but not a fierce rhythm, allowing her to concentrate on Kori's shaft. She loved the little groans and words of encouragement he offered as she sucked and licked, his fingers tangled in her hair. His eyes locked on hers and he stiffened under her attentions.

He came with force and she could only swallow his musky seed, his hoarse shouts filling the room. He slumped, chest heaving and pulled free. She savored his lingering taste, surprised at how much she enjoyed serving him this way. He moved away then, and took up a position behind her, settling her back against his chest. Hradi remained inside her, but motionless as he waited for Kori.

"Go ahead," Kori said. He pressed a kiss to Geira's head and somehow the gesture hurt as much as it gave her hope. Further thought vanished on the sudden movement of Hradi within her. Desire, held at bay, stirred to life, fast and sharp. She arched up toward him, meeting his slow thrusts.

Kori now cupped her breasts, caressing and stroking, catching the nipples with gentle pinches. She bowed her back, wanting more, her thoughts and body focused only on the pleasure awaiting her. Would they make her beg again? She didn't know if she feared or anticipated the very idea.

A squeeze on her clit nearly sent her over the edge, but it wasn't enough. She moaned, turning to catch

Kori's mouth, kissing him hungrily. His startled laugh soon changed to a low moan.

Hradi's hard cock sliding in her, combined with their caresses left her gasping, tumbled by the force of the joy shuddering through her. They kept touching her, fucking her, and just when she thought she'd reached the end, the bolts of delight continued, carrying her aloft as she cried out to all the gods.

The tumult slowly faded, her body trembling and weak in its aftermath. Her vision cleared and she blinked, trying with little success to steady her gasping breath.

"I think you liked that."

The laughter in Kori's voice brought a smile to her lips. How she longed to stay here like this forever. All too soon, the men pulled away from her, and Kori's cool master demeanor had taken hold.

"Clean yourself and join us near the fire." He gathered his clothes and left, Hradi close behind.

Geira stared after them, shivering now with sudden cold. She much preferred the flames of moments before, somehow now a distant memory. She refused to acknowledge the hint of tears burning her eyes. There was no shame in taking her pleasure.

She used the water Hradi had brought from the river to refresh herself before reaching for her dress. She wondered if Kori would allow her to make herself additional clothing. When she stepped around the wall, she stopped short to see Dota kneeling beside Hradi at the table. Her hands were bound, but she looked well-rested. Hradi handed his slave a hunk of bread and some dried fish.

Kori caught sight of Geira and beckoned her closer. He pointed to the floor beside Dota. Would she always be on her knees like this? She caught her friend's gaze, startled by the animosity there. She glanced up at the two men, deep in conversation. Torn between eavesdropping and Dota, she debated briefly to herself before turning to her friend.

"What is wrong, Dota?"

"You let both of them have you last night."

If she didn't know otherwise, Geira could swear Dota sounded jealous.

"I had no choice, as you well know. I find resisting makes things worse."

"Whore!"

"Enough!"

Kori's shout silenced Geira before she could respond.

"I'll give you back to Muli if you continue."

He directed his threat toward Dota. Geira glanced up at him, confused by the anger etched into his expression. She turned back to Dota. Her friend's face had turned a pasty white and she lowered her head.

"Please, if I may?" Geira asked. Kori gave her a curt nod. Geira reached out to Dota. "You must accept our fate."

She leaned in close to hug her friend. Lowering her voice to a whisper, she said, "We will speak on this later."

The angry glare Dota fixed on her baffled Geira. Did her friend truly think she had asked for this? The facts had to be made clear and soon. Unfortunately, Kori ordered her to stand and follow him outside.

She found the horses saddled once again. Where was he taking her now? In moments, he'd seated them both on the stallion. The feel of his chest pressed so closely against her reminded her of the way he'd held her as Hradi had tormented her last night and this morning. She closed her eyes and sucked in a deep breath to rid her body of its heated response to the recollection.

"We have a special ceremony in the village today."

Kori guided the horse toward the river and the village. Hradi and Dota once again rode beside them.

"Why don't you live with your father in the village?"

Why had she asked that? The question burst free

before she'd even realized it had formed.

"I prefer a quieter place to sleep."

She conceded the longhouse was often a noisy and chaotic place. She'd spent most of her nights in her village in a small hut built behind the longhouse, connected by a corridor that helped deaden the din.

"You are Jarl Thorfinn's son. Yet you live as a farmer?"

She must stop asking questions or he might mistake her interest for affection. But she hadn't expected to reside even this short distance from the village.

"My wife and I lived here."

A coldness crept into his voice with those words and Geira halted her next question. Another reminder now of her reason for being here wasn't welcome. Especially since she knew if Einnar hadn't killed Kori's wife, she would be back in Fellsskoger, as Einnar's bride. Why did she prefer being here? Her thoughts had grown so confused in the last day and night, she wondered if she'd ever sort them.

They reached the village in a short time. Warm shouts and welcomes greeted them as they rode up to the longhouse. Thorfinn stood speaking with several men, looking over a nearby building. The smith? The clan leader turned as Kori reined in his horse.

"Good morning, Father. Where is Thora?"

"Helping with the chores inside. She is growing into a fine woman."

Geira glanced at Kori, his pleased smile making her long for that attention from him. Though if she were honest, his intense scrutiny was as exciting as it was frightening.

"Summon her, so we may begin."

Still not understanding what he intended, Geira made no protest when he led her to the smoking fire of the blacksmith's forge. She looked around, a shard of alarm slicing along her spine to see the villagers gather round. She turned her gaze to Kori. His eyes seemed cold, his face a bland mask.

When Thora came up beside her father, a smug smile curving her lips, a sense of doom rose within Geira. Was he finally going to sacrifice her? She closed her eyes, a silent prayer for a quick and brave end.

"On your knees."

The words held an ominous tone. Her legs shook as she lowered herself to the ground, hoping she maintained at least a shred of dignity. She caught Dota's wide-eyed stare, saw the fear. Was her friend to be next? Had the men toyed with them both only to slaughter them now?

When Kori stepped behind her and gathered up her hair, twisting it into a long tail, she could no longer contain her trembling. Fear burned the back of her throat, her breath coming in harsh rasps. She clenched her fingers, hoping the discomfort of digging her nails into her palms might distract her. Foolish wish.

She lowered her head, eyes closing against the burn of angry tears. Better dead than a slave, she reasoned. Or tried to. Faced with her imminent demise, she knew she didn't really mean it. She *was* a coward, after all.

"With this, I claim this woman to be my slave. She is taken as revenge against my enemy and now my vengeance is complete."

The words shouted above startled her. Had she misheard? She looked up and realized what this ceremony was for. She nearly drowned in the rush of relief, her legs threatening to collapse beneath her. He wasn't going to kill her! Yet, a glimpse of what he held out for all to see chilled her once more.

He was going to mark her. The collar dangling from his left hand didn't worry her as much as the tiny brand in his right. It glowed red hot and her fear returned, though this time it was accompanied by a surge of anger.

She met his gaze, her own still blurred by the earlier tears. When her vision cleared, she found the same bland expression on his face. The roaring in her ears had died down and she made out the murmurings of the people surrounding them. She felt every stare, but ignored the uneasy sensations. Instead, she lifted her chin.

"Lower your head to receive my mark."

She thought about refusing, but feared he might be cruel enough to brand her on her face. Hands now clenched to contain her rage, she obeyed, biting hard on her lower lip. Once more, Kori moved aside her hair, fingers stroking lightly along the back of her neck. A sliver of awareness sparked, but was quickly scattered by the feel of one finger at the base. She sucked in a deep breath, concerned she might cry out. She must bear this bravely.

Heat grew against her skin, the brand nearing. For a moment, it hovered over her flesh then drew away. Why did he wait? The hesitation heightened her panic, but she managed to keep from fainting. She braced her shoulders, holding in a second deep breath. The shocking sear against her skin sent her eyes snapping open, and she bit down on her lip. The iron sizzled against her skin; it couldn't have been more than a few seconds, yet seemed forever. When Kori pulled the brand away, the tug on her flesh sent a scream to her throat. She prayed to every god she could think of to give her the strength to refrain. The bitter tang of blood coated her tongue from her teeth cutting her lip. Eyes squeezed shut, she fought the urge to weep. She had never known such agonizing pain. Flames took the place of the blood in her veins, sweat beaded along her brow. She fought her body's need to shake, her mind whirling. The sounds of the crowd faded, every one of her senses focused on the fire that ate at her skin. The acrid stench of burnt flesh surrounded her, rolling her stomach.

The throbbing burn continued. Something cool was placed against her wounded skin, but that hurt ten times worse. She gagged once, twice, and only Kori's hand on her shoulder kept her from falling over and retching.

After a few moments, the unimaginable pain began to fade. He'd put a healing salve on the wound, she realized, and turned to look at him. His mouth had set into a grim line. He asked for a bandage and stepped aside as a servant girl came forward, covering Geira's wound with a soft piece of cloth and securing it with another strip around her neck to hold the bandage in place.

"Kneel up, girl."

She straightened her back at the command, surprised at how easily she obeyed. Her legs still shook, but she possessed enough strength to gather her wits and hold herself proudly.

The thought she should fight him after what he'd done faded as quickly as it rose. The vow she'd made to him echoed in her head, oddly seeming stronger now that he'd marked her.

He wasn't finished yet. Her gaze settled on the collar he now held out. Slim and hammered into a smooth shiny circle, the metal gleamed in the sunlight. Despite the lack of adornment, she admired the skill of the smith, noting the smooth edges that would not mark or irritate her skin.

"This collar will ensure your status as slave is revealed to any and all, including other clans. You belong to me in every way. Mine to do with as I wish. For all time."

The words should terrify her, but when he leaned over and slid the collar against her throat, moving aside her hair as he connected it behind her neck, she found herself oddly at peace. The band of metal sat just above her bandaged wound. Kori's fingers brushed her skin when he closed the collar with a tiny lock.

Despite her intention to remain impassive, Geira's hands moved to touch the collar, seeming of their own volition. The cool metal quickly warmed under her touch. To her dismay, Kori fastened a chain to a hook in the collar. He tugged urging her stand.

"Give me your hands."

Too dazed to disobey, she did as he ordered. In a matter of moments, leather cuffs were fastened around her wrists. She raised a questioning stare.

"The markings of a slave. I will allow you to keep your hair. It pleases me, and you are here only to please me. As well, you have my protection. This collar and these bracelets declare this to all."

For some reason, the sensation of a malevolent stare caught her attention and she found Muli standing nearby. He watched everything eagerly, a malicious sneer on his ugly face. She looked back to Kori.

"Drink this."

She took the horn he offered, her thirst suddenly unbearable. The cool water soothed her swollen lips and parched throat. She handed the empty cup back, struck by the way he studied her. Desire flared in his eyes.

A calmness seeped into her arms and legs, lulling her into a realm she'd never felt. Flashes of the last week and how the events had left her defenseless in so many ways didn't anger her. Instead, an increasing peace flooded her senses. Recollection of moments of intense pleasure took hold in her thoughts. She tried to focus on her captor, blocking the morning sun as he stood over her.

For a moment, Kori's visage swayed in and out of clarity. Surely the pain had made her crazed, but she imagined she found affection and concern in his dark gaze. Unless… she didn't realize how deeply she longed to find confirmation of such emotions.

He gripped her arms, and his mouth moved, but she heard nothing other than a long dull roar. He drew her near and she rested her head against his chest. Her body seemed to have lost all sensation and she had the thought she floated, wrapped in the warm cocoon of Kori's embrace.

***

Kori watched Geira give in to the soothing elements of the herbs the healer had provided. Her eyes glazed over, the pain no longer assaulting her. Instead, as the man had warned, she had likely entered into a dream-like state. She could potentially communicate with the gods, and to disturb that would bring ill upon him.

And his family. He glanced at his daughter. He adored her. In appearance, she reminded him so much of Borga. But he disliked the hateful behavior she'd taken on since her mother's death. He understood her need for vengeance, and shuddered again knowing she had witnessed the brutal attack. He wanted his sweet and loving daughter back.

Was he mad to think Geira might be the path to that outcome?

His *ambátt* swayed when he released her from his hold. He'd not imagined he would take a slave who might be able to soften his daughter. Hell, if she'd been a spoiled shrew, he'd have no resistance to his daughter's contempt. Geira defied all his expectations and he didn't quite know how to react.

She'd born her branding well. He'd decided upon this permanent claim on her during the welcome feast. The notion that no matter what lay in the days ahead, she would always be known as his had taken hold. The pleasures they'd shared last night had only convinced him he'd made the right decision.

He would never say the words aloud, but from the moment he'd set his gaze upon her, she had become more than the mere slave he'd envisioned. He had to keep her – at any cost. What was wrong with him? She was the embodiment of his vengeance and yet, he wanted her to be so much more.

A surge of annoyance that she must have used her wiles to undermine him roused anger. Anger he needed to feel, lest he show his weakness for this woman before his entire clan. Before his father. His brother. His daughter.

His grip on Geira's arm tightened and she gave a pained moan, but he knew her wits remained addled by the herbs in the water. While he had planned to instruct her on her duties today, that would have to wait. His *ambátt* was in no shape for chores, and likely wouldn't be for some time.

He faced the crowd once more, holding Geira before him.

"Behold my slave. She embodies the restoration of my honor. Odin smiles upon me and my family once more."

He reached for his daughter, drawing her close beside him, the roar of cheers and applause filling the air. He accepted congratulations and blessings from his clansmen and friends. Several of the women sidled closer to him, invitation clear in their eyes. He thanked them for their good wishes, but felt no stirrings for any of them.

"Will I return home with you today, Father?"

Thora's question cut through his thoughts. He smiled at his daughter.

"Yes, Thora. There is much to be done to prepare for the winter. Your uncle Hradi will be staying with us for some time as well."

Thora clapped her hands in delight. "Two slaves to tend the farm!"

Kori studied her. "Geira's orders come from me."

She frowned at the reminder. "And the other?"

"She belongs to your uncle. You must speak with him about her duties."

A sulky pout crossed his daughter's face before she offered another warm smile.

"Very well. But this one will have much work to do in the house." She nodded toward Geira.

"Not today. After her marking, she must rest."

"Rest? She's nothing more than a slave, to be put to use. There is mending, and cooking to be done. I have several furs that need to be prepared. The garden needs tending. Winter is coming."

When had his daughter grown so much? In some ways, she became more and more like her mother every day, with the discipline to see to the needs of their home. Borga had been proud of their small farmhouse, and happy to live away from the great hall. In the years since her death, Kori had not paid much attention to the daily requirements of keeping hearth and home, leaving his daughter to struggle with the tasks needed to maintain their comfort. While many of the clan's women had assisted, he'd left her with too large a burden for too long. No wonder she remained bitter and angry.

No longer. Once Geira recovered from her marking, she'd be worked hard to ensure Thora no longer struggled under the weight of chores. He glanced down at his slave. She remained calm, docile. He noted her eyelids drooped.

He turned to Hradi. At his nod, his brother stepped forward, leading Dota. While Hradi also publicly claimed his slave, he did not brand the girl. She'd not been taken in vengeance, so he'd not felt the need to mark her as Kori had Geira. After the collar had been placed around Dota's neck, accompanied by more cheering and congratulations, Kori noticed his slave slumping in his embrace. The ceremony now over, Kori found himself anxious to return to his farm.

"Come, we go now."

He led Geira back to his horse, alarmed when she almost fell from the saddle a moment after he placed her there. With quick movements, he mounted behind her, securing her pliant body against him. Again, his cock stirred, but he pushed the desirous feelings aside. Aware of Thora riding beside him on her own pony, he headed toward his farm.

CHAPTER FOURTEEN

Awareness seeped into Geira's head. Her eyes felt heavy, her tongue thick and dry in her mouth. A throbbing at the base of her neck drew a moan of discomfort before she had the wits to contain it. Vague flashes of eager faces surrounding her, the smell of the smith's forge, cheers and laughter, assaulted her thoughts.

Recollection returned with sudden clarity. Kori had branded her, marking her as his for all time. She recalled very little after that, only a blur of returning to the farmhouse outside the village. He must have drugged her with the water after his claiming. How long ago had it been? She slowly opened her eyes.

The hole in the ceiling let in bright light, so it was daytime. The same day? She had no idea. She tried to sit up, the furs covering her heavy and suffocating.

"Finally awake."

She looked over at Kori who stood at the foot of the bed. Arms folded, legs wide, he gave her a fierce stare.

"You've been asleep since yesterday. It's time for you to begin tending your chores. But first, I must inspect your mark. Turn around."

What had he given her that had made her sleep so long? She obeyed his order silently, lifting her hair from her neck. The tug on the bandage ignited another burst of throbbing fire. She bit her lip, then let go at the sharp pain there as well. She realized she had wounded her lip during the branding and the swollen flesh remained tender.

At the first touch of Kori's fingers, moistened with salve, Geira sucked in a breath. The stinging pain lasted only a few seconds once he gently patted the ointment into her wound. Her tension eased and she remained still while he placed another bandage on her neck, securing it with a fresh strip of linen around her throat.

"It is healing nicely. If the pain worsens, tell me."

She nodded, waiting for further instruction. Sleep still muddied her mind and so much had happened that she needed to think on. Hunger gnawed at her, reminding her she hadn't eaten since yesterday morning.

Kori held out a hand. "Come, *ambátt*, tend yourself and break your fast."

He helped her from the bed, and despite her embarrassment, her weakness left her with no choice but to accept his aid during her ablutions. Finally feeling refreshed, she didn't resist when he led her to the table.

Cheese and dried cod sat upon a trencher on the table. Kori indicated she could sit at the table and eat. Once she had settled into her chair, he sat across from her.

"Eat well, you will need your strength."

She remained silent and stared at the food before her. The aroma of the cheese and fish made her mouth water. Cheeks heating at the thought he might recognize her hunger, she lowered her head and began to eat.

"There is barley that needs grinding. That will be your first chore. It has been a while since we have had fresh bread here. Meanwhile, Hradi and I will tend the fields and check on the cattle. It's almost time to move them down from the hill."

"Do you have others to help or will I be in the fields as well?" She hoped she hadn't sounded too resentful, but knowing she'd be required to use the stone mill troubled her. The hand mill was heavy and difficult to use. Her family had left that task to their own slaves. Now she was in their place.

He nodded, a hint of a smile curving his lip. "Yes, thralls help with that work. You are needed to tend the gardens, pigs and chickens. Thora will oversee the cooking, but you will aid in her any way she needs."

"What of Dota?"

He studied her for a few moments, the silence growing her uneasiness.

"Hradi agreed she will have chores of her own. You will divide the tending of the gardens and animals between you. Hradi has already shown her the garden and the pens."

So she would have help. After swallowing the last bite of cheese, she washed her meal down with ale and lifted her chin.

At that moment, the door opened and Hradi entered, Dota a step behind. Geira noted the collar her friend wore. She met Dota's stare, once again surprised by the hostility she found there. Today she must learn why her friend resented her.

"This one will beat the furs today," Hradi announced as he sat beside Kori.

"Geira will grind the barley and tend the hearth under Thora's guidance." Kori leaned close to his brother and lowered his voice.

Geira tried to make out his words, but missed most. One word she did hear was "separated." Her heart sank. They meant to keep her and Dota apart. The need to talk to her friend grew into a sharp ache. Knowing Thora's resentment, Geira doubted she'd be able to sneak outside. Geira suspected the girl's "guidance" would consist mostly of nasty comments and slurs against her.

As if she'd conjured Kori's daughter with her thoughts, Thora stomped through the door.

"It's about time she woke up!"

"She's been fed, and is ready to work now. She'll start with grinding the barley, then you can have her tend the garden."

She should be outraged at the way they spoke of her, as if she were little more than an animal. She supposed to Thora's eyes, that's all she was. Still, her main concern remained Dota. She needed her friend's alliance, not her hatred.

While it was clear she'd grind the barley here, under Thora's watchful gaze, eventually she would find herself in the garden. Then she might be able to speak with Dota. Geira met Kori's gaze. What thoughts hid behind those dark eyes? Hradi rose and led her friend outside. Beating furs was an exhausting task, and her heart ached for Dota. Then again, she faced her own trials with the grinding awaiting her.

Kori said nothing, merely nodded before stepping out of the small farmhouse. Geira rose, but before she could step away from the table, Thora had grabbed hold of her arm.

"Slave, get busy." She shoved Geira toward the center of the room, where a stone hand mill stood on a narrow table, a large pail beneath to catch the ground barley. Beside the table stood a large sack, filled with the barley stripped from their stalks.

Scooping a handful of grain from the sack, Geira poured it into the hole on the middle of the top stone. She sighed, clenching her fingers before reaching for the handle set into the upper stone. Her first tug barely moved the mill. Aware of Thora watching with a sneer, she pulled harder, finally making the top stone grind slowly against the bottom. The mill was heavy and it took some time to be able to make several complete rotations. Flour trickled out between the stones.

"Too slow! You'll be here for days! Let me show you what to do, slave."

Geira held up a hand. "I know how to work the stone. I had servants of my own to do this task."

"You follow my orders, or are you too stupid to recognize one when it's given? You'd better work harder, or I'll see my father whips you for your disobedience. You're the slave now. You have no voice of your own."

Geira pressed her lips together to hold back her retort. She would not give in to the girl's attempts to force her into an action that could end badly. Turning her back to Thora, she reached once more for the handle of the mill.

A few hours later, sweat poured down Geira's face. Her arms ached, but she'd managed to grind almost half the sack. After a short time, she'd developed a pattern to use one arm and then the other, so she didn't overtax either, but she still had little strength left. She paused to scoop up any stray flour and add it to the bucket, which was now nearly full.

"Hmph! Not bad."

She faced Thora, who stood with arms folded, the familiar scowl on her face. The girl was really quite lovely, with long curls of dark hair framing a heart-shaped face and eyes dark and piercing as Kori's. If only she possessed a kinder spirit. Wiping her hands on her apron, Geira waited for her next orders.

"I suppose you should tend the garden now. Come, I'll show you."

Silently, she followed Kori's daughter outside. The late summer sun blinded her momentarily and she put up a hand as a shield while she studied the layout. Two separate buildings sat upriver a little way, likely where the horses were kept. The nearby pens held goats and pigs, and a chicken coop lay a few steps beyond. Though small, Kori's farm was well-kept and thriving. Then again, being the son of the chieftain provided him the best lands and livestock and the money to support them.

She followed Thora behind the house, where a large garden flourished. She saw cabbage, beets, carrots, all ready for harvesting. At the far end of the garden Dota stood before a frame holding a fur, a large wooden paddle in her hand. Beside her, freshly beaten rugs and furs sat in a neat pile. She swung the paddle, sending dust and mites scattering into the air.

"Pull the carrots and the turnips. We'll do the beets tomorrow, the cabbage the following day."

Geira nodded in recognition of Thora's order and accepted the large woven basket. She made her way toward the patch of carrots, neatly planted in straight rows. As she neared, Dota turned.

The scorn lined into Dota's face brought a pang of hurt. She'd know her friend for years, had shared many laughs and secrets with her. The loathing directed at her now pained her more than she'd imagined.

"Dota, why are you angry with me?"

She glanced toward Thora, but apparently the girl didn't seem to care if the two slaves spoke.

"You're a whore!"

She should have known. Clearly, Dota had heard all that passed between her, Kori and Hradi the other night. How could she make Dota understand she only did as she had because she'd made an oath?

"I have no choice, if I want to survive." She tugged hard, but her exhausted arms had difficulty pulling the carrot.

"You gave yourself willingly to Kori."

Geira's cheeks reddened. Dota was right. She hadn't fought Kori very hard, not even that first time. Then again, he hadn't given her much choice, seducing her with his wicked ways.

"And if I didn't, he might well have killed me. I want to live Dota, and rebelling at every turn could cost my life. Besides, I did it for you!"

"For me? How could you whore yourself to them both for me?"

"So they would save you from Muli!" Geira longed to shake some sense into her friend. She dropped another carrot into the basket and stood. "I offered myself as a willing slave for you. Now I must find the best way to survive."

Dota stalked closer. "You liked it. I heard you, begging them. You wanted everything they did to you."

"And what is wrong with taking pleasure where it can be found? You were always the one to encourage wanton behavior, you've had several men in your bed already."

"They weren't enemies," Dota snarled.

"Einnar is the one who made Kori's clan our enemy. If I hadn't been given to him, we'd still be in Allesgat."

"See, this is all your fault."

Geira shook her head. "No, I didn't have any choice. You're lucky, your family didn't demand a marriage of alliance."

"Einnar was a good man and you are sleeping with his killer!"

Geira's annoyance surged. Didn't Dota understand? Had Muli beaten her so terribly, her wits had left her? And why did she care so much for Einnar?

"Dota, what aren't you telling me?"

"Nothing. Just tend your chores, and leave me to mine."

Dota turned back to the hanging fur, but Geira grabbed her arm.

"Tell me what you know of Einnar! Why do you defend him?"

"Why do you not? He was your husband!"

"For less than a day! And we shared no great love. In fact, I always suspected he wasn't as honorable as everyone said."

Dota's eyes widened. "He was a fine man, one of fairness and kindness."

"And what of how he murdered Kori's wife? Wanted to kill his daughter?"

"Lies!" Dota's voice rose to a shriek.

Geira suspicions solidified. She should be angry at the idea her friend had bedded Einnar, but couldn't find it in herself. She almost didn't care.

"He was cruel and mean. I saw it, Dota." How could she make the woman understand she had been tricked?

Dota shook her head. "You are wrong! He was a good man, one who deserved better than the likes of you!"

Geira's anger snapped into force. "You had sex with him, didn't you? That's why you care so much."

"He appreciated my… talents."

Dota clearly possessed no remorse for spreading her legs for Einnar. The betrayal stung, despite the fact Geira shared no love with her husband. Along with the rising anger, pity also grew prominent, sitting like an anvil in her gut. She looked over to where Thora had stood. The girl had disappeared. Good. The last thing she needed was for Kori's daughter to make things worse.

"He fooled you, Dota, like he fooled everyone else." Once again, Geira attempted to reason with the other woman. Why in the name of Hel did she try?

Anger twisted Dota's face. "You disrespect him by willingly cavorting with his enemy, his murderer!"

"If I'd known you wanted him, I would have let you have him. Be glad I didn't!"

"Still you slander him! I will avenge him, I promise you that!"

"Dota, he was not the man you think he was –"

The fist came at her so fast, Geira barely had time to duck. She dodged another blow, forced into repelling Dota's attack. Avoiding yet another strike, Geira landed a stinging slap to Dota's cheek. She held up her other hand, blocking her friend's next attempt, and turned. The forgotten basket now tripped her and she tumbled to the ground. She rolled to her back, but Dota stood above her, the large paddle in hand.

Geira held up her arms, trying to dart out of the way, but the basket and the vegetables hindered her progress. Eyes squeezed shut, she anticipated the blow, but it never came. Instead, a loud roar echoed in the garden.

She looked up to see Kori and Hradi holding Dota back. The woman screamed, curses spewing from her twisted lips when Hradi took the paddle from her and pulled her away. With an unsteady breath, Geira rose to her knees and attempted to stand. Kori's hands on her arms steadied her, gave her strength.

She swiped at the dirt on her dress and grimaced.

She had nothing else to wear. She held back a hysterical laugh at the inane thought. Her friend had just attacked her and all she cared for was the dirt on her dress. Despite her efforts, a mad giggle erupted.

"Geira?"

She looked up at the concern in Kori's voice. His worry proved her undoing. After all she'd been through in the last week, she had no more resolve. Tears welled in her eyes. Kori groaned and drew her close. Any remaining resistance shattered. She wept against his shoulder.

***

Kori didn't understand most of the words Geira blubbered against him, but he understood enough just by witnessing the fight between the two women. Clearly, his *ambátt* was deeply hurt by her friend's words and attempts to harm her. He would warn Hradi to use caution with Dota. The woman was dangerous. Then again, having endured Muli, Kori supposed any woman would turn angry and violent.

Kori lifted Geira into his arms and carried her inside. Thora stood over the meal fire, tending a stew.

"Did the lazy bitch get beaten?"

"Enough, Thora! See to our meal."

"But Father, I'm still waiting for the slave to bring the carrots so I can add them to the stew. The rest must be prepared for the winter stores. Her stupid fight means she didn't finish!"

Kori fixed a fierce scowl on his daughter. "Gather the carrots yourself."

Thora stomped her foot. "Why have a slave if I must still do all the work? It isn't fair that someone of her station should –"

"I said enough! When she is ready, she will help once more."

Thora continued to mutter under her breath but picked up a basket and stepped outside. He would deal with her later. For now, he had a shaking slave in his arms that was of no use to him in this condition. Kori strode into the sleeping room and eased Geira to the bed. Her weeping had mostly subsided, but hiccupping sobs still escaped. He brushed the hair from her face, her red and puffy eyes staring blankly beyond him. With her swollen lip and the bandage around her neck, she looked like a discarded waif. A pang of empathy knifed him.

"What happened?'

A few seconds passed before she spoke. "I only wanted to know why she was so angry. She blames me for all this."

"The blame belongs with your husband."

She nodded. "It does. I wish I'd defied my father and refused the marriage."

An odd hurt rolled Kori's gut. If she had refused, Einnar would have wed someone else. The idea of an *ambátt* other than Geira bothered him, more than he cared to admit. This slender woman had wormed her way into his affection, in a matter of days. She shouldn't. She was nothing more than a slave, to tend his home and see to his needs.

His gaze settled on the collar around her throat. It marked her as his, more visibly than the brand he'd placed on her. She would belong to him for all time, no matter her choice.

"Why does she blame you?"

Geira shrugged.

"Tell me."

He wanted to know, needed to know, in order to soothe her sadness. He bit back a curse. He shouldn't care about her moods. Yet, ignoring the feelings she stirred had proven a near impossible task to this point. He must harden his heart against her or she'd weaken him, in reality and in the eyes of his people. One day he would be the chieftain of the clan. Being enamored of his slave would be viewed as a sign of impotence he could not afford. He sensed a formidable task lay ahead.

He continued to toy with the ends of her blonde

hair. "Geira, tell me why Dota blames you."

Her eyes squeezed shut. The clenching of her fingers drew his gaze.

"She said... I gave myself willingly. That I enjoyed acting the... whore."

Anger burned in his throat. He held back the words of comfort the rush of guilt urged him to speak. She had been taken against her will. By him. He'd forced her to serve his brother as well, heaping further humiliation upon her. Her next words, a harsh and raspy whisper, near stopped his heart.

"She is right. I am a whore. I did enjoy it."

A surge of elation at the latter words chased his guilt. His instincts had been accurate. His slave liked his touch. But hearing her refer to herself as whore troubled him. She'd been innocent until he'd taken her. He remained silent, unsure of his next words.

Geira sat up, piercing him with a melancholy stare. "She was my friend for a long time. Now I fear she'll always hate me. I believe she dallied with Einnar."

Kori had no doubts Einnar would indeed use Geira's friend without remorse. The man had possessed no honor. Kori was again thankful he'd killed him. He held Geira's stare.

"Shouldn't that make you angry? He was your husband."

"For all of a day. You know we didn't..." She fell back to the furs. "You don't understand."

"Then explain."

She sighed, her hands wringing together. Her gaze darted to his time and again, moving away just as quickly.

"I... had doubts about my husband."

Smart girl. He waited for her to continue, nodding when her eyes locked on his.

"It's not your concern. But when you told me what he'd done to your wife... I thought it could be true."

"I know. I saw in your eyes that first night you believed him capable. You should talk with Thora. She can tell you just how evil your husband was."

"Thora wouldn't spit on me if I were in flames."

"She is angry over her mother's loss. You cannot blame her for that."

Her eyes narrowed and darkened with anger. "No, but I had nothing to do with it! And yet, you killed my husband and his clan, steal me away, mark and collar me."

Her voice rose, until she near shouted. Kori winced as she continued ranting.

"You claimed me as slave before all. I have been humiliated beyond what any person should endure, and now, I've lost my only friend." Her fists clenched and Kori braced himself, thinking she might attempt to strike him. Instead, she turned, laying on her side and facing away.

"A friend like that is not a friend I'd want."

She said nothing. Her words still rattled and echoed in his thoughts, but he had no choice. If he showed her kindness now, she would take advantage. That he could never allow.

"You seem recovered. It's time to finish your chores."

She gave a huff and rolled to her back, fixing him with a glare that might separate his head from his shoulders if it had been a sword.

"Yes. I must tend the garden," she spat.

He held out a hand to assist her, but she shrugged away, rebuffing him. He held back a grin. Her defiance would cost her later. Somehow, he knew turning her anger against her would reward them both.

He followed her outside. Hradi waited. Kori noticed Dota standing a few feet behind him, her wrists bound together. She looked less angry than she had before. Now, fear darkened her eyes.

"I'm taking her back to the village. I'll stay with her in the great hall until she understands her place and learns proper respect."

Kori's gaze remained on Geira. She hesitated a

moment before resuming her trek to the garden. He gave a smile and turned back to his brother.

"I understand. You'll return to help bring the cows down?"

"Yes, at sunrise."

Kori pulled his brother in for an embrace and stood back as Hradi mounted his horse, his slave before him. He waved as he rode downriver toward the village.

Kori made his way to the garden. Thora had cleared the carrots and Geira set to work on the turnips. He watched over them for a while, pleased to see his daughter mostly ignored the slave.

When he returned to his own tasks, he found himself imagining the coming night.

CHAPTER FIFTEEN

Geira cleared the table, lifting her own bowl from the floor. Despite the kindness Kori had shown this afternoon, he clearly remained determined to remind her of her place. Thora had thankfully been mostly silent, but from time to time, Geira looked up to find the girl scowling fiercely.

After wiping the wooden plates clean, she returned to the fire, stoking it to keep the house warm. In the days since she'd been captured, the weather had changed, heralding the arrival of autumn. Recollections of her own family's servants and how they kept the home comfortable for all assailed her with every move. Now she was the one responsible for seeing to Kori and Thora's comfort.

She tried to remain angry with Kori, but found herself blaming him less and less. Her outburst today had only convinced her this whole mess was her husband's fault. Truthfully, she much preferred Kori to her husband. She shuddered to recall the day she'd come across Einnar taking the servant girl. The act had been savage, but the girl hadn't resisted, at least not in any obvious way. But the recollection of the girl's grimace convinced Geira now, beyond any doubt, the servant hadn't wanted Einnar's attentions. When Kori stated what Einnar had done to his wife, intended to do to Thora, at that moment, Geira knew Einnar *had* raped the servant girl.

"Come."

Lost in her thoughts, she hadn't heard Kori step up behind her. She turned, sucking in a deep breath to see the heat in his eyes. She looked around the room. Thora had disappeared.

She placed trembling fingers into Kori's outstretched hand, allowing him to lead her to his bed.

Her heart raced in anticipation. She wanted this man, fiercely. No matter what the circumstances, she knew she would never refuse his attentions, enjoying them far more than she should. If only she wasn't a mere slave, to be taken on a whim. She wanted more from Kori, wanted him to care for her as more than a vessel to be used for his needs. She suspected he did care, a little anyway. Time and again she'd found him looking at her with affection. The bittersweet ache tempered her excitement. Yet, it wasn't enough to make her completely accept her position.

"What troubles you, *ambátt*?"

She shook her head. "I am tired. It's been a very long day."

He nodded. "And we shall rest soon."

He slid his hand through her hair, cupping the back of her head to draw her near. His lips descended on hers, hungry and demanding, stoking her eagerness once more. He did it so easily, with barely a touch or a glance, or a word. When he kissed her like this, nothing else mattered except giving in to the onslaught and taking her pleasure from it. If he would allow her.

He turned her, untying the laces of her dress and sliding it from her shoulders. He had yet to allow any other garments, and when the dress fell to the floor, she stood naked before him. Hands on her shoulders pulled her against him. Kori remained fully clothed, and the contrast was another stark reminder to Geira that she only held a lowly position in his life. It shouldn't hurt so much.

Abruptly, she found herself turned, her gaze immediately caught by Kori's dark eyes. The hunger in their depths soothed the ache, but stirred another. Another kiss, this one sensual and teasing, drawing Geira's desire to a higher pitch. She reached for the buttons on his tunic, opening them and drawing the garment from his body. His under shirt kept her from touching his flesh. She reached for it, surprised when Kori caught her wrists.

"You have a reprimand awaiting first."

Her eyes widened. What in Thor's name had she done now? She shook her head in confusion.

"Why?"

"You need a reminder of your place."

"Kneeling at your feet isn't enough?"

He chuckled, but the sound roared ominously through her.

"You just proved why you need to be punished. You are to show me proper respect. I am your master. Every time you defy me, by word or action, you pay a price."

"But what did I say? What did I do?" She mulled over the events of the day. No, he couldn't possibly mean after... when he'd been so kind and understanding? She met his gaze. "You are truly merciless."

Something flickered across his face, but vanished in a moment. Instead, his lips pressed together for a few seconds before he spoke.

"You should know by now what behavior is expected of you. As your master, I will care for you as you need it, but you are to show respect at all times. You didn't do that today."

"I see. So I am not even to have any thoughts of my own?" Despite her effort to remain calm, she spat the words at him, sneering.

He caught her arm and hauled her against him. "I am beginning to think you enjoy what I do to you, so you speak to me that way apurpose."

She didn't answer, the sudden truth sucking the breath from her lungs. She sassed him at every turn because she wanted him to take her in this way. Wanted the torment he bestowed upon her because it also gave the most delightful pleasure. She jerked her arm free, backing away. Her flight was halted by the bed, the furs soft against her now-heated skin.

A slow grin crossed his face. He reached for her once more, easily subduing her evasive moves, and pushed her back to the bed. He climbed up, straddling her, pinning her arms beneath his, and spreading her legs with his. Her heart raced, breathing heavily. She *did* want this, enjoyed his rough lovemaking. Her pussy heated and grew wet, dampening her thighs with desire.

In that moment, she knew taking her pleasure, even if it meant taking it on his terms, didn't make her weak. She raised her chin.

"Then do with me what you will."

His eyes widened and he gave a hearty laugh. "Be careful what you dare."

"I will endure."

Her breasts tingled, the light rasp of his shirt sensitizing her skin. Damn him! She wanted him to truly touch her. He knew it as well.

They remained motionless for several moments, until Kori grasped her wrists and hauled her closer, his mouth demanding and masterful. When he drew away, her breath rasped between her lips. Her nipples tightened almost painfully to hard peaks, her pussy hot and desperate for the torment Kori would inflict.

***

Kori rose and tugged Geira to her feet. He seated himself on the bed and yanked her down across his lap. She screeched her outrage and tried to rise, but he quickly caught her hands and hooked her bracelets together behind her. He gripped her wrists and pressed them into the small of her back then caught her flailing legs between his, immobilizing her. Cursing at him, she vowed to bring the wrath of the gods down on him.

"You made an oath," he reminded her. "That you would submit willingly. Lying is cause for further chastisement."

She stilled, the only sound her heavy breathing. He smiled, caressing her ass with his free hand. She jerked under the gentle touch, clearly not expecting he would arouse her first.

With slow gentle strokes, he continued to caress her, sliding his hand down into her warm cleft. Her juices, wet and hot, coated his fingers and her hips jerked toward his touch. He probed further, finding the hard knob of her pleasure. She let out a low moan when he circled it, squeezing gently to coax a sharp cry of need.

Satisfied, he withdrew and raised his hand. He wasted no time, slamming hard into her bottom and savoring the way she jolted under the blow. His cock, already steely as his sword, lurched. Her squirming tormented him and he nearly rolled her to the bed to take her at that moment.

Instead, he fought his lust back under control, resuming his spanking. He landed several hard blows, finally wrenching a hoarse scream. He continued, savoring the heat rising in her flesh, the way her pale skin grew red from his blows. He paused, trailing his fingertips along her ass. She gave a delightful wiggle and moaned. He caressed harder, her voice deepening in pitch. A quick slide into her sex and he found her wetter than ever.

"My little *ambátt* likes to be spanked."

"More."

The whispered moan nearly eluded him. He hadn't expected a response, definitely not that one, but relished it just the same. He obliged her.

Each blow on her ass sent her hips rolling against him. He thanked Odin he'd left his hose in place. His achingly hard cock would surely betray the depth of his passion. Her flesh grew dark red, and despite her sobs, she raised herself up, meeting each strike of his hand.

He paused, caressing, the heated skin of her twitching ass scorching his palm. Another slide into her pussy and he withdrew drenched fingers. He sucked them one by one, savoring her musky, spicy taste.

He released his hold on her bound wrists, helping her to stand. She swayed toward him and he caught her, pulling her close. She snuggled into him, her hands still bound behind her back. He lifted her chin, studying her tear-streaked face. Heat flamed in her eyes and she pressed her lips against his. Startled by her boldness, he barely thought to respond, soon taking control of the kiss.

Holding her chin, he swept his tongue deep into her mouth, her moan vibrating through him. He wanted, needed more. He clutched her closer, but it wasn't enough. Might never be enough. Hating the time it took to let her go so he could strip out of his clothes, he paused when he reached for her again.

Standing before him, chin high, eyes meeting his squarely, she looked like a wild Valkyrie, her hair floating in tumultuous waves around her head. Her breasts, full and lush, drew his hands before he had awareness of moving. She arched toward him and he pulled her close, devouring her mouth. He gave half a thought to releasing her hands but knew if she touched him, he would erupt like an untrained lad. Instead, he lifted her and laid her on the bed, taking several moments to savor the way she squirmed against the furs.

The firelight bronzed her skin, giving her a sensuous glow that dried his mouth. Thor's teeth, she would be the death of him. To die in her arms would surpass falling during battle. With quick movements, he straddled her body, delighted at the way she opened her legs to let him nestle against her. Her hot slick flesh cradled him and it took all of his will to refrain from sliding into her.

He kissed her again, a brief taste before dragging his mouth down her neck. She whimpered and threw her head back, thrusting her breasts against his chest. He drew away, noting the way she continuously tried to free her arms, caught beneath her. He grinned, enjoying the feel of her helpless to his whims. Judging from the way she panted, her eyes glazed with lust, she enjoyed it as much as he.

"What do you want, *ambátt*?"

She moaned, the quivering of her body sending little jolts of pleasure to his cock.

"Take me." The words came out on a low moan.

"Not yet. Your body belongs to me. I wish to savor it."

Another whimper, more a whine, of both frustration and eagerness. He grinned then caught one breast in his hand, squeezing and caressing, rolling her hardened nipple in his fingers. Her cries grew louder. He lowered his mouth to suck the tip of her flesh into his mouth, her moans turning to little shrieks. He sucked and licked, teasing her by drawing away and tracing a wet circle around her nipple. She squirmed wildly beneath him, half-pleading words falling from her parted lips.

He ignored her pleas, turning his attention to her other breast. If he hadn't been atop her, she might have lurched right from the bed. Her hips bucked toward him, as if she tried to force him to enter her. He drew back, squeezing her nipple hard. Her cry echoed in the room, fueling the lust controlling him.

"Be still!"

"I… please, Kori!"

"Patience, *ambátt*."

She shook her head, frantically, telling him her patience was at its end. He grinned. Tormenting her this way gave him a surge of pleasure so great, he almost came right then. He lowered his mouth to her flesh once more, sliding along her ribs and lower across her belly. Each tremor and cry sent another jolt to his cock. Her skin tasted of honey and musk, intoxicating him further.

He caught her hips to still her frantic movements, using his knees to keep her legs spread wide. Pausing, he stared at her, taking in the desperate need lining her face. He intended to make her mindless, though he feared he would end up the same. He didn't care. Losing himself in her this way filled his soul as it hadn't been in over two years.

The realization gave him pause, but his desire for the woman beneath him chased the errant thought. With his fingers holding the slick flesh of her pussy open, he lowered his head.

***

Geira nearly screamed as Kori's tongue slid along her sex. She was already hanging on the edge of a climax so intense, she feared giving in. Not that she had a choice. Only Kori would decide to give her that pleasure. The very notion intensified her need. She wanted him to continue tormenting her in this manner, even as she desperately hungered for release. Her arms ached with the need to hold him against her, but somehow, the helplessness only spiked the yearning holding her fast in its grip. His hot mouth on her pussy, tongue seeking and teasing, nearly drove her heart out of her chest.

Unable to do more than surrender to the onslaught of lust, she closed her eyes, lifting her hips as Kori drove two fingers deep into her. She wanted his cock inside her, knew he wanted the same, but damn the man! He took delight in torturing her this way. And yet, so did she.

He drew away and she couldn't help smiling in response to his devilish grin. Moments like these gave her a strange hope, one she didn't dare acknowledge. Instead, she focused on the storm Kori stirred in her body.

He withdrew his fingers with a lingering caress that sucked the breath from her lungs. Lids drooping heavily over her eyes, she gasped as he put his fingers to his mouth, sucking them clean. A wink and a chuckle and his body covered hers. She panted with excitement, anxious for him to take her.

With fingers tight on her hips, he lifted her. She cried out at the feel of his hot flesh filling her. For several moments he remained motionless, studying her. In his stare she found a hunger that matched her own, a fire that only the two of them knew. He lifted his hand, sliding his fingers slowly across her cheek, grasping her chin and holding her still for a fiery kiss.

At the same time, he moved within her, slowly,

making her feel each inch of his hard shaft. Her body quaked, his tongue sliding against hers in a sensual rhythm that matched that of his cock. Nothing mattered but the way he claimed her, binding her to him with his body more securely than he could with his marks.

Just when she thought she would explode with pleasure, he stilled and broke the kiss.

"Please... Kori, I can't bear it!"

He remained silent, reaching beneath her to free her arms. She ignored the sharp tingling and wrapped herself around him, holding on as he began once more to move, this time hard, fast. She approached rapture in moments, crying his name as she rocked under the explosive delight. The roaring in her ears near drowned out his shout, but the pulses of his climax set off another eruption of sheer bliss that left her unable to hear or see, only able to feel the waves washing through her.

Kori slumped against her and she held him close, savoring his weight atop her. She felt oddly safe, cherished. She almost protested when he rolled from her, sliding his cock from her body, but then he pulled her near, settling her against him. His fingers idly toyed with her hair, adding to her feeling of contentment.

With nights spent like this, the long winter months didn't seem to stretch out so bleakly anymore.

CHAPTER SIXTEEN

Geira shivered as she made her way behind the barn, the sack gripped tight in her hand. She had only a short time to complete her task. A light snow fell, the flakes glinting in the darkness. The solstice soon approached.

Watching frequently over her shoulder to ensure no one watched, she found herself again worrying about going to the village for the Jul celebration. When Kori warned her the longest night of the year would be spent in the longhouse with his family and clan, she'd worried about how his clan would look upon her. Though the past months had not been the atrocity she'd feared the night of her capture, she still found herself uneasy surrounded by the villagers. Most ignored her, but there were a few that went out of their way to taunt her, or otherwise, when Kori was out of earshot.

What she hated most about their deliberate torment was the whispers mocking Kori. Most were careful not to be overheard, but she had heard some speculation that he was weak to care so much for a slave. Those who dared speak that aloud were few, and easily quieted by their fellow clansmen. Still, why did Geira want to so fiercely to defend him? She'd not forgotten her plans to escape, but several months lay ahead before she could act on those plans. In the meantime, she'd done her best to prove herself loyal. By now, he surely believed that devotion real.

As do you. She ignored the voice that insisted on making itself heard when she least wanted or needed to hear it. She pulled the cloak tight about her, glad for the warmth of the wolverine pelt around her head. Kori had kept his word, having a cloak fashioned for her, the hood made of the wolverine's fur. Geira smiled to recall the way Thora had shouted and raged against such a fine garment. Kori had held firm, insisting Geira had earned it for facing the beast so bravely. He'd been delighted in the way she initiated the night's passion.

She sighed, pushing the thoughts from her mind. The task facing her must be done quickly. No time for pondering such things now. Nearing the oak behind the barn, she withdrew the small bowl and dagger from her pocket. At the base of the tree, she knelt and reached into the sack. The squirrel squirmed wildly in her grip, scratching and hissing, but she held its neck firmly, giving the animal no leverage. She lowered the creature to the ground, securing it in place before slicing its throat. The squirrel twitched in its death throes. Geira's stomach rolled, but she forced down the urge to retch. Such an act ion would disgrace herself and taint the offering. She raised the animal over the bowl, easing her tight grip. Blood poured into the bowl, and the sliver of moonlight told her when enough of the squirrel's life had filled the vessel.

She pulled more items from her pocket. After sprinkling the herbs she'd snuck from inside into the blood, she arranged the small twig between two tiny rocks. With quick motions, she struck a third stone against them. She made several attempts before a spark ignited the twig. She dropped it into the bowl, pleased with the way the herbs flared before the tiny flame flickered out.

"Odin, accept my meager offering. I seek knowledge and pray you will guide me."

She clasped her hands together, begging the lord of gods for compassion. "Tell me if my father lives, send a sign so I may know my family is well."

She repeated the prayer several times, closing her eyes and focusing all of herself on gaining an answer. A burst of excitement shook through her. Was it a sign Odin had heard? Accepted her offering? Or did he mock her measly sacrifice?

She remained still for a bit longer, shifting her pleas to Thor in the hopes he would deign to give her a sign. After several more minutes when nothing happened, she opened her eyes. The snow had grown heavier, adding to the thin layer already covering the ground. Knowing she would receive no sure answer now, she dumped the blood into the dirt near the tree trunk. A scoop of snow and no one but the gods would know of her sacrifice. Though the ground was hard, she used the bowl to scoop a small grave for the squirrel, dropping the carcass into the hole and covering it with dirt.

Rising, she tucked the bowl and dagger back into her pocket along with the fire stones. Satisfied she'd completed her task before any would miss her, she turned to the house. Kori awaited her and the notion set her heart to racing.

***

As always, Kori concentrated on the woman kneeling beside his chair. Ever since he'd informed her of the plan to celebrate Jul in the village, she'd been tense. The only time her anxiety seemed to lessen was during the long nights. Tomorrow would herald the longest of all, the height of Odin's Wild Hunt. The feast ahead would last for several days. Kori's eagerness for the celebration surpassed what he'd felt in the years past. This occasion gave him the opportunity to share some revelry with Geira. He must be careful, lest the rumors of his weakness in regard to his slave grow stronger.

A knock on the door startled him. Who would be out now? Geira started to rise, but Kori touched her shoulder, urging her to remain. He rose and reached the door in two quick strides. Pulling it open, he gaped at Hradi.

"Brother, what are you doing here?"

Kori moved aside to let Hradi in. His brother rubbed his hands together and walked toward the heart, pausing to study Geira for a moment. He gave Kori a grin.

"If only my slave was as calm and agreeable."

Kori chuckled, noting the way Geira's shoulders tensed. "I am lucky. Are you here to spend the night?"

Hradi shook his head. "No, just returning from the night's hunt. Odin and Sleipner led us on a merry chase last night, but we slayed several stags for the feast. I merely wished to rest a bit before returning to the village to help prepare."

"Make yourself comfortable," Kori said, returning to his seat. "Geira, pour us ale then await me in bed."

He accepted the flagon Geira handed him and waited until she had disappeared into their sleeping room. He leaned over, tapping the horn against Hradi's.

"The feast will be a success," Hradi said. "Odin smiles on us again. With a strong sacrifice at Ostara, the coming year will be fruitful."

Kori stared into the fire, sipping his ale, trying to ignore the warning tone in his brother's voice. Odin's blood, Kori had much to be thankful for this Jul. Still, not participating in this hunt had roused more whispers. He needed a successful sacrifice on the solstice to silence the gossip and waiting for Ostara was the last thing he could afford. The risk that all he'd succeeded in these last months might crumble into dust lay like a lump in his gut. His thoughts wandered to the woman awaiting him. Surely she had ensorcelled him somehow, making him appear weak.

No longer. At the feast tomorrow, he would quiet the whispers and remind all who was the slave. And who was master.

***

Sol gave her final gasp across the sky, sinking into oblivion. Geira held her breath, watching as the last of the sun goddess' light winked out. Máni now ruled the heavens. Kori guided the horse toward the village, the babbling of the river against the rocks of the shoreline echoing Geira's heartbeat.

The remnants of her sacrifice were well hidden and she hoped to soon receive some sign from the gods. Perhaps when she slept tonight, Odin would appear in her dreams and give her the answers she sought. Tonight would be very long, the height of Odin's Wild Hunt, and she wondered if she'd sleep much during the feast. Kori was unusually silent, and she sensed a tension in him she hadn't felt in some time. Was it due to fact they were to spend the next several days in the longhouse, rather than at his farm? Geira worried about being surrounded by Kori's family and clan, but had kept those concerns to herself. She had no choice in the matter anyway.

"A fine feast has been prepared." Kori's words broke the silence. "My father has planned a large sacrifice to ensure the coming months will be peaceful and prosperous."

"I have no doubt."

Despite herself, an eagerness to be part of the celebration grew within, warming her. Recollections of past Juls celebrated with her family flashed in her thoughts, tingeing the excitement with a whisper of sadness.

They reached the village quickly and many people rushed to greet Kori. He dismounted then helped Geira down from the horse. Slinging an arm about her shoulder, he greeted his clan, chatting easily while they made their way toward the longhouse.

"Kori! It's about time you arrived!" Jarl Thorfinn's booming voice carried over the din. He strode to them, the people falling aside to let him pass. Kori released his hold on Geira just as Thorfinn grasped his son in a brief hug.

"Come, the sacrifice awaits."

Kori took Geira's arm once more when Thorfinn led them to the altar set up alongside the longhouse. The stone top supported by hefty logs looked big enough to hold a person and Geira shivered, wondering if it ever had. Several bronze bowls sat upon the stone, three small and one large, two ceremonial daggers arranged among them. A flame burned bright in the pit beyond the altar.

"Stay here."

Kori stared fiercely at her until she nodded. He and Hradi joined Thorfinn before the altar. The crowd fell silent.

"Bring the sacrifices!"

Thorfinn's voice rang out over the gathering. To his right, men led three goats to the altar. Geira clasped her hands before her, watching as each man with the aid of two others, positioned the animals properly. The only sound to break the reverent quiet was the bleating of the goats. Three quick slices silenced the animals, their blood gathered into the smaller bowls.

Around her, the crowd pressed in, their excitement muted by the solemnity of the ceremony. Her heart raced, caught up in the anticipation buzzing through the villagers.

A fourth man led a horse to stand before Thorfinn. The jarl picked up the larger bowl as the handlers wrestled the animal to the ground. Clearly, the mare had been given herbs to calm her, for she barely resisted and soon lay on her side before the stone. Thorfinn knelt before the animal and quickly opened its throat. Blood quickly filled the large bowl and Thorfinn stood, replacing it to the altar top as the men moved the animal's carcass away. The animal would be drained, as would the goats, the lifeless bodies to be burned in offering, their blood used for other ceremonies designed to please the gods and bring prosperity.

Murmurs and quiet blessings rustled through the crowd. Geira recalled a similar sacrifice her father had made last Jul. Oddly, watching Kori's father now roused a sense of peace and calm, despite the pounding of her heart. For a moment, excitement that echoed what she'd felt as a child overtook her. The jarl's sure and steady arrangement of the bowls captivated her, even as her gaze darted again and again to Kori and Hradi, flanking their father. Thorfinn spoke an incantation, arranging rune stones about the altar.

Finally, he bowed his head and sprinkled herbs into

each bowl of blood. He then dipped his finger into one of the smaller ones and turned.

"Odin, accept our sacrifice and grant us a prosperous year." He stepped toward Kori and drew the warm blood across his son's forehead. He repeated the prayer and motion with Hradi and the second bowl. With the third, he applied the blood to his own face.

Lastly, he dipped both hands completely into the large bowl with the horse's blood. He raised them up to the sky then turned to face the crowd. The murmurs grew louder and Geira found herself pushed toward the jarl when the clan surged forward, eager to be blessed. Her own anticipation easily matched the thrill pulsing among the gathering. Pleas to the gods to accept the offerings whispered through the crowd, adding to the fervor which soon had everyone, men, women and children, dancing and jumping and praying for blessings.

"May this worthy sacrifice bring us all the rewards Odin sees fit to bestow!"

Thorfinn shook his hands wildly, spraying the assemblage with the blood. Geira bowed her head with the others, showing respect to the sacrifice, a shivery feeling of blessing suffusing every part of her when several drops spattered her hair and dress. Hope that this, combined with her own private entreaty to Odin, would ensure an answer to her prayer flared like a beacon within her.

Silence hung over the crowd for several moments before cheers rose up, soon reaching a deafening roar. After shaking much of the remaining blood across the gathered clan, Thorfinn rinsed his hands with the sacred ewer. Once cleaned, he took a flint and quickly sparked each of the smaller bowls. A flare illuminated each for few seconds, the herbs floating on the blood catching in a brief flash of light before winking out. Thorfinn clapped his hands and faced his clan.

"Our sacrifice has been accepted. The value of the offering will be foretold in the morn, when Sol returns to us to chase the night."

More cheers erupted and the throng moved toward the longhouse. Kori pushed his way through the crowd, enclosing Geira in his embrace. He guided her free of the crush, until she stood beside him and Hradi at the altar, waiting for the villagers to enter the hall.

With the courtyard clear, Kori guided Geira to the longhouse. Smoke from the fires fogged the hall and Geira blinked to soothe the sudden burning of her eyes. The noise and laughter assaulted her senses, the din more intense inside. She leaned in close to Kori, relieved when he tightened his embrace. After a few minutes, her uneasiness calmed completely.

Around the hall, several pine trees stood, hung with sweets and images of the gods. The scent of holly battled with the smells of roasted pig and stewed vegetables. They made their way to the throne where Thorfinn had taken up a stance. A broad grin broke through his white beard.

"Now the feast can begin!"

At those words, several women brought platters of meats and vegetables and pitchers of ale and mead to the tables. Thorfinn gave another small prayer of thanks to Odin and Thor for their success this past harvest, and everyone piled their trenchers high.

As usual, Kori motioned for Geira to kneel beside him. The affectionate way he ran his fingers through her hair soothed her while she waited for him to feed her. He didn't usually do so at the farmhouse, but before his clan, she suspected he wanted to make clear his role as her master.

She looked around, the din of raucous laughter and shouted merriment hurting her ears. She'd gotten used to the quiet of home and… Home? When had she begin to think of Kori's house her home? When had she grown so comfortable in her position? So caught up in the startling realization, she didn't notice the morsel of meat Kori held before her. She looked up into his confused expression.

"What has you so far away from here?" he asked.

She shook her head, not wanting to tell him of her thoughts.

"Missing your family, I suppose."

Though the words were directed to her, she sensed he merely spoke his thoughts aloud. She nodded. Let him think what he wanted. She leaned forward and accepted the food. She held his gaze and deliberately ran her tongue along his thumb, drawing an arched eyebrow and a quirk of his lips. She held back her own smile, knowing he understood she taunted him as he so often did her. When he offered a horn of mead, she hesitated a moment before accepting it.

"Thank you."

He continued to feed her and she used each bite to further tease him. The way he looked at her left her heart racing, her breathing shallow. After she swallowed another bite of stewed turnip, he ran his finger along her lower lip, his dark eyes intense upon her. His touch sizzled through her.

"Have you had enough? There are tarts and sweetbreads, if you'd like." The low timbre of his voice sent another shiver of anticipation along her spine, spreading through her like Sol's warmth.

She suspected his kindness tonight was borne not only of their shared desires, but of the spirit of the celebration. Nevertheless, she enjoyed his indulgent mood, one he rarely showed in front of others. Tonight, kneeling beside him, she felt the familiar bond that had grown between them. Sometimes, she could almost forget her station, if only for a little while.

"I'd like that."

He gave her a generous smile and waved over one of the women.

"Bring some tarts."

The woman nodded, giving Geira a look of contempt before attending her task. Geira fought the urge to return the glare, turning her attention back to Kori. He no longer watched her, talking quietly with his brother and Leif. What had she expected, that he would defend her? She had hoped though, that he wouldn't dismiss her so easily. The sting pierced her heart. She shook her head. Foolish again.

Despite the momentary souring of her mood, Geira soon found herself swept up once more by the festive atmosphere. She studied the boisterous villagers. Laughter and good-natured taunts hung in the air and Geira held back a laugh when two of the men rose from their chairs, staggering as they made their way to the clearing in the center of the hall. Amid shouts and insults, the two began a half-hearted fight, neither gaining an edge, both laughing too hard to land a solid blow.

"Leif, you should know better than to fight Bjorn when you've had so much ale!" Kori shouted. Geira laughed out loud. The gaiety expressed in the hall was too infectious to resist and when the bard broke out in song, she found herself tapping her fingers to the music. Several people rose and began to dance and for a moment, Geira longed to do so with Kori. She looked away from the revelers, and found herself looking up at Dota, who placed a platter of tarts on the table.

What did she read in her friend's eyes? Not animosity as she expected, but no sign their bond of friendship existed either. Dota simply stared blankly at her before Hradi ordered her back to her place with the other slaves who served the clan. Her pleasant mood ruined for good, Geira lowered her head in an attempt to hide the tears burning her eyes. She resisted Kori's attempt to force her to look at him and thankfully, he did not press the issue.

"How's the whore working out?"

The voice above her made her gut churn and any remaining appetite for sweets disappeared. She refused to look at the man taunting both her and Kori.

"She's a delight."

Despite the words of satisfaction, Kori's voice held a note of warning. Unable to resist, Geira finally lifted her head. The anger flashing in Kori's face gave her a moment's gratitude that he didn't direct that rage toward her.

"I hear you are alone again. How long did it take you to kill your slave?"

Geira bit back her gasp. The woman given to Muli in place of Dota was dead? Daring a glance at the evil man, she suppressed a shudder and inched closer to Kori. His fingers sliding through her hair calmed her panicked heartbeat.

"She was weak! You tricked me, all of you!" He stepped closer to Geira, sneering. "All because of this one. She deserves a good whipping!"

Kori stood, knocking his chair to the floor. Geira moved to a crouch. Around them the celebration stalled, the din fading away.

"Back away, Muli. If you are drunk or foolish enough to dare me, be prepared to be humiliated."

"You think you can take me. You'd best watch your back." Muli spat on the ground beside Kori.

"Enough!" Thorfinn's bellow drew all eyes to him. "Muli, go sleep off the ale. Kori, sit down and finish your meal. This is a celebration, a feast to prepare for the longest night! I'll not have this foolishness ruin it!"

For several more seconds, Muli, fists clenched at his sides, glared at Kori. He gave what sounded like a growl then turned away, stalking out of the hall. Kori remained standing a few moments longer, then straightened his chair and resumed his seat. He turned to Geira.

"Don't fear him."

She lifted her chin, determined to hide her apprehension. "I don't. He's no better than a rat."

Kori's exuberant laughter warmed the cold shill surrounding her heart. He ran his hand through her hair and reached for a tart. He offered it to her, and though she had no appetite left, she accepted it and nibbled at the sweet bread filled with custard.

Once more, the bards broke out in song and the

laughter and sounds of celebration resumed. Children ran between the tables, their games reminding Geira of her own childhood. Longing for home rose once more, muting her enjoyment of watching them. Again, she prayed for some sign that her family still lived. Surely Odin would be generous this night and grant her plea.

Before long, Thorfinn stood and announced it was time for the children to gather before the central fire. The bard stood before them, urging the children to silence.

"I have a tale to tell you all, so listen carefully, so Odin rewards us!"

The giggles and jabbering continued for a little while longer, until the entire hall was now quiet and focused on the bard. The flame-haired man, taller than Kori and with a long red beard, walked among the gathered young ones of the clan.

"Tonight is the longest night of the year. The most important night of the hunt. Who knows the name of Odin's horse?"

"Sleipnir!" one of the children called out.

"Yes, you're right. And he has eight legs and moves faster than Sol in her chariot chased by the wolf. We must make hay sacks for Sleipnir, so he can carry Odin on his hunt with strength and stamina."

The bard stilled, straightening his back until he stood tall, his head cocked as if he listened for something, Geira grinned at Kori, enraptured by the tale everyone already knew so well.

The bard cupped his ear. "Can you hear the sound of the lur horn? Odin and his band of hunters approaches!"

He made a sudden spin and lunged toward the children, some of whom squealed with laughter, while others ran to their mothers. Geira laughed and leaned against Kori's leg. When had she grown so comfortable this way?

"Listen carefully, children." The bard once more wove among the children. "We haven't much time.

Odin rides with the Valkyrie and the fallen warriors who reside in Valhalla. They will be upon us soon."

The bard made his way through the hall, winding up and down the tables, the children one by one falling into line behind him. As he made his way to the door, the hall slowly emptied, parents accompanying the children outside. The men and women would likely return later, once the babes had been settled into bed to await the rewards Odin would leave.

For a moment, Geira stared longingly at the mothers who hugged their daughters, the fathers who lifted their sons to their shoulders. While she had once wanted children, she no longer possessed that desire. No child of hers would be a slave. She supposed she should be relieved she'd so far avoided that calamity. Someday, when she was free again, and maybe married to another, she would welcome a babe. But not now. Not when she was held as a slave.

The bards continued their songs and poems, the words growing more ribald with every flagon of ale consumed. Geira stifled a yawn, heat flooding her cheeks when Kori chuckled.

"Come, we retire now."

He led her behind the hall, where they would bed down for the night. Silence hung over them as he guided them into the bed carved into the walls of the longhouse. Kori paused, hands on her shoulders.

"Happy Jul, Geira."

She blinked, not expecting the blessing. Gathering her wits, she answered. "Happy Jul, Kori."

He smiled and pressed a brief kiss to her lips. He released her shoulders, pointing to the bed. She climbed in, surprised he did not remove her dress. Part of her recognized gratitude, for the longhouse bustled with activity, and would all through the long night. She had no wish to be bared before all of his clan. But she worried Kori wouldn't share his passion tonight and the idea left a bitter disappointment. She settled beside the wall, turning into Kori's arms without a moment's hesitation when he slid in beside her. The sounds of the feast continuing made an oddly soothing music and Geira snuggled closer, the dismay growing when he made no attempt to touch her in any other way. Geira closed her eyes.

Yet, sleep eluded her, the steady thump of Kori's heart beneath her ear reminding her of the pleasure he usually gave so freely, but now withheld. Or maybe it was the people constantly walking up and down the corridor that kept slumber at bay.

It seemed a long time passed before Kori's hand slid along her back, the motion bringing back awareness, accompanied by a giddy joy suffusing every part of her. She lifted her head, the flames from the fire illuminating his face and revealing the yearning in his dark eyes. Without hesitation, she offered herself to his demanding kiss, wrapping herself around him as he rolled her to her back.

CHAPTER SEVENTEEN

The morning sun came through the holes in the ceiling, brightening the entire house. Hints of spring appeared everywhere, though the cold had once again tightened its grip on the area. Geira stretched, wishing for just a few more moments to snuggle into the blankets. At moments like this, the bed was the one place she felt truly secure and safe, the heat from Kori's body surrounding and comforting her. Instinctively, her fingers moved to the mark on the back of her neck. Stroking the raised scar brought the familiar comfort, the knowledge she belonged to this fierce man. The sense she betrayed her own had long ago dimmed to a murmur in her thoughts.

She heaved a sigh. These past months had turned into a surreal dream, one she knew she shouldn't delight in, but she did anyway. When had she given up hoping to awaken back in her home, with her family around her? How had this place turned into a replacement home?

She tossed back the furs. Sitting up, she took a moment to study Kori as he still slept. She loved being in his arms at night, savoring his embrace as she awakened each morning. He'd shown her depths of passion she'd never imagined existed, except perhaps in Valhalla. He'd protected her from many in his clan who sought to take advantage of her status. Especially the times Muli confronted her whenever they were in the village. As a result, the contempt Kori directed toward her had lessened considerably.

His eyes opened, clearing quickly as he focused on her. A soft smile curled his lips and he reached for her, pulling her across his chest. She giggled, straddling him. His hardening cock stirred against her sex and she wiggled, drawing a hoarse groan.

"You'll be the death of me, *ambátt*."

Though he called her slave, the word had become an endearment, one she relished hearing. Her heart raced and she reached between them to curl her fingers around his hard shaft. Another groan, and his arms came tight around her, holding her close for a bruising kiss.

She fought to remain in control of her senses, wanted to tease him as he so often did her. She pulled her mouth from his, grinning, and began to stroke his hard flesh. He gripped her hips, the touch rough and harsh, just as she liked it. Her pussy swelled, anxious to be filled, but she focused on touching Kori. His reactions as she slid her fingers across his skin, scraping her nails against his nipples, were as intoxicating as his touch and his kiss. He gave a hoarse groan, his hold on her tightening as he thrust up against her hand. He released her then to reach for her breasts, caressing and stroking, squeezing. She trembled atop him, but held him back when he moved to enter her.

"No."

"You refuse my demands?"

"Not as you think. I will see to my master's pleasure in my way."

"Very well. Proceed."

He gave her a devilish grin and stilled beneath her exploring touch. Holding back her own smile, she resumed her teasing caresses, loving the way his shaft throbbed in her grip, hot and hard. Without giving him any warning, she lowered her head, licking the tip with her tongue. His shout shuddered through her, but she held herself as still as she could, using only fingers and mouth to torment him. His fingers tangled in her hair, pulling, but the tug only added to the chaos assaulting her wits.

How she had come to love the musky taste of him. When she took him fully into her mouth, the fingers in her hair tightened more. She rather liked the hint of pain. In the past months, she'd learned to crave whatever sensation he chose to bestow upon her, pain or pleasure. Often both together. If she'd imagined last summer she would become a willing slave to the man who'd spirited her away, she would have laughed at the idea. Yet, here she was, keen on serving him, and pleasing him, in any way he chose. Pleasing him was a reward of its own, and even now, she recognized the way her desire intensified in response to his delight.

Cupping his balls, she stroked lightly, making Kori tremble and sending that shivery feeling through her veins. She would savor that sensation for the rest of her days, knowing it only happened when she and Kori were intimate.

Turning her complete attention back to her task, she sucked hard on his flesh, using her tongue and lips to make him taut with need. Another stroke of his balls and she sensed he was close. She wanted him inside her when he came, wanted to feel the heat of his body within hers at that moment. Lifting her head, she grinned at his glare of frustration.

"Geira…"

His husked voice sent another shiver along her spine. She ignored the warning, positioning herself above him. His eyes lit with excitement, and he guided her to him. The tip of his cock rested against her cleft. She hesitated but a moment, then sank swiftly, impaling herself completely.

They moaned together, the sound like music floating in the room. For several moments, Geira remained still, content to savor the feel of him filling her. All too soon, the urge for more overcame her, and she began a slow slide against him, leaning forward so he could cup her breasts once more. When he raised himself up and sucked the tip of one breast into his mouth, she cried out, pumping faster against him. Heat spiraled through her, her body caught in the throes of passion. As she often did, she wished this moment would last forever, when she and Kori were in perfect synchronization with each other, as if their souls spoke to each other on a plane she barely realized existed.

His mouth on her breast, his hand on her hip, his cock hard and driving within her soon had her nearing the pinnacle. She forced her eyes open, finding Kori staring at her. She seemed to float above him, the pleasure so intense that when it exploded in a fireball, she nearly wept. Breath sucked from her lungs, she could only gasp and moan as she and Kori rocked together. Shuddering waves of delight seemed to go on for ages and she never wanted it to end.

When the flames had settled to glowing embers, she collapsed against him. Under her ear, his heart raced, testament to his own consuming passion. At moments like this, she felt almost his equal, cherished and cared for. She fought the burn of tears to know it was only a dream, one she feared she'd never attain.

A deep breath and she forced the thought from her head. He did care, even if he didn't show it in many ways outside of his bed. That knowledge had kept her from insanity these last months. That and the fact spring would arrive soon, and with it, her chance for escape.

Kori's fingers slid in her hair. "Freyr must have haunted your dreams last night."

She gave a soft giggle, savoring the gruff words. "Perhaps. Or maybe I wished to please my master, as he often does for me."

She lifted her head, meeting his gaze. An affectionate smile curled his lips.

"You never fail to amaze me, *ambátt*." He pressed a kiss to her forehead. "Come, we have a busy day. I must ready the fields for planting."

He eased her from him and stood. Once again, he was her stern master. She likely wouldn't see his affection again until tonight.

***

Geira set aside the mending and walked to the fire. She poked at the tinder, stirring the flames. If only the cold would lift and allow spring's warmer temperatures to gain a foothold. He tease of warmth of the few days past had once again vanished. She resumed her seat and picked up the tunic she repaired for Kori. The door opened and Thora stomped in, her usual scowl in place. The contentment born of this morning's love-making evaporated in her presence.

"Fetch me something to eat!" The girl swept off her cloak and threw it to Geira.

Catching the garment before it landed on the fire, Geira tossed it on a chair. "Fetch your own meal. There is plenty still in the pot."

Geira nodded to the stew and turned her attention back to her mending. Thora grabbed her arm.

"You're the slave, I want you to do it."

"Your father has made it clear I am not your personal maid." She jerked free of the girl's grip. It was rare Thora laid hands on her. After the time Kori had caught his daughter about to slap Geira, the girl had stopped daring, keeping her torment to taunts and slurs. Obviously something had her in a foul mood today judging from the sneer on her face.

Thora yanked the tunic from her hands. "This can wait. You are still the household slave and you will serve me."

Geira stood. "That is your father's. I must have it finished before he returns from the village."

"There won't be a tunic to mend if you don't fetch my meal." Thora dangled the garment over the flames. "He won't like that you were careless enough to let this fall in the fire."

Anger surged through Geira's veins. She'd endured this hellion's torment, mostly in silence, long enough. She'd kept her need to fight back suppressed these past months, but her control shattered. She reached for the tunic, but Thora held it further out of reach.

"You brat! That belongs to your father, and don't think I won't tell him you did it! He will believe me."

"Ha! You're a slave, nothing more. Nothing you say will ever be believed. By anyone!"

Lost in her rage, Geira slapped Thora across the

face.

Stunned, the girl froze and Geira took the opportunity to grab the tunic. Thora covered her cheek with her hand. She took a step toward Geira, fist raised. Geira lifted her chin.

"I will strike you back ten times as hard. None would blame me!"

Thora lowered her arm a little. "You whore! You'll pay for that!" She grabbed a hunk of Geira's hair and pulled hard. "On your knees, slave."

Geira caught Thora's wrist in her hands, trying to break free of the painful pull on her scalp. She kicked at Thora, catching her on the shin. Thora yelled and released her hold.

"I'm going to find my father. He'll see you punished for disobeying and daring to strike me!"

"You provoked this! You and your childish antics!"

Thora shook a finger at her, face reddened with rage. "You're nothing but a slave. He'll kill you for this!"

Thora grabbed her cloak and stomped back out into the cold. In the silence, with the fight leaving her shaky, Geira fell into her chair. Kori's tunic lay forgotten on the floor. Would he be angry? Thora was his daughter, Geira a mere slave. Yes, she had struck the girl but months of constant berating and taunting, daring Geira to cross the line had become too much. Surely Thora planned this, hoping for a chance to see Geira punished. How many times had Kori dismissed Thora's requests to penalize her? More than Geira could count. But she knew with certainty, this action would not be ignored. He might believe she'd been forced into it, but her actions constituted a crime, considering her position.

In an effort to distract herself from dwelling on whatever penalty Kori might mete out, Geira busied herself with the remainder of the mending. The chore took more time than she preferred. The ever growing apprehension made her clumsy. She pricked her finger more than once, wasting time on preventing her blood from staining the cloth. Finally, she folded the last tunic and placed it atop the neat pile.

She walked to the door, pulling it open. The remnants of the winter air provided soothing cold. She hadn't realized she'd grown so warm. With slow steps, she made her way outside and to the garden. From here, she could see the fields and the river. Kori and Thora were nowhere to be seen. She glanced at the sky. Sunset remained hours away. Where was Kori?

***

Kori blocked his brother's blow and swung around kicking, catching Hradi in the gut. The taller man stumbled back, then let loose a loud laugh before storming toward Kori once again. Raising his shield, Kori thwarted Hradi's attempt to bury an axe in his chest.

"You can do better than that, brother!" Kori taunted, dodging a punch. He swung his sword, narrowly missing Hradi's ear.

Hradi's brow furrowed. "Are you trying to kill me, man?"

Kori laughed, chest heaving from his exertions. "No more than you're trying to kill me."

Around them, the sounds of battle training filled the square. While the chances of a raid during the winter months were slim, they must always be ready to defend their home, especially with spring upon them. The crunch of a boot behind him made him spin about, blocking Muli's attempt to strike. While these exercises were meant only to keep their skills sharp, Kori suspected Muli might make another attempt to ambush him. The fool refused to relinquish his bitterness at having Dota taken from him. The sneaky bastard wouldn't hesitate to deliver a blow meant to injure.

"You'll not best me today, Muli!" Kori jumped back at Muli's next swing, then advanced, slashing heavily at the beefy man, not giving him a chance to raise his sword in retaliation. Muli retreated, holding up his shield.

"I give!" Muli threw his sword down, signaling his surrender.

Kori grinned. "You always do. Save your underhanded tactics for a real battle. You'll not enter Valhalla by going down during a mere practice."

"You couldn't kill me even in a real battle." Muli spat on the ground. He focused on Hradi, standing behind Kori. "How's the whore? How many times has she tried to castrate you?"

Kori kept his focus on Muli, holding back a smile when the man's grin faded at Hradi's growl.

"She treats me most sweetly," Hradi said, his voice tight with anger. Kori knew his brother still resented Muli for his mistreatment of Dota. Kori's sympathy had passed the day Dota had attacked Geira, though he believed his brother when Hradi said she had realized her error. He wondered how much punishment the woman had endured before recognizing her mistake.

Muli snorted. "If you don't beat her regularly, she'll try to slice your throat. Like she did to me."

"Shame she didn't succeed. Unlike you, Muli, I can convince a woman to want to serve me properly."

Kori held Muli back when he charged. The hefty man tried but failed to break Kori's grip.

"Don't do it," Kori warned. "You're barely tolerated these days. Don't think my father won't banish you. Or worse."

"Fine." Muli jerked against Kori's hold once more and Kori released him. He bent to pick up his sword and stalked away, muttering under his breath.

"He nearly killed the other one we gave him twice already." Hradi slammed his axe into the dirt, retrieved it and repeated the action.

Kori nodded, keeping his gaze on the retreating man. "Be vigilant. He wants her back and he's getting desperate."

"He won't get near her." Hradi's fists clenched, his jaw tight. "He'll never touch her again."

Kori grinned. "So that's how it is, then?"

"What?"

"You've grown fond of your slave."

Hradi smiled. "She is much changed. You haven't been to see her at all?"

Kori shook his head. "No, since she attacked Geira I have no desire to speak with her."

"She wants to make amends for that. I will bring her one night."

"I will ask Geira first."

Now Hradi laughed. "Since when do you give your slave a choice?"

He glared at his brother. "I have no use for a weeping slave who can't perform her chores."

"If you say so, brother."

"I do."

Kori turned and walked toward the smith to see if his new axe was ready. He didn't like the way Hradi mocked him, but he truly didn't want Geira upset by Dota's presence. He did care for his *ambátt*, probably more than he should. How could he not? These past months, watching her determination to make the best of her situation had roused his admiration and respect. She'd been stoic under Thora's constant taunts and ill treatment. She was brave and strong. The way she came alive in his bed only intensified his never ending need for her. He couldn't imagine his life without her. And he didn't have to. He owned her and she bore his mark to prove it. Now if only he had some way to know if he'd captured her heart and soul as well. For she had certainly captured his.

He smiled as he walked, not even the chill in the air bothering him.

CHAPTER EIGHTEEN

Geira paced near the garden. Each passing moment only increased her dread. Why hadn't Kori returned yet, ready to beat her for fighting with Thora? She paced, rubbing her clammy palms on her dress. He usually returned from the village long before now. Or maybe it only seemed hours had passed.

A shriek broke through the quiet air. Heart pounding, Geira turned, trying to determine where it came from. Another scream, this one accompanied by a plea for help. Thora! Geira ran in the direction of Thora's shouts, into the forest behind the house.

Was Thora hurt? Was she with Kori? Was *he* hurt? She quickened her pace, not wanting to examine her fear for his safety.

"Please, help! It will kill me!"

What did she mean? Now running, Geira held her skirt up as she jumped over a fallen log. Her foot caught, sending her tumbling to the ground. She rolled and righted herself, leaping up and running once more. Panic gave her speed and when Thora's latest scream sounded to her right, she halted.

"Thora?" she called out.

"Over here! Help!"

Geira dodged through the trees. She spotted Thora's chestnut hair, dark against the backdrop of snow and bare birch trees. Geira headed toward the girl, stopping short to see what had frightened her.

A large wolf, hackles raised and ears pinned back, growled menacingly at Thora. She slowly backed away as the animal advanced on her.

"Thora, I'm here!"

Thora's gasping sobs echoed in the quiet air. "Get it away from me!"

The wolf turned, now aware of Geira. She froze.

Another terrified sound came from Thora and the wolf resumed its slow stalking of the girl.

Odin's blood, what could she do? Geira glanced around, spying a long, thick branch nearby, half as tall as herself. She inched toward it, not wanting to draw the wolf's attention again before she had a weapon. Why hadn't she thought to bring something from the house? Another deep growl sounded from the wolf, and it took another menacing step toward Thora. With caution, Geira bent and curled her hand around the branch. She'd need both hands to hold it, and hefted it upward.

"Over here, you cur!" She waved the branch, gaining control over the unwieldy wood, despite the weight. Her palms slipped but she adjusted her grip, holding the limb tightly.

The wolf changed direction, now moving closer to Geira. Thora chose that moment to attempt to flee.

"Thora, hold!"

Damn, the wolf had focused on Kori's daughter once again. Geira gave a low whistle, and took several steps toward the angry animal. What had Thora done to provoke its attack? The wolf didn't appear hungry. Were there others around? Wolves ran in packs and if... she forced the thought aside.

The wolf growled at Geira, sitting back on its haunches. Geira held her concentration, ready for the animal's attack. She had only once chance.

With a howling bark, the wolf leaped. The seconds it took for the animal to be close enough to swing at seemed to last hours. Hoping her judgment was accurate, she swung the heavy branch around.

With a sickening thud, the branch connected with the wolf's head. A loud crack echoed, the small tree limb breaking as it made contact. With a whine, the wolf dropped to the ground, legs twitching for a moment before it stilled.

Only now did Geira allow fear to take over, and her legs trembled. She collapsed to her knees, leaning against the broken branch to keep from falling on her face. Hands on her arm urged her to stand once more. She looked at Thora.

"Come, we must go!"

Using the branch for support, Geira wrapped her other arm around Thora. The girl didn't seem to mind, even embraced her back. Every now and then, a soft sob escaped. Geira could barely breathe, flashes of the wolf lunging at her coming again and again. She tightened her grip on the wood, just in case. If, Odin forbid, the wolf rose and stalked them again, she would need the weapon. Using the broken branch as a kind of crutch, she led Thora back toward the farmhouse.

"You saved me."

The soft words were hard to hear, though Geira detected surprise in the girl's tone. She paused and looked into Thora's eyes.

"Of course I did. You didn't think I'd let you die?"

Thora hesitated, her blue eyes brimming with tears. "Why wouldn't you? I've been horrible to you."

Geira nodded. "You have."

Thora lowered her head. "When I saw you, I thought you'd walk away and leave me. And…"

Geira didn't hear the rest of the mumbled words. "What?"

Thora lifted her head meeting her stare. "I wouldn't blame you."

Geira searched for the right words. She still possessed anger over the way Kori's daughter had treated her. Yet, she suspected Thora's regret was real and the girl truly did want to make amends. She sighed gave Thora a small hug.

"I wouldn't let anything happen to you. Even after the way you treated me."

"Truly?"

Geira nodded. "Truly."

"I am sorry. And thank you."

"You're forgiven." She paused, thinking of the girl's cruel words. "Thora, I understand that losing your mother hurt you very deeply. And you need to lash out at someone for it. The person who did it is dead, and I am the closest target you have."

"He… what he did to her… I can still hear her screams. I wanted to kill him myself, but I had no weapon."

Geira realized Thora's need for vengeance had consumed her over the last few years.

"Thora, I didn't do anything to hurt you. And I never would. But know this, I care for your father, and I know it would destroy him if anything would happen to you. I did it as much for him as I did it for you."

Thora nodded. "I don't even know how it found me."

"You were looking for your father."

Another nod, accompanied with a sniffle. "He wasn't here. I suspect he went to the village. I was still angry. At you. So I decided to find a place to wait for him to return."

Geira nodded. She well imagined the snit the girl had worked herself into. "In the forest?"

Thora shrugged. "Yes. No, I… I don't know. I was just wandering, really. But then I heard it growl, and… I just screamed."

"I'm glad I got there in time." Recalling her own confrontation with a wild animal, she suppressed a shudder to think what the wolf might have done to Thora. She raised her eyes to the heavens, thanking all the gods for giving her the strength and courage to succeed.

Finally, they reached the farmhouse. Geira halted, panicked to see Kori waiting, hands on hips, his expression tight with anger. Oddly, she had the sense his rage was directed at her. She glanced at the branch she still held, the blood from the wolf shining bright in the sun, and then at Thora's disheveled and dirty state. Now she understood. Would he believe the truth?

Thor, save me from his wrath.

***

Kori's gut twisted with a mixture of fury and pain. What had the two unkempt women been doing? He feared the worst, their appearances suggesting they had fought. Terror dulled Thora's eyes. The sight alarmed him, as did the way Geira gripped his daughter's arm. Yet, Thora didn't seem to be trying to break free. The large branch Geira dragged troubled him a great deal as well. The idea his *ambátt* had turned on him, hurt his daughter, caused an unfamiliar ache. Anger soon drowned it.

He stalked over to them and pulled away the large branch. It had blood on one end. He looked Thora over, but she didn't appear injured.

"What have you done?" He snarled the words at Geira, surprised when she didn't back away. Instead, she lifted her chin.

"Nothing! I saved her!" She held herself straight and proud. At any other time, he'd find the sight of her intoxicating. But this time…

How he wanted to believe her, but his daughter shook, hands trembling fiercely, obviously from fear. Despite Thora's mean treatment of Geira, that a slave would dare take up a weapon against her master's family required a severe punishment. The thought of administering it brought a bitter taste to his tongue.

"Saved her, eh? Get inside. I'll be along to tend to you."

"But –"

"Do not argue!" His bellow echoed in the silence.

Face pale, Geira nodded. She hurried past him and slipped into the house. He scowled and faced his daughter.

"What did she do to you? Where are you hurt?" He gripped her shoulder with one hand, the other tipping up her face. A bruise had formed on her cheek. His anger toward Geira intensified.

"I'm not hurt, Father. She spoke the truth. She saved me."

Had he misheard? He listened as Thora began to

speak, haltingly, telling of the argument that led to her wandering the woods. His daughter made clear the fact she had provoked Geira. He forgot that the moment Thora related her encounter with the wolf. Senses spinning, he leaned against a tree.

"Where is the wolf? Did she kill it?"

Thora shrugged. "I don't know. We left as soon as the animal went down."

The idea the wolf might still live troubled him. He pushed Thora to the house.

"Go inside. Your uncle should be here any minute and we will find the wolf and make sure it's dead."

She nodded and turned.

"Thora!"

She faced him, biting her lip in apprehension. "Yes, Father?"

"We will discuss your fight with Geira later."

She nodded and disappeared into the house.

Kori shook his head. His daughter had almost caused her own death today. His anger at thinking Geira had hurt her was gone, replaced with relief and gratitude. He must thank her. Before he punished her. She had struck his daughter, no matter if she was provoked. That required retribution. Though in truth, her rescue of Thora heavily outweighed her earlier actions and absolved her of any wrongdoing. He grinned. Didn't matter. She knew by now he could find the simplest infraction and make her enjoy every moment of chastisement. Thor's teeth, half the time, she provoked him intentionally, the devilish gleam in her eye betraying her motive. His cock hardened. He would have her begging for a long time tonight.

He entered the house, not seeing her in the main room. He could hear Thora moving about on the opposite side of the house. Kori moved to his sleeping room. Geira sat upon the furs, her back to him, head down. From here, he could see her fingers twisting nervously in her lap. A little shudder passed over her. He stood for several moments watching her. He ached to hold her, to soothe her, to tell her what was in his heart. He would, eventually. Not yet.

Silently, he made his way around the bed and sat beside her. She gave a little gasp when she looked up, eyes wide. He said nothing for several moments, studying her in the glow of the fire. Terror whitened her face.

"Thora explained it all. Hradi and I will find the wolf to ensure it's dead."

Her entire body seemed to melt with relief. Tears welled in her eyes. He scowled.

"You weep?"

She nodded. "I am relieved."

"Yet, you still struck my daughter."

The way her eyes widened again stirred him in so many ways. He gave her a leering smile. How he loved teasing her this way. Damn his soul to Helheim, he loved *her*! Keeping the realization from his face grew into a struggle he quickly won. Better to focus on other matters.

"You will be punished for that. Tonight."

In the room's coppery glow, he made out a flush creeping into her cheeks. When he covered her hands with one of his, she gave the most delightful tremor. Her breathing quickened and he knew she anticipated the upcoming punishment as much as she feared it.

"But surely the fact I saved her…"

"I will consider it when determining your punishment."

She sucked in a breath, her lips twitching. Hradi's voice booming from the next room prevented him from kissing her. He stood.

"See to the meal, and tend to Thora. I will return."

She nodded, still silent, and followed him to the main room. He greeted his brother, thoughts on the coming task.

"There's a wolf in the woods we must find. Geira injured it but I want to ensure it is dead. A wounded wolf is more dangerous than a healthy one."

"What was she doing in the woods?"

"She saved Thora." Kori caught her stare and almost laughed at the surprise on her face. Didn't she realize that despite the fact she would be punished, he was proud of her for what she'd done?

"You did well, *ambátt*. I am pleased."

The smile that brightened her face tempted him to drag her back to his bed. Instead, he caught his brother's curious stare. He idly wondered if Hradi had truly attempted to take his own slave yet. Kori had suspected Hradi had only made his declaration in an attempt to anger Muli. But his brother hadn't made mention of joining Kori and Geira in weeks. Sharing a bed with Dota could be a reason. He'd find out soon enough.

"Come, let's find the beast. Geira, you have chores."

"Yes, sir."

He left the house without a backward glance.

***

Geira stoked the fire and stirred the stew in the pot. Then she made her way toward Thora's sleeping bunk. The girl lay on her bed, staring at the ceiling.

"Are you all right?" Geira asked.

"Yes." Thora sat up. "I must say I'm sorry again."

Geira sighed and sat beside Kori's daughter. "It's not necessary."

Thora nodded. "I'm sorry that you're a slave now."

Geira nodded. "Me too. Especially since even though I married Einnar, I didn't love him. My father wanted the marriage and I had little choice. When I arrived in his village, a week before our wedding, I had suspicions. There were things that troubled me. When your father told me why he'd taken me, I knew he spoke the truth. My husband was not an honorable man. But he's dead now. And I know you still want to hurt him."

"I do. I want the chance to kill him, to make him suffer as he made my mother suffer."

Geira slipped an arm around Thora's shoulders and drew the girl close.

"Your father saw to it. His wound did not kill him instantly, and the cottage was set afire." Geira suppressed a shudder. "I'm sure his death was not easy."

"Good."

Geira held back a grin. The girl was as bloodthirsty as her father. Geira suspected Thora also possessed the kindness that Kori had shown on so many occasions, though she'd yet to see it. Maybe now that she and the girl had reached an accord, she would get a glimpse of the daughter Kori spoke so lovingly about.

Geira looked around. She truly did feel at home here. If only she could stand beside Kori as his equal, rather than a mere slave. Facing the rest of her life with no rights still made her ill. She knew enough of the area that she could escape, once the warm weather took root. She'd heard Kori speak many times about going on quests in the summer months. Her chance would come. She would be free again.

"Geira?"

Thora's questioning stare brought Geira's attention back to the girl.

"I must ensure the dinner is ready. I'm sure your uncle will be joining us."

"Did he bring your friend?"

A bolt of hurt ran along Geira's spine. She shook her head. "Dota is no longer my friend. I have not seen her in months."

"She's wrong, you know."

Geira moved into the main room. "What do you mean?"

"She blames you. Everyone heard her that day."

At the reminder, Geira's shoulders slumped. "I know."

"But that's just stupid. No one plans to be taken as a slave."

A mad giggle threatened at the words. Thora was right. And for once, the insult wasn't directed at her. The realization lightened her heart.

The door swung open and Geira turned. In his

hands, Kori held two wolf cubs, Hradi held one.

"Oh!" cried Thora. "Puppies!

"This is why the wolf attacked. You got too close to her babies." Kori stepped inside and placed the cubs on the floor. Hradi held his pup closer.

Laughing, Thora lowered herself to the floor. The pups immediately trotted to her, and her infectious giggles filled the room. Geira looked over at Kori. A broad grin curved his mouth, eyes sparkling with laughter. Her own amusement burst forth. She sobered, recalling the cubs' mother.

"The wolf?" she asked.

"Close to death. I finished it to end its suffering."

A swift pang of remorse rose in her throat, but she forced it back. The wolf had only been protecting her babies. Now they had no mother. But if she hadn't struck the wolf, it would have hurt Thora. Or worse.

"What will you do with the pups?" she asked.

"I haven't decided. Hradi will keep the one."

"Can I keep these, Father? Please?" Thora's voice took on an excited edge.

"They are wild animals, Thora."

"I will train them. You'll see." The pleading note in her words grew stronger. She batted her eyelashes at her father, her face lined with a desperate plea. Kori's stony expression faded and Geira recognized the moment he lost this debate.

Still, he gave a skeptical shake of his head. "It's dangerous."

Geira caught Hradi's eye, holding back a smile when he winked. Though he'd not been near hers and Kori's bed recently, she still shared a comfortable camaraderie with him. That he also found the exchange between father and daughter amusing anchored that fondness further.

She looked away, realizing what she would miss when she left. The day fast approached and she must plan. She turned to tend the fire, a sudden wave of dizziness making her sway. She forced it back, determined to see her chores completed before she served the evening meal.

Even as she poked at the flames, her legs grew weak, her knees trembling. *Must not fall.* She repeated the words silently, over and over, but her weakness soon overcame her and her legs buckled.

As if from far away, she heard Kori's shout. Her vision blurred as his strong arms came around her. The room went dark.

***

Kori cradled Geira's limp body against him. What had befallen her? Had she been hurt in the encounter with the wolf? The lighthearted mood of moments ago lay shattered at his feet.

"She looks so pale."

"Thora, step aside." Kori turned, carrying his slave to his bed. He laid her out carefully. "Fetch some mead. And a cold wet cloth."

A few minutes later, his daughter pressed the requested items into his hands. He gently wiped Geira's face with the cloth, relieved when her eyes fluttered open.

"Are you ill?"

Her hazed eyes narrowed in concentration, confusion clear in their pale depths. He slid an arm about her shoulders and eased her up. He held the cup to her lips.

"Drink."

She took a few tentative sips then pushed the cup away. "I'm fine."

"You fainted, and almost fell into the fire."

"Must have been too much heat."

He didn't believe her. Her movements remained slow and shaky, weak. What ailed her? He thought of the illness that had spread through his clan several years earlier. Many had died. Had Geira developed a sickness such as that? The thought of her death left a sharp ache in its wake.

"You will rest here until I send for you."

"But –"

"Thora will ensure the meal is ready. You will stay here."

She nodded. He wanted to stay with her, but had too many chores to tend before nightfall. Much of the crop fields remained unready for planting. While the winter's cold had lingered, spring hovered in the air.

He stood, pausing a few more moments to study his *ambátt*. His. He never tired of reminding himself of his luck in finding her. He thanked the gods every day for his good fortune. Leaning over, he tucked the furs around her and pressed a gentle kiss to her forehead.

"Rest. I will be back before dinner."

He felt her stare on his back as he strode away.

CHAPTER NINETEEN

Geira stared after Kori, wishing he would stay a little longer. Despite the affection he showed her, he always made it a point to remind her of who she truly was. A slave. Belonging to him, a possession. The knowledge reinforced her determination to escape in the coming weeks.

She tried to formulate the basis of a plan, but found herself too weary to focus. Aside from her fatigue, she now felt fine. The earlier illness seemed to have passed. Odd. What had she eaten in the last day that might cause such sickness? Nothing unusual. Perhaps the terrifying excitement of the day had somehow made her ill. But that didn't make any sense.

What else could cause such an abrupt sickness, one that vanished as quickly as it rose, leaving nothing but exhaustion in its place? A chill ran over her. No!

Even as the thought took root, she tried to deny it. But she couldn't. The puzzle pieces started to fit together. The weariness, the abrupt rising of her symptoms, how much time had passed since her last flow… all that could only mean one thing. She was with child. Kori's child.

A bright spark of joy burst, but she refused to savor it. She could be wrong. But if she wasn't… the excitement sputtered out. Her child would be a slave, just as she was. Yet oddly, that foolish hope of something more with her master strengthened. *Stupid girl! He'll never care for you as more than a slave. Not even a babe could warm his heart to you.*

She rested a hand on her belly, imagining the life growing inside. A fierce need to protect this child overtook her fatigue. She sat up. Many slaves had their children wrenched from them. Not her. She would keep her baby. In order to do that, she had no choice but to leave.

Somehow, she must find a way back to her home village, her clan. Family. They would welcome her. Protect her. Keep her and the child safe. Wouldn't they?

Or would they think as Dota did, that she had brought it on herself? Had made herself a whore for her enemy. Maybe they would see she'd had no choice, in order to survive. Then again, perhaps they would rather she had died.

She clutched at the furs, the sensation that the bed lurched beneath returning. Was this an omen from the gods? What message did they send?

She had little time to think on that. She must soon leave Kori, before her condition became obvious. If he knew she carried his child, he would never allow her to go, would hunt her until he found her. She vowed her child would never be a slave, would live as a free man or woman. In order for that to happen, Geira needed to take the first opportunity when it arose. Which meant she needed to start preparations now. Her only chance of packing what supplies she would need for her journey would be during the day, when Kori tended the fields, or visited the village to discuss clan business with his father.

She threw back the furs and stood, determination giving her strength. A wave of sickness rolled over her, but she forced it back. She must hide any and all clues that might lead Kori, or Thora, to realize the truth.

She stepped into the main room. Thora tended the stew on the fire. She looked up when Geira approached.

"Are you feeling better?"

While pleasant, she found it odd to have the girl treat her with courtesy and concern, rather than anger and hatred. She'd best not grow accustomed to it, since she didn't plan to be in this house for much longer. She nodded and moved toward the girl, relieved her step stayed steady. Collapsing again would ensure she would be kept under close watch.

"I am. If you like, I will continue cooking."

Thora shook her head. "Father said you must rest. Sit."

Gera automatically moved to take her place on the floor beside Kori's chair.

"No, sit here!" Thora pointed to the chair she usually used.

"I cannot."

"You can. You have earned it."

For a moment, Geira wondered if the girl had figured out the secret, but then realized Thora referred to the wolf. She held back a laugh at how she'd nearly panicked. She must use greater care. For her plan to succeed, no one must have any clue of her intentions or condition.

As Thora tended the house and again offered profuse apologies for her behavior, Geira took the time to look around. How would she be able to store supplies without drawing notice? Weapons would be difficult to obtain, but she'd need an axe or a dagger, at the very least. If only she dared steal one of the small boats Kori and his men had used when they had attacked Fellskoger. Even if she did, she wasn't much of a sailor. Frustration nearly choked her. She still didn't know exactly where she was in relation to her father's village. All she knew was they were much further upriver from Fellsskoger than she'd thought in the first days of her captivity. As the months had worn on, Kori had spoken more and more freely before her. She suspected he never imagined she would flee. She must recall all he'd shared.

Getting past the village without notice would be most difficult, but once she'd done that, perhaps she could lose herself in the mountains for a few days. Little by little, her plans took shape. She could do this. She must. To save her child.

The door opened and Kori stepped inside. The anger on his face startled her. What had happened to the caring and concerned lover? Even after all this time with him, she'd not become accustomed to the way his moods changed as easily as the wind.

"Why are you not abed?"

"I needed to be up and about. My illness has passed."

"You disobey me again?"

Damn him to Helheim! Did he know what effect those words had on her? Just the sound of his voice had her nipples tightening to hard points. He leaned in close and his recognizable musky scent washed over her, stirring the familiar fluttery sensations in her belly. Her pussy tingled, already preparing for whatever devilish game he might be planning.

"You must be disciplined for ignoring my orders."

The husk in his words told her exactly how he would punish her. She turned, meeting his stare evenly.

"I will withstand whatever punishment I must face."

He grinned. "We shall see."

When he stood, she thanked Odin for the chance to recover, gain control over the trembling in her fingers. She must take greater care lest she do something stupid and reveal what caused her to faint before. She made no effort to leave her seat, and he didn't seem to care Thora tended the dinner. He sat across the table from Geira, carving a small piece of wood with his favored small knife. He kept his attention on the blade.

"I must thank you for saving my daughter."

"I would never let anything happen to her, if I could prevent it."

He nodded, gaze still glued to the wood. "Even after she has treated you badly, you still rescued her."

"She is your daughter."

"You are devoted to me so much?"

She hesitated. What did he ask, exactly? Yes, part of the reason she saved Thora was because she knew losing his daughter would devastate Kori. Geira would do whatever she must to prevent that. She cleared her throat and raised her chin.

"You are my... master. I serve your family and

protect them as I would you."

Her heart raced, feeling as though Thor's hammer itself crashed against her ribs. Kori pierced her with a stare so intense, she was convinced he saw the thoughts and questions in her head.

He remained silent but nodded. "Yet before you saved her, you struck her."

Now she understood. Did she dare speak in her defense? Judging from his scrutiny, he wouldn't believe anything she said. Would he?

Damn it! Apparently, the bond she'd thought had grown between them was one-sided. He still saw her as nothing more than a slave. How she wanted to believe the concern and affection he showed was genuine.

The suddenness with which he grabbed her hand startled. His gentle squeeze seemed to indicate he knew exactly the path her thoughts had taken. She held his stare.

"I am sure you were provoked."

Her eyes widened. She glanced over at Thora, who seemed unusually busy stirring. Had she admitted her role in the tussle? The girl refused to look up, so Geira returned her focus to Kori. His dark eyes penetrated her soul. What if he learned of her plans to flee? What if he knew of the child?

His eyes narrowed. She'd raised his suspicions, the opposite of what she'd intended.

"Did my daughter lie when she accepted blame for the fight? After the way she's treated you, I wouldn't believe it. Except you did save her life. And perhaps she feels grateful enough to swear for you."

His words left her more confused than ever. Did he mean to trap her, or free her? If only he didn't keep his face so bland and expressionless. Still, she met his stare steadily. "Do you truly think I would attack your daughter?"

He said nothing for what seemed a lifetime. Surely, after all this time, he knew her well enough to know she could never hurt his daughter. Didn't he? Coldness surrounded her heart.

Finally, he shook his head. "No, not without provocation."

Warmth returned, but slowly. She almost let out the sigh of relief. But still, speaking the truth of Thora's actions could come back to worsen Geira's situation. "I... well, I did not make the first contact. But..."

"What?" His fingers tightened around hers again. Reassuring. Soothing.

She lowered her eyes. "I wanted to hit her. And..."

"And?"

She raised her gaze to his once more and shook her head. Confusion took deeper root when the corners of his mouth twitched.

"You find this amusing?"

His lips parted in a full smile, the one that always stole her breath. "I do. Admit it, Geira, it felt good to hit her. Didn't it?"

She covered her open mouth with her free hand. Her gaze darting between Kori and Thora, who still refused to face them, soon left her dizzy and unsettled. She took a deep breath, forcing back the threatening nausea. How could she admit to him that she did want to strike his daughter, had refrained from doing so many times until today?

"I've wanted to hit her myself many times."

"Father!" Now Thora spun about, her cheeks red.

Kori laughed. Geira finally let her breath free. Again, she wondered at his aim with this discussion. And again, she remained silent when Kori faced her again.

"I do understand, *ambátt*."

The tingle along her spine intensified. She waited for him to continue.

"I must punish you for your actions, but all else you've done has gained you a great advantage." He leaned closer, his voice lower. "I think you will like what I have planned to satisfy... the law."

Her eyes widened at his meaning. He lifted her

hand to his lips, brushing them across her fingers. She trembled, her senses unable to get a firm grip on what was happening. If she didn't know better, she'd swear he courted her. What had brought about this change? A shiver of fear seized her heart. Did he know? Or was all this simply gratitude for saving his daughter?

Kori released her, leaning back in his chair. He continued to watch her in a sensually casual way, keeping her body hungering for his touch. The time to retire seemed days away.

***

Kori nearly laughed at the confusion in Geira's face. He'd come to adore that look, almost as much as he adored keeping his promises. She would beg him tonight. He hungered for the sound of her voice, pleading for release. The pitch of her whine when he denied her. Simply thinking of it tightened his balls. He would enjoy her tonight. As well as see to her pleasure. Watching her face melt into bliss while her body rocked under him, her nails scratching his back as her climax assailed her was a gift from the gods.

Thora setting trenchers of fish and turnips on the table distracted him from his thoughts. Geira still appeared confused. He supposed she wasn't used to sitting with them like this at meals. Keeping her kneeling at his side had been more for his own pleasure than to humiliate her or remind of her place, but he found he rather liked facing her during the meal. Noting how she ate slowly, he wondered if her illness still lingered. Silence reigned over them, until finally, the meal was complete and Thora cleared the remains. Geira moved to stand, as if to help, but Kori waved her back to her seat. The yapping of the wolf cubs broke the heavy silence.

"Thora, see to your animals. Set them in the barn for now."

"Yes Father. Would it be all right if I stayed with them? At least for tonight."

He gave his daughter an indulgent smile. "Yes. But

until they are trained, they must spend the nights there. Surely you don't intend to stay with them every night."

Thora shrugged. "Why not? The weather has warmed enough."

He contemplated her for several moments then nodded. "Very well. But you will still tend all of your chores. If the pups interfere, they will have to go."

Thora leaned over and kissed his cheek. "Thank you!"

For the first time since Borga's murder, Kori finally caught a glimpse of the loving and carefree daughter Thora had once been. Oddly, he found himself thankful for her encounter with the wolf. Facing her possible death had likely brought on the regrets most people felt moments before they died. His heart ached that his daughter had already experienced that feeling more than once. Now, for the first time in years, he felt as though his life had somehow settled similarly to the peaceful one he'd once lived.

When Thora had slipped out into the night, Kori stood. He walked over to Geira and held out a hand. The way her fingers trembled when she accepted stirred him. He couldn't wait to make her entire body tremble like that.

He drew her close, tilting her chin back to properly kiss her. Today had been a long and eventful day, with many hours yet remaining. Somehow, the balance between them had shifted. The need to show her how important she had become to him grew with each passing second. He claimed her with his mouth, telling her without words that he planned to possess her for the rest of her days. Her tongue dancing with his sent a sizzle of lust straight to his hardening cock.

He drew away, panting heavily. How easily she undid his control. Sometimes he wondered if she knew how devastating her allure was to his senses. He studied her flushed face, lips swollen from his kiss, eyes glazed with desire. From the very first night he'd stolen her away, they'd shared a passion so intense it near scorched him every time he touched or kissed her. He'd sworn that night to have her loyalty to him, in all ways, and now, he knew he'd achieved that goal. Only he found himself as devoted to her.

Shaking his head to clear it from the silly thoughts, he led her to the sleeping room. He indicated she should turn so he could open the laces of her dress. Within moments, she stood bare before him, her skin glowing in the firelight. He caught her wrists, briefly running his fingers over the bracelets before hooking them together. Her eyes widened.

"Punishment, remember?"

She nodded, still silent. He kissed her again and pushed her back against the furs. With quick movements, he secured her connected wrists to the headboard. She made no protest, just watched him steadily as he stood and removed his own clothing. He chuckled at the way she slid her tongue along her lips when his cock sprang free, hard and ready.

"Soon enough, *ambátt*. But first, you must pay for your crime."

A soft whimper escaped her, accompanied by a quiver that rippled over her skin. His fingers itched to touch her. Still, he waited until the intensity of his need had fallen back under his power. With careful movements, he rolled her to her belly. He ran a hand over her rounded buttocks. This would not truly be punishment, for either of them. He enjoyed reddening her ass, as much as she savored his doing so. He stroked her flesh, loving the way it trembled under his touch. He dipped a finger to her pussy, not surprised to find her already soaked. Her low moan drifted over him, spurring a tantalizing shiver and making his cock throb.

He gave her no warning, simply drew back and spanked her. Each blow drew a sharp cry, but not one of pain. One of desire. Passion. For him. Damn the woman, she'd enchanted him from the start. He possessed no defense against her magic.

He paused, once more sliding into her sex. Her flesh twitched and her hard clit revealed how intense her need had become. In the quiet of the night, her harsh rasping breath sounded like a roar of pleasure.

He gave her a few more harsh spanks then stopped. Her pinkened skin called to him. He took his time stroking her warm ass. When he turned her to her back, she cried out. A tear rolled down her cheek. He leaned over and licked it, savoring the tang. She turned catching his lips with hers. Instead of reprimanding her for her boldness, he obliged her, loving the way she swept into his mouth with her tongue, her motions frantic. He laid a hand on her chest, stunned by the way her heart pounded. When he drew away, their mingled gasps for breath rasped his ears like a rough caress.

"Kori…"

His name on a sigh drove his need to a painful state. He fought the urge to take her now, to slake his desire in her body. He wanted to wait, wanted to torment her and savor her before he allowed himself the pleasure. With a roll of his shoulders he leaned back.

"Patience." His voice, thick and heavy, betrayed his passion.

He took his time exploring her, finding the sensitive spots he knew would spark the most intense reactions. Circling her nipples, stroking the underside of her breast. The hollow in her arm. His seeking hands slid over her skin, soft and damp with a sheen of desire. He lowered his head, teasing her nipple with his tongue before sucking the hardened peak into his mouth. Her musky sweet scent called to him, spurring him on, scraping his teeth against her sensitive tip. Her cries grew in pitch, her entire body overcome with tremors.

He moved his mouth along her belly, grabbing her hips as he nuzzled her mound. She undulated toward him, offering herself to his ravenous mouth. The first stroke of his tongue along her swollen pussy locked her body rigid, but when he repeated the motion, she went into wild gyrations. Grinning, he continued to taste her, thinking how he wanted to glut himself on her. Her juices coated his face, and he caught the hard bud of her clit between his lips, sucking gently.

She shrieked, squirming and crying against his urgent mouth, until she finally gave a hoarse shout, her body rippling beneath his with the force of her release. Her hot cream poured from her body and he lapped up every bit, like a man starved for months. Each stroke of his tongue drew another cry and quiver, keeping her riding the crest until she finally collapsed weakly against the bed. With one last slide of his tongue, he eased away.

Her eyes fluttered open and she gave him a dreamy smile, one that revealed her contentment. His cock nearly exploded at the sight, without being anywhere near her.

He reached up and freed her wrists, anticipating the moment she threw herself at him. He didn't have long to wait before she wrapped herself around him, pressing her hot and slick cleft against his cock. He groaned, all restraint now gone, and entered her with one swift stroke.

He remained still, savoring the way her muscles clamped around him. If he didn't take care, this would end before he wanted it to. He gritted his teeth and grabbed her hips, holding her still.

"You tempt me beyond my endurance."

A soft giggle next to his ear set his heart into another uneven rhythm. Finally, the last vestiges of control gone, he moved within her, closing his eyes at the glorious feel of her slick sex surrounding him. He kept his movements slow, wanting to enjoy the sensations for as long as possible.

But need soon won out over restraint and he increased his pace. His mouth crashed onto hers, swallowing her cries as he pounded roughly into her. Her nails scratching along his shoulders shattered the last of his resolve and he erupted, calling her name as the intense pleasure momentarily blinded him. On and on the waves of pleasure exploded within him, carrying him from one pinnacle to the next until he had nothing left. Shaking arms gave way and he pressed atop her. She clung to him, arms tight about his neck, legs locked around his waist. If only they could stay like this forever.

He tried to ease free of her body but she didn't allow him, instead tightening her hold on him.

"Stay."

The word, husked with the remnants of her passion, shivered through him. He nodded, burying his face in her neck. When had he last felt so content?

CHAPTER TWENTY

Geira cleared the last of the morning meal from the table and prepared to venture outside to tend the garden. Today marked the third week of warmer weather. The time had come for planting. And more. Sometime in the coming days, she must make her escape. She placed a hand on her belly, still flat. That wouldn't last much longer. She worried each time Kori took her at night, fearing he might be able to discern the changes in her body. Her breasts had grown tender, and she feared he'd notice. Oddly, Kori's touch soothed the ache, even when he handled her roughly. Even now, thinking of how he had spent hours tormenting her the night before sparked a sharp pang in her sex. The familiar heat and wetness rose insistently.

He had truly made her his slave, slave to the way he mastered her body. How she wished she could stay and serve him for the rest of her days. Each night this last week, there had been an intensity in his lovemaking that hadn't been present before Thora's encounter with the wolf. Something had changed that day, and though Geira couldn't quite name what specifically had changed, it wreaked havoc with her emotions. The thought of leaving strangely left her afraid and sad.

She sucked in a breath. How could she possibly want to remain a slave, forever in thrall to him for every moment of her life? Damn her soul to Hel, she couldn't let this happen! The past weeks in particular had lulled her senses until she didn't even realize how deeply she'd accepted her position. Reveled in it. No matter how she tried to tamp down the dark hope, it refused to go away, poking her again and again. Surely, she'd lost all her wits.

The door flung open and Kori stepped inside. Thora's laughter as she tended her wolf pups drifted in behind him. The cubs had grown quickly in the last weeks, but had shown no signs of aggression toward any of them. In fact, they'd become quite protective in the weeks since Kori had brought them home. Thora had a gentle touch and sweet nature when caring for the animals, and they seemed to adore her as much. Geira couldn't believe the change from the sullen witch to the kind and loving girl. The last weeks had been peaceful and calm, and she and Thora had actually become friends. She'd never imagined she would enjoy their time together. Instead of nasty and hateful remarks, they shared fun and intriguing conversations. Geira learned that Kori used to play silly games with his daughter when she was small, and that he'd taught her how to hunt.

"We go to the village." Kori's words drew her from her reverie.

"Why?" She bit her lip, wishing she hadn't blurted out the question. Kori's smile soothed her worry.

"There is much business to discuss and I won't leave you here alone."

He'd had no qualms leaving her here with Thora before. Did he suspect her intentions? She forced herself to remain calm, her expression bland. She nodded and reached for her cloak. Silently, Kori led her outside to his horse, climbing up behind her once he'd settled her in the saddle. Beside them, Thora sat astride her own horse, the wolf pups barking and prancing beside them excitedly.

The ride to the village took little time. It had been several weeks since Geira had been in the town. Aware of others stopping in their business to stare at them, she held her head high. The collar she wore around her neck proclaimed her to be Kori's and she was proud of that.

Again, she found herself appalled by her thoughts. She was the daughter of a brave chieftain. How could she be proud to be Kori's slave? The long winter had surely frozen her ability to think. The time to flee fast approached.

They reached the longhouse, where Jarl Thorfinn stood, surrounded by several other men. Geira caught Hradi's warm smile and recognized many of the others. She'd never spoken with any of them, deemed too lowly to be worthy of their attention. Her gaze drifted to the edge of the gathering. A shudder came over her before she could suppress it. Muli watched her with angry eyes, threat clear in his stare. He spit on the ground then turned and walked away.

Kori slid down and helped her from the horse. He took her chin in his hand.

"Stay with Thora for now. I will send for you shortly."

His words held an ominous note and she wondered what he intended. She recalled the day he had brought her here to claim her, branding and collaring her. She sucked in a breath to realize this day had a similar feel to it. What did he plan now? Various ideas tumbled through her thoughts, spurring panic that set her heart to racing.

She spotted the chain looped onto his belt. Dread dried her mouth. Fear seeped into her veins, fear he might guess her plans and do whatever necessary to prevent her flight. Her breath hitched in her throat. She wasn't ready to leave today, had not finished gathering what she needed for the long journey. For now, praying he didn't intend to hinder her was her only option.

She followed Thora to the back of the longhouse, where the kitchens lay. The other women paused briefly to stare, then resumed their preparations. Apparently, a large feast had been planned. Why? She and Thora set to work helping.

As she worked, she became aware of someone staring. She looked up and caught Dota's eye. A pang of regret for losing her only friend arose, setting the nausea rolling once more in her stomach. It was only the child causing the illness, not Dota's contempt. But as she held Dota's stare, she realized the other woman looked on her with affection. Puzzled, Geira beckoned her over.

"Are you well?" she asked when Dota neared. She shouldn't care, but she did, pleased to see Dota did indeed look healthy.

Her friend nodded. "Yes. And I must apologize to you."

"For what?" Though she pretended indifference, a surge of excitement passed through her. Did she dare hope Dota would once again be her ally? She might even be able to help Geira escape.

"For thinking you... calling you... I know you did not plan any of this, and did not give yourself willingly. I know you did what you had to, to survive. I... I'm sorry I attacked you." Dota twisted her hands before her and lowered her head.

Her obvious shame dissolved any bitterness Geira felt toward her friend. Tears burned her eyes.

"Dota, I would have done anything to save you from this. I intend you no harm, I never have."

Dota nodded, raising her head to reveal dark eyes shimmering with tears. "I know. I am sorry."

"You are forgiven. I know you didn't really mean it."

"I did, when I said it. But I was afraid and I..."

"Yes. I think both of us were."

"I am also sorry for bedding with your husband. Hradi told me all about what Einnar did."

What had Kori's brother told Dota that convinced her of Einnar's evil acts? Or was this all a well-rehearsed act? While Geira held affection for Hradi, she knew the man could be ruthless and cruel. She'd overheard enough tales through the winter to convince her they couldn't all be false. Though she knew Hradi to be a generally honorable man, she also recognized he was capable of treating Dota with contempt. Had he coerced her into making the apology? Not that she cared anymore. She only wished Dota didn't foolishly think so highly of Einnar.

"It was before I was wed, anyway." Somehow, Geira felt the need to assure her friend she didn't hold any animosity over that. "And there is much about Einnar you didn't know."

"Can you forgive me?"

Geira blinked back her tears. The genuine regret her friend appeared to reveal was enough. Were her words truly sincere? She realized she must accept the apology, and appear gracious. Soon enough, she would know the truth.

"Of course I can." She reached for Dota and hugged her, remaining silent when the woman shuddered. Suppressed sobs or something else? Finally, she released Dota.

"Tell me, how are you faring?"

At the question, Dota's expression brightened. "I've learned to survive as well, and… I am well. I find Hradi to be… an understanding master. Not nearly as terrible as I'd feared."

Something about the glow in her friend's face told Geira the pair's intimate relationship proved as satisfying as her own with Kori. She sucked in a breath. Was that a pang of envy rising along her spine? She did still harbor an intense attraction to Hradi. She wouldn't deny him should he and Kori decide to repeat that one unforgettable night. But she had grown to love Kori and…

The thought crashed to a halt and she swayed, the breath sucked from her lungs. Love Kori? The man who'd taken her from everything she'd known and made her a slave? How could she love him? She would never be anything more than a possession to him. Not his equal or partner. Then why did the fervent hope she could stay with him always linger? He'd weakened her over the winter, his possession of her body stealing her heart and mind as well. Her soul. Unacceptable. She could no longer pretend she might mean something more to him when clearly he held her in such low regard. Her decision to flee strengthened.

A shout from outside sent the women running to the square. From the excited exclamations from those around her, Geira realized someone approached the village, sailing up the river.

She sought Kori and found him standing with his brother and father in the center of the square. She hurried to his side.

"Who comes?" she asked.

Kori shrugged. "I don't know that raven banner."

Geira shielded her eyes against the sun and looked at the lead vessel heading toward them. She recognized the half-circle banner, a black raven woven against a white background, long black fringes falling from the edges.

"It's my father!"

The hope she'd harbored since the night of the raid had proven true! Her father lived! When she made a move toward the shore, Kori grabbed her arm to halt her flight. She turned, stomach churning to see anger etched into his face as he stared at the incoming vessels. At the same time, she recognized panic. His dark gaze settled on her. She never expected to find fear there.

Several moments passed, what seemed like an eternity. Neither spoke. So many confusing thoughts rambled through her head. Excitement at knowing her father lived, had come for her. Anguish at the idea of being rescued. Worry for Kori's life. And her father's.

"He will demand my freedom."

Kori gave a terse nod. "I will not let you go."

Did she dare hope he meant his words, intended them because he wanted her, but not as a slave? Perhaps something more? The wish taunted, and she closed her eyes against the wave of sickness rising with more force.

"Geira? What's wrong? Are you ill?"

She opened her eyes to find Kori studying her intently. She shook her head, clenching her jaw to hold back the urge to retch. A deep breath, then another, and finally her jumpy belly settled.

"I… my father lives, Kori. He survived! And now…"

How did she explain that she wished him no harm, wanted him safe, just as she wanted her father safe. She looked toward the longships, nearer now than ever, and the sight of her father standing at the bow filled her heart with joy. Just behind, her brother Brosa stood, and then…

Her heart seemed to slam to a halt. Einnar! How had he survived as well? Panic stole her breath this time. She knew what he was capable of and knew he would not be pleased to find her healthy and comfortable. She grabbed Kori's shirt.

"My husband! He lives!"

Kori gave a single nod, his mouth set in a grim line. "Don't worry, *ambátt*. He will not survive this day."

Her head spun, thoughts whirling with the possibilities of how the day might end. Too many terrified her. Her legs trembled and she leaned against Kori for support.

"I don't want to go back to him."

She muttered the words into his shirt. Beneath her hands, his heart raced. He worried as well. Fingers on her chin tilted her head back.

"Geira, you will never go back to him. I will protect you from him."

Geira held his stare silently. His oath echoed in her ears. The affection in his eyes deepened, and he leaned down, brushing a soft kiss across her lips.

"You belong to me, Geira. As I belong to you."

Stars danced before her eyes as his words sunk in. He'd not proclaimed his adoration or love, but she understood he *did* love her. With that realization, she knew. She belonged here. With Kori, however he would have her. She wanted him beside her to raise their child. She loved him with all her heart.

"I… there's something you should know."

He gave her a gentle smile and placed a hand on

her belly. "You carry my child."

She gaped at him. "How...?"

"I touch every inch of you each night. I remember the changes when my wife carried Thora. Your body has changed in similar ways."

"Kori, I —"

"Not now, *ambátt*. I must face your father and your... husband first." For a moment, his face dissolved into revulsion before he composed himself, a bland and calm expression settling over him. He turned, nodding to his brother. "Take her and watch her."

He pressed another kiss against her mouth and turned to stand beside his father.

Geira's gaze darted between her father and Kori, not daring to settle on Einnar again. Aware of Hradi's arm sliding around her waist, she realized she had been caught. While his embrace appeared casual, Geira knew Kori's brother would never relinquish his grip. She twisted her hands before her, praying to Odin and Thor and every god in Valhalla to keep Kori safe.

***

Kori stood beside his father, ready to draw his weapon. He'd known Geira's father would come, though he didn't know when. He'd made no mention to Geira that he'd recently learned the man still lived, nor that he had exchanged messages with her father, not wanting to give her hope for no reason. Nor did he want her to demand she be returned to her family. Today's plans had been made in the hope of securing his claim to her before Sturlasson arrived.

The boats came to the dock. Just as the message he'd received a few days past had warned, Soren Sturlasson had launched a raid to reclaim his daughter. No mention had been made of Einnar, however, indicating the barely civil tone of those messages had been a ruse. His foe's survival came as a shock. He'd been certain he'd left the man for dead. While he disliked being wrong, he had little time to dwell on his failure. Today he must ensure Einnar never walked

Midgard again.

"You will have to kill him, to settle this once and for all." Thorfinn never took his gaze from the boats at the dock. "Sturlasson is the reason we aren't now under attack. Einnar has no men of his own, so he must depend on Geira's father, who I suspect doesn't want a war."

"Then why are his men armed for battle?"

Thorfinn shrugged. "Probably because he anticipated reclaiming his daughter would not be easy."

"You know what was to happen today."

Thorfinn nodded. "Yes. And it will. I'll explain it to Soren. I've met the man before. He's smart and mostly reasonable. Einnar likely filled his head with lies over what happened when you raided Fellskoger. If you truly wish to proceed with your plan, I expect Sturlasson will demand some sort of repayment."

"Such as?"

Thorfinn shrugged. "Gold, most likely. But we can make an alliance as well. Your plan fits in well when I direct the discussion that way."

Kori nodded. He looked over at Geira, wishing he could soothe the panic from her face. It wasn't good for the child if she remained agitated. He offered a smile, but it did little to calm the way she fidgeted under Hradi's strong embrace.

Soren Sturlasson stepped out of the boat, followed by his son and son-in-law. All three men wore stony expressions, but Kori studied Einnar. The contemptuous sneer turned his stomach. He wanted to see the other man's eyes widen in the last moment before death, as he thought he had before.

Once more, he silently cursed not taking the time to ensure his enemy's death. The thought of Geira in the other man's clutches set his teeth on edge. He gripped the hilt of his sword. His father's hand on his arm held him in place.

"Calm yourself."

Kori nodded, forcing his rage back under control.

The three men approached, a respectable number of warriors hanging about ten feet back. The men of his village surrounded the town square, ready to advance if necessary.

Sturlasson stopped a few feet away from Kori. "Kori Thorfinnsson, I accuse you of kidnapping and murder. I demand you return my daughter!"

Kori remained silent at his father's urging. Thorfinn stepped forward.

"Kori took vengeance against Einnar for murdering my daughter-in-law."

Soren seemed surprised by this and gave Einnar a sharp look.

"It's a lie!" Einnar spat on the ground. "I've never even laid eyes on your wife!"

"No, it's not a lie! I was there! I saw you!"

Thora stepped up beside Kori. Before she could run further, Kori grabbed her arm. At her feet, the two wolf pups had taken on a protective stance, growling along with their mistress' shouts.

"Easy, Thora."

"It's true. I was right there! Trapped in that hut while you… I saw you rape her, watched you strangle her, then cut her throat." She turned to Kori and her grandfather. "When he was finished, he looked at me, and I knew he meant to… If Uncle Hradi had not come in and fought him off, I would be dead too!"

Shouts demanding justice erupted in the crowd, as Thora recounted the day her mother died. Kori had heard it all before, but now, seeing the tears streaking down his daughter's face ignited the pain as if Borga had just been murdered today.

Soren stalked over to Einnar, grasping the man's shirt in his fists. "I should have listened to my instincts. Should have known the dread in my daughter was because… "

He shoved Einnar away from him. The other man stumbled back several steps before righting himself.

"She's a stupid child! She doesn't know anything."

Einnar's agitation grew apparent, his eyes wild with anger. And madness.

Soren raised his sword. "You have humiliated me before my clan. I defended you, saved you. I should have let you die in the fire!"

Einnar gave a maniacal laugh. "I cannot die! Sword and fire have failed to stop me. You will fail too!"

"You no longer have the support of my men." Soren spit on the ground at Einnar's feet. "You face your justice alone. May the gods condemn your soul to Hel."

Einnar's face twisted with rage. "You break our agreement? You swore an oath before the gods –"

Brosa leaped in front of his father, sword in one hand, the other twirling a hand axe.

"The gods know the blackness of your heart. They'll have their vengeance."

The two men stared hard at each other, but the madness in Einnar's stare fueled Kori's determination to see the man dead. He made a move toward the pair, only to be checked once more by his father.

Soren turned to Kori. "My daughter is innocent in this. This vile excuse for a man is the cause of it all. You cannot hold her responsible."

"She is compensation for my loss."

Yet, Kori knew Soren was right. Geira held no blame in any of this. Still, he refused to let her go. How would her father react when he learned of Kori's plan?

"Perhaps we can reach an agreement." Thorfinn stepped forward.

Kori kept even with his father as they approached Soren.

"The only agreement I will accept is the return of my daughter. I will pay any bounty you choose." Soren's sword remained at the ready.

"No!"

Kori heard the cry behind him, recognized Geira. Fear rang through her voice. He refused to turn, though his longing to comfort her continued to grow. There must be some way to please everyone, without resorting to killing her father.

His grip on his sword tightened, but he still didn't withdraw the weapon. He thought of how he'd wanted her family to be reduced to begging for their lives, and now... Now he wanted her family to accept him, as she did. His desire to see them all dead had long ago ceased to exist.

"I demand you free her!" Sturlasson's voice grew louder, the calm of moments ago evolving into anger. His stare focused on Geira across the square.

Kori sensed, and understood, the man's worry and fear for his daughter. He truly didn't want to fight Soren, but feared he had no choice. If he did... he refused to consider the possibility, knowing he would lose Geira forever, even if he kept her beside him.

"Set your men upon them!" The scream came from Einnar, who stalked up behind Soren, sword at the ready.

"This is all because of you!" Soren shouted at his son-in-law. He shoved Einnar again, and the two men tussled before the older man drew a dagger and placed it to Einnar's neck. "She wouldn't be here now if you had any honor. You disgust me. I should have left you to burn! I'd kill you now, but his claim on your life is much stronger than mine."

Soren jerked his head toward Kori stood. Kori's grip on his sword tightened. Einnar broke free of Sturlasson and turned to face Kori. His enemy sneered, his gaze darting over Kori's shoulder. An evil smile curled his lips and Kori knew the man had seen Geira. Einnar leaned in close to Geira's father.

"I will have her back! I will save her and when I do, you will again reward her to me. This time, as *my* slave."

Another cry behind him, but Kori's focus had narrowed dangerously on Einnar. Rage tinged his vision red and he drew his sword. He would never let Geira fall into this man's clutches again.

"You'll see! You'll all see! After I kill him, then you will know how powerful I am!" Einnar's proclamation possessed a desperate madness.

Several moments passed, heavy with silence broken by several chuckles and mocking taunts, from all assembled. Kori ignored the murmurings, resting his other hand on the axe in his belt. Einnar tossed his shield aside and stalked toward him, sword raised. Kori gave a grim smile, aware of his father stepping back.

He took in the sight of his enemy, still and poised. He would let the fool make the first move then proceed accordingly. Einnar was a powerful warrior and, though he'd been grievously injured last summer, appeared to have recovered completely. A brief moment's annoyance at his previous failure seeped into Kori's awareness but he forced it aside.

Einnar ran the last few strides, sword high above his head. A war cry echoed in the square when he charged. Kori remained still, easily lifting his own blade to block the strike, the metal screeching harshly.

He shoved the other man away, answering with a swing of his own sword. Einnar danced back, narrowly avoiding the thrust, snarling in anger.

"You stole my bride!"

"You killed my wife!"

Kori let Einnar circle him, bouncing on the balls of his feet. Each time Einnar dared to lunge or swing, Kori blocked the move. He remained calm, not making any real advances, allowing the idiot to tire. Again and again, Einnar lunged forward with a slice of steel, but Kori blocked each attempt. His ears rang from the constant shriek of steel.

Around them, the crowd grew excited, shouting encouragement and cheering Kori, while at the same time jeering Einnar. Had Kori heard Geira telling him to kill his enemy? He didn't dare let his concentration wander.

Einnar's step grew sluggish. The time had come. Kori charged forward, slashing toward Einnar's neck.

At the last moment, his enemy evaded the move, rolling to the ground and coming up behind Kori. Before he could turn, the slice of the blade into his arm burned through him. The smell of blood scented the air. Kori let out a grunt of anger and pain and spun about.

***

Geira's nails dug into her palm, breaking the skin. So many times she wanted to grab Hradi's sword and charge after Einnar herself. So far, Kori had done nothing but defend himself. What did he intend? She had no idea how to fight such a battle, but shouldn't he be attacking?

"Ease, Geira. Kori knows what he's doing."

Hradi's words beside her ear drew her attention for just a moment. Hradi nodded toward the combatants.

"Look how he's tiring him out. Soon, he will strike."

She was drawn again to the macabre dance the two warriors engaged in. But she realized Hradi was right. At that moment, Kori made his charge. Geira held her breath, stunned when Einnar evaded Kori's blow.

Einnar rolled behind Kori, rising to slice at his opponent. Geira screamed as the sword landed on Kori's arm, drawing blood. She would have run into the melee then if Hradi hadn't tightened his hold on her.

"Kori!"

At the sound of her calling his name, both men stopped. The hatred and malice in Einnar's stare sparked terror. She shrank back against Hradi, looking to Kori.

He gave her a nod. She bit her lip, tears welling as she prayed to all the gods in Valhalla to keep him safe. Einnar took that moment to charge Kori once more, but this time, Kori ducked the sword and rose, landing a solid punch to Einnar's nose. The crunch of bone was drowned by cheers as Einnar went down with a howl, holding his face, blood spurting between his fingers. Still, when Kori moved to take another swing, Einnar lifted his sword to block it.

"Kill him, Kori!"

"He's yours now!"

"Finish him!" Geira shouted.

Sensing Hradi staring at her, she lifted her gaze to him. He laughed. "You are a bloodthirsty woman."

She hadn't realized she'd screamed those words aloud. But she couldn't find humor in this, even if Hradi appeared to think it merely a game.

Einnar rose once more, but now his gait grew sloppy and unsteady. His legs seemed to barely hold him. Kori moved closer, but even in his weakened state, Einnar managed to deflect most of the blows. Kori thrust again, and again, each move biting into each of Einnar's arms. Sweat poured down his face as he toyed with Einnar.

"How does it feel to die slowly? To suffer agony and wish for death?"

Geira understood. This was his way of forcing Einnar to suffer as Kori's wife had. Death was inevitable, but how much would Einnar bear before he begged for it?

"She was mine!" Einnar seemed to regain some strength with those words, standing straighter and raising his sword.

"Now she's mine. And she always will be."

Einnar took one last lunge. As Kori blocked the attack, he spun about, now behind Einnar. Seconds hovered like dark storm clouds as Kori completed his move. The momentum drove his sword against Einnar's neck. A second later, Einnar's head tumbled to the ground. As if an obscene puppet, his body remained upright for another breath before collapsing.

Geira sucked in air, nearly lightheaded. Loud cheers erupted, and suddenly free of Hradi's grip, Geira ran toward Kori, hoping to reach him before the crowd did. As she neared, he turned. Blood and sweat splattered his face and clothing. He swayed, clutching his arm, before falling to his knees. Excitement gave way to panic. She threw herself to the ground before him, examining his wound.

She bit her lip. Deeper than she'd imagined. Tears burned her eyes.

"I need bandages and salve. Some thread to close the gash." Her fingers frantically covered the injury, blood staining her hands. Kori's blood. Panic set her heart to racing.

Kori's fingers stroked across her cheek. "Geira, I am fine. A minor wound."

As if the reassurance dissolved the last of her strength, sobs of relief overtook her and she wrapped her arms around him. He returned the embrace with his uninjured arm, holding her tight. She never wanted him to let go.

An anguished howl cut through the cheers. Geira turned to see Dota fighting against Hradi's hold.

"Einnar!" the woman cried.

She still had feelings for the dead coward? So stunned she nearly forgot to breathe, Geira's gut rolled to realize her suspicions had been correct. Dota's apology had not been sincere. Beside her, Kori sucked in a deep breath, his arm tightening on her waist. She met his concerned gaze, then looked to Hradi.

Kori's brother's face mottled red with rage, his lips curled in disgust. Yet, when his gaze flicked momentarily to her, Geira realized how deeply Dota had hurt Hradi with her reaction to Einnar's death. How she longed to offer her comfort. All she could do now was give him a nod. He returned the gesture then focused once more on the woman struggling in his arms. In a swift motion, Dota's wrists had been fastened behind her back. Still, she continued to bemoan Einnar's death, sobbing. After several moments, she calmed, straightening her spine and turning to Geira.

"This is all your fault!" she shrieked.

"Silence!" Hradi bellowed. Geira sensed he wanted to hit Dota. Instead, he dragged her from the crowd, warning of all the ways she would pay for her treachery.

Geira met Kori's gaze. "She lied to me. To all of us."

Kori nodded, silence hanging between them for several moments. "I am not surprised, not after the way she treated you when all you tried to do was help her."

"She was my friend."

Kori shook his head. "She was not. She betrayed you in so many ways." He gave a soft smile and ran a finger along her lower lip. "You have a tender heart, Geira."

Tears stung her eyes but somehow she held them back. "What will happen to her?"

"It isn't your concern. Hradi will deal with her and I suspect he may well sell her now."

A brief moment of sadness for her former friend's fate tugged at Geira's heart before she forced it aside. The regret was only for the loss of the friendship, not for anything Dota might endure in the coming days. Grateful that Kori truly loved her, she hugged him tight again.

The crowd around them stepped back. A shadow fell across them. She lifted her head, a cry of joy to see her father.

She gave Kori a questioning stare. He nodded.

"Greet your father."

She carefully stood, suddenly aware of all she'd endured this past winter. For a moment, she couldn't meet her father's stare. Would he be disappointed in her? His fingers on her chin lifted her face.

"I am happy you are safe. You look well."

"I am, Father. I've missed you."

He smiled and opened his arms. Geira flung herself against him. She'd feared him dead, and to have him back seemed truly a gift from Odin himself. His strong embrace roused a sense of safety she hadn't known since she was a child.

"What about me?" She looked up to see her brother Brosa studying her, a broad grin on his face. She let him pull her from her father and enclose her in a tight embrace. Tears of joy spilled down her cheeks. Images of the games they'd played as children flashed through her thoughts when his warmth engulfed her.

"I thought you were both dead."

Brosa shook his head, finally releasing her from the suffocating hug. "We were in the forest when the attack happened. They never found us."

"You didn't come to save me."

"We had no choice, outnumbered as we were. Our only chance to survive, to save you, was to remain hidden, waiting for the right moment." Brosa lowered his head, toe kicking in the dirt. "We waited too long. After it was over, we thought everyone was dead, including you."

Soren bowed his head. "I thought we were too late, until we found Einnar."

Geira wiped her eyes. "I thought Kori killed him."

"He would surely be dead if we hadn't found him. He gave us a tale about what happened, but we didn't know who had taken you. Or where. Clearly, he lied. If I could kill him again myself, I would."

Once again, her father pulled her close before setting her away to study her, she supposed checking for any injuries or signs of ill-treatment. If he lifted her dress and bared her bottom, he might find a bruise or two. Heat scorched her cheeks and she averted her face until it passed.

Turning to study her father, Geira read the confusion in his eyes. When Soren looked past her, towards, Kori, his face tightened in anger.

"I demand you free my daughter at once!"

Geira failed at concealing the wince of discomfort when her father's fingers tightened on her.

"No, I will not."

Did she dare meet Kori's gaze, which she felt fully upon her as if he touched her with his hands? She remained still.

"She is my only daughter."

The hint of a plea in her father's words seemed a

fist squeezing Geira's heart. Yet, she wanted to assure him she was fine. Wanted to stay in this village, with Kori, however she may have to do so.

"She is my only... *ambátt*."

Geira closed her eyes, the sound of his endearment bringing the burn of tears.

"She is innocent in your claim of vengeance. Hasn't she endured enough at your hands?"

The strange urge to tell her father she hadn't suffered nearly burst free. Somehow, Geira contained the words.

"I plan to keep her."

So many doubts lingered over the intent in Kori's words. Did he still mean to keep her for vengeance? Or was it for the child she carried? She turned, studying him. He met her gaze with warmth and a smile.

"I cannot allow that!" Soren's shout dimmed Kori's smile.

"Not just as an *ambátt*. But more." Kori held her father's stare.

"What?" Geira and her father spoke at the same time. When Kori's gaze returned to her, she sucked in a breath. Did she dare hope...?

"Before your father's arrival, I had planned a special... ceremony."

Her confusion grew. None of the thoughts rambling through her head made any sense. "I don't understand."

"I planned to free you Geira."

Had she misheard? The roaring in her ears seemed to drown out all else, but she knew he kept speaking because his lips moved. He wanted to free her? A moment of despair rose up, but she forced it back, refusing to let him see it. She lifted her chin, wishing her heart would stop pounding so hard.

"Did you not hear me?" Kori asked.

A chuckle from her father left her more bewildered than ever. She looked around at the sea of faces surrounding them. They all seemed to be waiting for her response.

"I'm sorry, Kori, I'm just confused. Can you explain it further? Please?"

He shook his head, but a grin curved his mouth. "Very well, *ambátt.*"

A shiver of desire passed along her spine. He winked, as if knowing how his endearment melted her heart instead of causing shame and fear.

"I planned to release you from your slavery."

"Why?"

"Because I want you to be my wife."

Geira stared. Had he just said...? This must be some sort of mad dream. Had he poisoned her porridge, so she couldn't clearly grasp the truth before it was too late?

"Our arrival seems to have interrupted his plan." Soren tightened his embrace.

"What?" The world tilted, and she clutched at her father to steady herself.

"If we'd been a few days later, you would already be wed."

Fragmented thoughts assailed her, but she realized her father was right. If he hadn't arrived today, Kori and she might be wed right now. She looked from Kori to her father and back again, her muddled thoughts near impossible to comprehend.

"But even if... Einnar was with you."

Her father chuckled. "Well, he's dead now. You are married no longer."

"I didn't know I was still wed until now!" She rubbed her forehead. Confusion still reigned. Logical words eluded her.

"Yes, I know. But it doesn't matter anymore. And now that I am here, Jarl Thorfinn has proposed an alliance with our clan."

She gaped at her father, unable to find her voice. She must look like a fish gasping for water.

"Tell me, Geira, do you want to wed this man?"

She struggled to calm her breathing. The hope

she'd buried deep burst free in a wild rush of joy. This couldn't all be a dream, could it? Her gaze focused on Kori, but still no words formed. Her thoughts raced frantically and she couldn't grasp a single one for more than a moment.

"Tell *me, ambátt,* do you want me as your husband?"

Her thoughts still chaotic, she shook her head. At the grief that crossed his face, she realized how his gesture appeared to him. She stepped toward him, nodding, and still unable to find to words to express what she felt for him. Her heart's desire had been given to her, but she still wasn't sure it was real. If only she could stop panting, maybe she could talk. She grabbed Kori's arm. Touching him calmed her, gave her a moment to gather her thoughts and find her voice.

"Yes, Kori, I do. I want to be your wife. To stay with you forever."

Several heavy seconds passed before his grin returned, wider than ever. He caught her in his arms, swinging her around. His mouth sought hers in a hungry kiss, and she held on tight, responding with all the love in her heart.

He wanted her to stay! As his wife! She wanted to laugh and weep with the joy suffusing her. When he set her down, she stumbled, leaning against him.

"Does this mean I must give up my collar?"

Bewilderment furrowed his brow. "You still wish to wear it?"

"It tells everyone I belong to you. I am proud to wear it."

He stared a few more moments, then shook his head. "You amaze me *ambátt.* And I love you for it."

"As I love you. In taking me as your slave, you freed me."

He grinned. Leaning close to her ear, he lowered his voice. "And you have made me a slave in return. But I will take your collar."

"Why?"

"Because my wife must have a collar befitting her station. I will have Leif work on it."

She shook her head. "No."

"You refuse me?"

She grinned. "I want this collar as it is. So yes, I refuse."

In a whisper, he said, "You will be punished for that."

"I hope so."

He silenced her laughter with a hungry kiss.

THE END

Also Available:
Norseman's Deception, Book 2
in The Norsemen Sagas

Thank you for taking the time to read Norseman's Revenge. I hope you enjoyed it, and if so, please consider telling your friends who have similar reading tastes. If you did like it, I'd love it if you wouldn't mind posting a short review. Word of mouth is an author's best friend and more appreciated than you know.

About the Author:

I'm a proud born-and-bred Jersey Girl with Brooklyn roots. And I still live where it all started - I married my very own alpha male many eons ago, and have an amazing college-age daughter, and a pre-teen son who both charms and frustrates me at every turn. Free time is always a luxury and I spend the bulk of what time I manage to scrounge up lost in the worlds of my own making. I love to read and write hot, sexy and emotional stories about people both glamorous and not-so-glamorous. Be warned - some of my characters are even downright un-heroic, which is part of what makes them so interestingly sexy, in my opinion!

On the rare occasions I'm not taking advantage of that valuable free time by writing, you can catch me poking around in my other favorite twisted historical worlds of Sleepy Hollow, Reign and the History Channel's Vikings. I'm also a huge fan of Harry Potter, Highlander, Charmed, and DragonBall Z! Yeah, a strange fandom medley, but each one features some of the sexiest villains ever. Did I mention I love villains?

And of course, let's not forget my beloved NY Rangers.

Find Gianna online:

Magically Kinky!
A Kinky Twist on History!
Men Who Take What They Want and The Women
Strong Enough to Enjoy It!

Website: www.giannasimoneeroticromance.com
Blog: http://giannasimone.blogspot.com
Twitter: @Gianna_Simone
Facebook:
www.facebook.com/GiannaSimoneRomanceAuthor
Goodreads:
https://www.goodreads.com/author/show/4493720.Gian
na_Simone
You can also find me on Pinterest, Google+, LinkedIn!
I love hearing from readers - don't hesitate to reach out
and say hi!

MEDIEVAL WARRIOR'S LEGENDS

WARRIOR'S POSSESSION: Upon her father's death, Lady Gillian Marlowe is ordered by King Edward I to wed Royce Langley, the Earl of Montchester. Worried she is being offered up as little more than a sacrifice in a political game, Gillian is surprised to find herself intrigued by her arrogant and infuriating husband.

Tasked with ridding the border along Wales of rebels who seek to unseat the king, Royce finds subterfuge and secrets everywhere, even with his beautiful wife. Though he only agreed to the marriage because of the king's order, he finds himself both fascinated and incensed by Gillian at every turn. She tries his patience, defies his orders and places herself in danger. To keep her in line, he spanks her, binds her to his bed and uses dominating sexual games to torment her, in an effort to get her to reveal her secrets. But even that is not enough to subdue her stubborn determination to stand beside him and defend her home and people.

Discovering his wife enjoys the same dark pleasures as Royce does only stirs more confusion. He has sworn never to fall for a woman's wiles, but his wife captivates him and stirs a desire deeper than any he has ever known. Trusting her is another matter, as he fears Gillian may bring about his downfall with her continued secrets, which he views as an attempt to undermine his authority.

As the rebel attacks increase and danger lurks everywhere, Gillian falls under suspicion as the traitor, despite her vows of loyalty. Royce must overcome his mistrust and find a way to maintain his possession of Gillian as they battle the enemies both within and without, if there is any hope for them to save each other.

Includes: Male domination, bondage, spanking, anal sex and so much more!

Amazon: http://www.amazon.com/Warriors-Possession-Gianna-Simone-ebook/dp/B00ZS51HJ0

WARRIOR'S VENGEANCE: Near the Scottish border during the reign of Edward I, Marissa Langley, daughter of a powerful English earl is captured by a band of marauding Scotsmen. Completely at their mercy, she is desperate to escape. When the leader of the group saves her from certain rape, she believes she will be freed.

But Ian MacCallum is no savior. He takes her for his own, seduces her then makes her a submissive. Her collar and chains are part of his vengeance on her father—the man Ian claims is responsible for the death of his beloved wife and son.

But her immediate death is not Ian's plan. He subjects her to daily suffering and punishments and goes so far as sharing her with another clansman. Yet, her spirit will not be broken. He finds himself drawn to that core of strength within her; finding it most exquisite as it cannot be violated.

When danger from within his clan threatens her, Ian protects her, discovering at the same time that he does not want to lose her, ever.

Marissa makes her own discovery: she comes to crave Ian's torturous touch. When she learns the source of his hatred, she is certain he is wrong. Her father would not commit atrocities. She waits for the moment when she can escape and prove her father's innocence. But that would mean leaving Ian when she is no longer sure she wants to be free.

Includes: Bondage, collars, spanking, multiple partners and so much more!

Amazon: http://www.amazon.com/Warriors-Vengeance-Gianna-Simone-ebook/dp/B0088QRBIC

WARRIOR'S WRATH: In 14th century England, a long-kept secret devastates Rowan Langley. Anger sends him on a quest for truth. He trusts no one, keeping others away, except fellow knight Gerard.

Aeron Dawkyns, fleeing Wales and a charge of murder, lives on the street, pickpocketing. She steals Rowan's coin. Later, Rowan catches her attempting to steal his horse. She has a choice – sexual slavery, or be handed over to be hanged. She chooses Rowan and Gerard.

Serving an angry Rowan has dark pleasures Aeron learns to crave. She feels safe, despite the knights' wicked games. When Rowan drags her back to Wales, she fears that safety will be destroyed.

Rowan learns Aeron's plight and vows to hunt down her enemies, promising to protect and keep her. Yet he worries he's no better than her enemy. Still, he craves his slave's touch, as much as he craves her heart.

Staying with Rowan becomes Aeron's heart's desire – but could mean her death.

Includes: Bondage, spanking, multiple partners and so much more!

Amazon: http://www.amazon.com/Warriors-Wrath-Gianna-Simone-ebook/dp/B00IOBPTZI

THE BAYOU MAGISTE CHRONICLES

CLAIMED BY THE DEVIL: Helene Gaudet finds the perfect Dom in an internet chat room. It's as if he can read her mind – and he knows how to make her beg. When they agree to meet in the real world, Helene realizes why her Dom knows her so well – he is none other than Devlin Marchand, the same man who handed her over years ago to a dark sorcerer – to be killed.

She thought she was free from suffering – including a rageful ex-husband who cursed her, leaving her unable to bear children. She wants to forget the past – but her lust for Devlin is so intense after each tormenting, releasing encounter, she doesn't want to leave him.

Devlin wants to repair his past wrongs – but guilt over his past betrayal is multiplied when he learns the curse that has dogged Helene for years comes from the trove of magic created by his very own family. Devlin fears the tentative relationship they've built will be destroyed – and he cannot allow that.

Can they overcome the past to have a future together?

** Contains lots of explicit Magically Kinky! love scenes of the paranormal kind, including magical sex toys, potions, bondage and spanking, and more!

Amazon: http://www.amazon.com/Claimed-Devil-Bayou-Magiste-Chronicles-ebook/dp/B00ETR8GI8

CLAIMED BY THE MAGE: Lily Prentiss wishes she could ignore her inborn healing magic so she can live life on her terms, not follow the path her Magiste family chose for her. But when she stumbles across Aidan Marchand in the excruciating throes of evolving into a Mage, her touch is all that stops his pain and she can no longer deny her powers. When the sexy Dom seduces her into willing submission, she finds she doesn't want to resist and actually enjoys giving up control.

Aidan has more to worry about than just his rapidly maturing powers – his business partner is blackmailing him into funding a venture that involves kidnapping young girls both magical and mortal, and selling them as sex slaves. Even as Lily's touch eases Aidan's pain, he knows staying with her puts her in danger from his enemies. But the gift of her sexual submission helps him even more than her healing magic...so how can he let her go?

** Contains lots of explicit Magically Kinky! love scenes of the paranormal kind, including magical sex toys, potions, bondage and spanking, and more!

Amazon: http://www.amazon.com/Claimed-Mage-Bayou-Magiste-Chronicles-ebook/dp/B00F6IKGGO

CLAIMED BY THE ENCHANTER: Regine Marchand loves being in control – and the role of domme is the perfect way for her to exert that control. An accomplished equestrian, she has her goals of championship in sight and no one will get in her way. Her life and future are in her hands, she doesn't need to depend on anyone for success and happiness.

Cameron McIntyre is fascinated by the cool façade Regine displays, but he senses the depth of her passion lurking under the surface. Despite her protests to the contrary, he recognizes in her a desire to submit and be dominated. But when he is forced to suspend her from competition due to performance enhancement spells used on her horse, he worries he may drive her away, instead of back into his arms. Believing her innocent of the charges, he vows to help her uncover who set her up while convincing her that submission to him is what she truly wants and needs. Submitting to the tall Irishman brings a new level of pleasure Regine has never known, at the same time making her question everything she knew about herself.

Regine is unaware an enemy from her past has targeted her for revenge. Together she and Cameron must discover who wants to knock her out of competition for good, possibly killing her in the process.

** Contains lots of explicit Magically Kinky! love scenes of the paranormal kind, including magical sex toys, potions, bondage and spanking, and more!

Amazon: http://www.amazon.com/Claimed-Enchanter-Bayou-Magiste-Chronicles-ebook/dp/B00ENNUGD6

CLAIMED BY THE ZYNDEVINE: In 13th century France, attacked by those carrying out the Papal Inquisition, *Magiste* Enchantress Chantal Belliveau is thankful for rescue from certain torture and death. But she never expected it to be at the hands of Henri Marchand, one of a powerful pureblooded line of ancient *Magiste*, the Zyndevines. Henri holds the key to her survival, but the danger he poses to her heart and soul could turn out to be even more perilous.

Henri is part of *Il Resistasse*, a handful of powerful *Magiste* fighting the atrocities the Catholic Church inflicts on their race. Saving Chantal becomes more than a simple rescue - the innocent young woman with half-trained powers enchants him more than he has ever been before. That she enjoys the dark side of pleasure he inflicts on her makes him question his determination to never give another his heart.

Chantal is horrified when Henri invokes an ancient spell, the *Possede Puissant*. The incantation leaves her little more than his possession. While she finds herself enjoying his dark and wicked sensual delights, she determines to free herself. Still, the security she finds with Henri encourages her to stay by his side, claiming spell or not.

Resentment toward her from Henri's family convinces Chantal she must ultimately break free of Henri's possession. But when the Inquisitioners attack, Henri convinces Chantal to embark on a journey to a new land, a journey that may well mean the survival of the entire *Magiste* race but the loss of her freedom forever.

** Contains lots of explicit Magically Kinky! love scenes of the paranormal kind, including magical sex toys, potions, bondage and spanking, and more!

Amazon: http://www.amazon.com/CLAIMED-ZYNDEVINE-Bayou-Magiste-Chronicles-ebook/dp/B00YB65GS0